Other Books by C.S. Humble

THE BLACK WELLS SERIES

BOOK 1 - **ALL THESE SUBTLE DECEITS**

BOOK 2 - **ALL THE PROSPECT AROUND US**

BOOK 3 - **ALL THAT MANKIND FAILS TO BEAR** (2024)

BOOK 4 - **ALL OUR STRANGE GLORY** (FORTHCOMING)

BOOK 5 - **ALL FOR THE FIERY HUNT** (FORTHCOMING)

THAT LIGHT SUBLIME TRILOGY

BOOK 1 - **THE MASSACRE AT YELLOW HILL**

BOOK 2 - **A RED WINTER IN THE WEST**

BOOK 3 - **THE LIGHT OF A BLACK STAR** (NOVEMBER, 2023)

A Red Winter in the West

A Red Winter in the West

THAT LIGHT SUBLIME TRILOGY

Book Two

~

C.S. Humble

CEMETERY DANCE PUBLICATIONS

Baltimore

2023

Cemetery Dance Publications
132B Industry Lane, Unit #7
Forest Hill, MD 21050
www.cemeterydance.com

The characters and events in this book are fictitious.
Any similarity to real persons, living or dead,
is coincidental and not intended by the authors.

Trade Paperback Edition

ISBN:
978-1-58767-925-4

Part I:
THE SURVIVORS

&

Part II:
THE MOST FEARSOME HAND
OF A FEROCIOUS ORDER

&

Part III:
THE LAST OBELISK

For my grandfathers

And we, who marked the scene sublime,
Beheld a shining band
Press upward to the mountain top,
As to a Promised Land;
Their faces kindling with the light
That played about its crest—
And two, more glorious, led the way,
In spotless garments dressed;
Some wearied on the way, and these
The stronger lifted up,
And held unto their parching lips
Love's overflowing cup—
And thus refreshed, they buoyantly
Pressed forward in the van,
And leaped and danced for gladness, where
The purpling river ran.

— M.H. COBB, *THE MOUNTAIN IN THE WEST*

Prologue

PRESCOTT, ARIZONA

WESLEY BURROWS SAT at the table rubbing the raised skin on his cheek where, only a few years ago, a wayward bullet had left a pink puckered star. He looked at the cards in his hand. Three jacks and a pair of sixes looked back at him. He let a look of feigned disappointment mask his face. He sighed with a deep melancholy even though the cards were good. They were very good.

Were they good enough to beat the dentist? Time would tell.

The blue evening moon lifted its tired head up from the stony Arizona horizon. Cool beams slanted through the saloon's wooden blinds, emblazoning stripes across the dentist's dark suit.

They were the only two left at the table now.

Wesley "Six Scars" Burrows with his full house and a dentist. A goddamn dentist wearing a calm, smooth smile. Black suit and gossamer moonlight gave the man a panther's sheen.

The piano player, his bowler hat drunkenly tilted on his bald head, was playing a sad, lonely song. The meager crowd, huddled around sagging wood tables grumbled with tired conversations.

They were mostly Arizona cowboys smoothing their wrinkled cares away with whiskey and a few misty-eyed working girls and fellas. Every one of them was mumbling either to themselves or someone else. All of them either seducing potential customers or pouring the guts of their own sad confessions into their foam-rimmed mugs.

Wesley was playing cards...and still laying low.

The cards, he thought. The cards and the game calmed his mind, soothed his worries. Wesley's mind relaxed, lulled down into memories. Memories of all the things that had brought him here. He wished now, more than anything, that he'd never fallen in with the Culliver gang. Wished he'd never held up that wagon train with all those women and children.

He'd never forgive Cy Culliver, that black-bearded son of a bitch. Never.

They never should have done what they did, and it was Cy that had made them do it. It was Cy's fault that the Marshal's posse discovered the gang's hideout, and it was Cy's goddamn fault that Jenny and Mark and Toby had been shot to hell in a muddy gulch.

Cy had probably survived. That's what he did. Time after time, Cy lived to see another day.

Wesley had run. That's what *he* did. He ran, wishing he had a chance to find Cy. If only fate would afford him the opportunity to walk right up behind Cy Culliver, put his pistol to the back of his head, and say...

Wesley didn't know what he'd say. The gun, Wesley thought, would do all the talking. He wished for that chance. Wished for it badly.

But that was behind him, he told himself. There were only the cards, the dentist, and the chips on the table. Tonight, the here and

A Red Winter in the West

the now, was the table game. Tomorrow, when the red dawn rose, there would be the trail.

The long journey to Colorado.

If he couldn't kill Cy, he would settle for reaching Colorado where Richard his brother lived. Wesley would lean on him. Take his hospitality. When your only sibling comes riding in, looking to make a fresh start in a fresh place, well, family couldn't turn away family. If their father had taught them anything with the discipline of a razor strop, it was that in this life, the only people you can rely on were your kin.

It was an immutable truth of the ever-changing world.

Wesley would ride north to Mormon country in Utah, then cut east through Grand Junction. It was dangerous country, filled with Natives and cutthroats, but it was too risky to ride up the more comfortable, populous path through Santa Fe.

A train was out of the question as well. Though that way would certainly be easier, Wesley couldn't chance his picture being posted at one of the ticket stations where rangers loved to lay in wait for the more dim-witted outlaws who'd thought shaving their beard and hair would disguise them enough. Fellas like that swung from a noose every day.

His best chance was on horseback, off the beaten path, heading north.

Wesley looked at the stack of chips, now diminished. Only an hour ago they had stood like indomitable pillars. A little fortune big enough to get him out of Prescott and all the way to Colorado Springs.

"Five hundred to call?" asked Wesley, letting his voice shake a bit at the end. The tremor was a ruse. All part of the show.

The dentist's eyes sparkled, widening at Wesley as he took a deep pull from his cigarette. Big, green, and luminous, they were eyes less fit for a man than a predator. A cougar's eyes.

"The same five hundred as it was two minutes ago, my young friend," said the dentist. There was a slow, easy way about the man, the languidness of a big, bloody-muzzled cat, sunning itself after a fresh kill in the afternoon. The dentist was relaxed, glutted on the chips he effortlessly took from Wesley Burrows.

"We're friends now, huh?" Wesley arched an eyebrow at him.

"You've been so generous to me over the last, what? The last seven hands? Hospitality like that, I don't see how we could be anything else." He winked at Wesley.

Wesley smiled, charmed. "It ain't generosity, so much as it is my hatred of money. As you can see"—he gestured at the few remaining chips in front of him—"I just can't stand the stuff."

The dentist smiled back. "Your hatred of currency notwithstanding, it's still five hundred to call."

"You're awful eager to see the game done."

"I have business elsewhere this evening. But don't feel rushed on my account. By all means, take your time. Consider the cost while you still remain in the game."

"Business? At this hour?"

"At the current rate of this hand, I'm starting to wonder myself if I'll make that appointment or any other this week."

"Well, I wouldn't want you to be late." Wesley gave the man a hard, cruel smile and slid the short stack of chips to the center of the table. They fell over, splashing into the pot. "I'm all in. That's eight hundred to you."

The dentist looked away from the pot, a dash of amusement on his lips. He took a sip of whiskey from a small, sterling cup. "All in. Now, I thought you said—"

The doors of the saloon clattered against the wall. Wesley did not turn to look but kept his eyes on the dentist.

A Red Winter in the West

The dentist did look away, though, his glassy stare scanning the door, his placid demeanor uninterrupted.

"Friends of yours?" asked Wesley.

"They don't look charitable enough."

"Law?"

"Two tin stars joining our little cosmos." The dentist's eyes went back to his cards. "Arizona rangers most likely."

Slowly, as if with no care in the world, Wesley leaned his elbow against the arm of the chair and cupped the starry scar on his cheek in his palm, hiding it from sight.

The sound of boots *thunked* over to the bar, where a low conversation began. This one between one of the rangers and the bartender.

"Why, Wesley," the dentist remarked quietly. "What is this new trepidation I see? You lose chips without a care in the world but when the law arrives…"

Wesley slanted an unhappy smile at the dentist.

"Well," said the dentist, "I suspect one of us will be leaving soon. So, in the interest of brevity, I guess I'm just going to have to call."

"Knock that playing off, pianoer!" A heavy voice called from behind Wesley, confident, carrying the unmistakable authority of a lawman.

The piano's sad tune died.

"It's pianist," said the little man, turning back in his seat to level his beady eyes at the lawman. "Pianoer ain't even a word. I'm a pianist."

"No one gives a shit, peckerhead," said the lawman. He addressed the room: "Listen, I'm a warranted officer by the Arizona Territory here on official business."

Here it comes, Wesley thought.

"We're looking for a man. Young fella, got a big pucker of a scar on his right cheek. Name's Wesley "Six Scars" Burrows. Wanted for horse theft, robbery, murder, and worse."

The dentist raised an eyebrow at Wesley. "Looks like they're *your* friends." His voice was low.

The lawman boomed again. "Anyone here seen a man like that?"

Out of the corner of his vision, Wesley saw a table of cowboys look over at him. One of them, a sun-cracked crow of a man without any sort of brotherly affection for what, as far as that son of abitch knew, was a wrongly accused man, pointed at the table where Wesley was playing.

Goddamn you.

Boots *thunked* their way toward Wesley.

He felt the gravity of their presence directly behind him. A rough hand shoved him, shocking his head forward. His hat pitched onto the mess of chips at the center of the table.

"You, gambler. Stand up. Keep those hands holding them cards while you do it."

The dentist gave Wesley an apologetic look, setting his own cards face-down on the table.

Wesley sagged in woeful resignation. He should have cut his losses and run when he had the chance. But, once again, he was undone by an absolute curse of bad timing. Three hours ago, he had had all the money he needed. He could have walked away. Almost did *twice*. But then the dentist showed up, announced himself as a high roller, and started bleeding the kid's chips. And now, just as Wesley was close to winning it back, the law had caught up with him.

The prospect of winning it all would cost him everything.

The dentist surprised Wesley—hell, surprised everyone—when he spoke up: "Gentlemen, if you don't mind, we're just finishing up here."

A Red Winter in the West

"Game's over," the man barked. "I said stand up, boy."

The saloon hummed to life with the mumblings of the patrons urging Wesley to obey, the bartender going so far as to say, "Go on now, boy. This here is a law-abiding business!"

It was with a delicate gesture that the dentist quieted the room. His eyes, almost glowing, seemed to reach out in a way that Wesley could not understand, but could feel. It was an invisible pressure, an eerie weight.

"Officers," the dentist said, smiling. "With all due respect, allow us the small courtesy of finishing our business."

A floorboard groaned under the shifting weight of one of the law men, cutting through the tense silence in the room. "This boy's got a debt with the law, mister."

"He that dies pays all debts," said the dentist. He turned to look at Wesley. "That's Shakespeare, Wesley."

"I know," said Wesley. "*The Tempest.*"

The dentist nodded approvingly, his smile shone bright. The invisible pressure lifted momentarily. "An educated man. Well." Then, he looked again to the officers. His eyes widened, and the weight returned, heavier than before.

"It's a crime to impede an appointed officer of the La—"

The dentist lifted a single finger and gently pressed it against his lips. He shushed the lawman like a mother soothing a squalling child. "Now, Wesley," he said. "You're all in, and I've called."

Wesley's mouth was dry. His heart hammered in his chest. He wasn't sure he wanted to win anymore. But what Wesley Burrows wanted didn't seem to matter much at the moment; he was compelled to do what the man required. The dentist's voice and eyes penetrated Wesley's will.

Wesley thumbed his trio of jacks and pair of sixes down onto the table, face-up. "F-Full house."

"Now," said the dentist as he glanced at his own cards with a solemn nod. "If you would be so kind…"

Wesley reached over and flipped over the dentist's hand.

It was a flush.

A straight goddamn flush.

"L-Looks like you win, mister," said Wesley.

"All right, game's over," the lawman said. "Get up, kid." There was a tremor in the lawman's voice. He reached for Wesley all the same.

The dentist spoke, a killer's confidence in his voice, his big cat-like eyes pinned on the lawmen. "Stay right there, Wesley."

Wesley obeyed the dentist.

All fed up with the dentist's impudence, the lawman closest to Wesley went to skin his gun from his leather. "I said get up, you skinny son of a—"

What happened next seemed to happen slowly, slow as a noon-day dream. The liquid of time thickened.

A group of cowboys sitting at a table across the room scrambled from their seats, sending the cardtable clattering to the floor before the oncoming gunfight. A spray of poker chips, red and blue and white, filled the space between three flipping beer mugs spilling their foamy yellow innards into the open air.

He heard the swift *click-click-click* of the lawman's hammer draw back, priming to fall and unleash killing thunder. Wesley squished his eyes shut and lifted his hands to cover his ears.

"Be still," said the dentist.

The world obeyed.

A trio of mugs shattered on the wooden floor. The poker chips splattered in the river of glass and beer. The sound broke

A Red Winter in the West

Wesley's nerves, and he let out a whimpering yelp. But there was no gunfire.

The room was silent.

After a moment, Wesley opened one eye. The world blurred back into view. He turned to the lawman behind him. The man was completely motionless, still as a statue. Except for his eyes. The man's irises were wide, ballooned into black pools, frantically shifting back and forth. Left and right, maddened with panic.

The other lawman, unmoving save for his fingers twitching just an inch above his revolver, let out a low, strained groan. The veins in his weathered hand bulged from the struggle taking place between his mind and his body. The bartender, the cowboys across the room, even the working girls and boys, all of them were frozen.

Everyone except the dentist.

He leaned back in his chair, a look of annoyed consideration on his face. He picked up a silver dollar from the mess of chips, and when he did, the most peculiar thing began to happen. Where the man's flesh touched the metal coin, tiny drifts of smoke began to rise. It gave off an acrid smell—the sickly sweet aroma of cooking meat.

He sighed.

"What to do, Wesley," he said, displeased. "What. To. Do."

"Wh-what did you do to them? Why are they…why are they like that?"

The man waved away the question. "How old are you, Wesley Burrows?"

Wesley's face twisted at the question. "Huh?"

"How old," each word was slowly paced out, "are you?"

"I…I dunno. No one ever told me."

The dentist clicked his tongue. "What a shame," he said. "People say that age is just a number. They've said it as long as I can remember. It's said plainly enough in English, rudely in Greek, more eloquently in French. It's said in other languages too, ones you've never even heard of." The man leaned forward, moonlight slanted against his eyes. "They're wrong. Age is more than that. I know that as a truth, Wesley. You see, I am very, very old. Old enough to know just how young you are. So young and so afraid. So young you don't even realize the depth of your current peril."

A thought clutched Wesley's mind, the choking grip of fear. A dark epiphany that sent a rail of ice down his spine. "You're the Devil," he said.

The dentist had a laugh at that, a slender, joyless sound.

"Oh my God," said Wesley. "You are. You're the Devil and you've come to take me to Hell." He began to breathe rapidly, each inhalation a stuttering wheeze. "I don't want to be in Hell! I want to—"

"Shh, Wesley. Calm yourself. You do not need to fear the Devil. I have lived lifetime upon lifetime, and never once have I spied Satan's form or anything that might be considered his work. I don't think he even exists."

Wesley's lips began to tremble. "Then who—who are you?"

The man tossed the smoldering coin back into the mess of chips. The flesh of his fingers was charred black, still smoking, but he took no notice. He tilted his head. "My name is Sigurd, Wesley. Sigurd of Antioch. When I was like you…" He paused. "Well, to tell you the truth, I have never been like you, but I was once a man, such as you hope to be. A king at thirteen, I ruled a battle-hardened people with my brother kings, and we made such war together. Cutting a red line through our enemies, I was a terror such as the world had never seen. Until one day, while in a far-off city now lost to time, I met a truer king than I. A king who ruled over not just a kingdom, but over life

A Red Winter in the West

itself. I have witnessed the rise and fall of countless empires as the most able soldier in an endless army. A force irrepressible that reaved and conquered. I loved only ever one woman—a timeless beauty. Her name was Abella. Three years ago, she was taken from me."

Sigurd's perfect teeth clenched, and he spoke through them with an old anger. "Three years is less than a yesterday to me, Wesley. So you must understand that my heart is still freshly wounded. The passing of time, to the timeless, offers no comfort to grief."

The man's eyes were everything now, glowing like emeralds set in a porcelain bust. There was a weight to them, a gravity pulling Wesley closer and closer.

Wesley swallowed. He tried to think of some response, something he might say to get out of the shadow of the manlike creature before him.

"Are you guilty of the crimes these men announced, Wesley? Do not lie to me. I will know if you do."

Though the room was silent and still, inside Wesley's mind a bell of alarm was clanging. Over and over, red and loud and furious. He could move…perhaps he was quick enough to go for his gun. He didn't do that, however; for some unknown reason, he was compelled to answer. "I am."

"You are," Sigurd said. "When I walked into this saloon tonight, I saw you and I knew you were a guilty man. But I believe in mercy. I believe that all guilty men should have a chance at redemption. A chance to rise above their station and cling to a higher purpose. I have a choice to make, Wesley, and it can only be made after you make a choice of your own."

Sigurd winked.

From out of the quiet stillness, the pianist suddenly brought the instrument back to life. He played a slow, melancholy tune.

"I could let these innocent lawmen do their duty. Allow them to take you in and give human justice to those you wronged. And that justice would see you hang at the end of a rope. Your suffering would be their reward."

"I don't want to die," said Wesley.

"He who dies—" Sigurd said, one finger lifted into the air.

"Pays all debts," Wesley finished.

"I can save you from this debt, Wesley. All mortal debts. If you will choose to come with me."

"I don't understand." His voice felt so far away, a distant sound.

"None of you do. And due to that ignorance, many of us hold a deep swell of pity for you."

"Who—?" He was unable to finish the whole question.

"The people of the kingdom." Sigurd rose. He was so tall that it seemed to Wesley as if he were unfurling out of the chair. "Be my friend, Wesley. Come with me to Abilene. There we will confront those who killed the woman I loved—the people who tried to kill me when I demanded justice of my own."

Wesley was drowning in the deep ocean of Sigurd's eyes.

"I—"

"You," said Sigurd.

Wesley felt only one sensation in Sigurd's embrace. "I'm afraid."

His eyes felt so heavy.

Sigurd approached. "Naturally." His pale lips brushed Wesley's ear. "The best safety lies in fear." From behind his great form came a billowing curtain of fog swirling into reality. Sigurd's skin grew paler, brighter than before.

"Embrace me," said Sigurd. "Leave these mortal woes behind, at only the small price of a life already forfeit to these...these cattle."

A Red Winter in the West

Wesley looked at the frantic, terrified eyes of the lawman, still frozen. He turned back to Sigurd, who stood like a creature of myth, now fully revealed in his dark glory.

Wesley stepped into the cold comfort of Sigurd's shadow. "Are you going to hurt me?" His voice was small, almost child-like.

"Yes," Sigurd said, curling a pale, graceful hand over Wesley's shoulder.

"Will I die?"

"Only once and never again. Will you come with me, Wesley? Will you be a friend to me?"

There was only one answer, no choice.

Wesley spoke a word.

Sigurd became a blur.

Pain like nothing Wesley had ever known before swallowed the light of the saloon.

The world dimmed.

Wesley fell into darkness.

Part I

THE SURVIVORS

"*The Nine are not like the false gods of fire and war and covenants measured across the ages. Time cannot mark them, but their imminent return shall indeed mark the time.*"

—Principe of the Society of Prometheus,
Lucio Gandolfi, *Illimitable Primacy*

Chapter One

LUBBOCK, TEXAS

EVERY NIGHT IN his dreams, Orrin Adolphus watched the monster kill his mother and father. The dream was always the same. An event playing over and over in sleep with the same punishing clarity as it had in waking life. He saw the bristling hide, the flashing claws, and the wide lupine smile.

He saw the haunches and shoulders rising and falling, muscles rippling like a fierce wind on dark water. The creature circled them with a predatory gait in careful anticipation. The attack so quick, so absolute in its finality. His mother's head was torn from her shoulders with a single snarling bite. The stump of her neck sprayed blood along the yellow wallpaper, walnut floor, and Orrin's white dress shirt, transforming the colors of home, boy, and world to red.

Of all the many voices he heard screaming, it was the wild keening of his father that he remembered most vividly. The boom of the shotgun was clear, too. So was the flesh of the creature absorbing the gun's volley, shivering at the impact, bloodless. The creature's claws unfurled in a looping swipe, taking his father at the waist. The spray, like scarlet curtains caught in a whirlwind, splattered against him. Blood wetted Orrin's face, tasted hot and bitter in his mouth. It stung his eyes, half-blinding him. Blood. Blood everywhere. Bloody light and a dark, growling shadow.

A braver boy, Orrin thought, would have picked up the shotgun. He wanted to do just that.

As in life, Orrin was not brave in the dream. Terror seized him. Possessed him.

The beast, savoring its fresh kill, turned its back on him, unafraid. It leaned over the destroyed bodies, sniffing first, then eating. Crushing bone and flesh, it tore away his mother's arm and swallowed it one huge mouthful. Next to her, his father's flat eyes, flecked with blood, stared up at the ceiling, never to blink again. The bodies, shredded of its animus, laying on the Adolphus parlor carpet where the beast slowly consumed them.

The carpet had been a gift. His father had it shipped in from New York, Orrin remembered the strong cowboys bringing it into the house and his mother's elation at the sight of it being rolled over the freshly polished wooden floor. The carpet, all black and cream with golden tulips stitched into the fabric, hadn't rolled out flat at first, its edges curling up. Though the carpet's initial unveiling hadn't been perfect, the happy sound it had produced from his mother had been. For all of his years, no matter how long he lived, Orrin would never forget that sound. Now, in the dream, that cream-colored curl of fabric reminded him of the lazy furl of skin peeled away from his father's ribs. Orrin would never forget that either.

Without fear of the boy, the creature ate.

Orrin watched, motionless, as the beast lifted its head from the meal and slowly, so very slowly, turned its gaze to him. And with one cold black eye, it took the very measure of him. Blood dripped from

A Red Winter in the West

the great muzzle. A wet gray tongue snaked out from behind shining teeth, licking the snout. Big and black, like orbs of starless night, the eye weighed him. There was a total confidence there, a complete knowledge of the child's incapability to conjure a threat.

Gunfire peppered the air outside. At this, the beast dipped, surprised. These were the first sounds to interrupt the wails of those being massacred in the street. People were finally fighting back, shooting at the pack of beasts with their pistols and rifles and shotguns.

The beast leaped toward Orrin, unfurling those massive paws and the razor-edged nails. There was nothing he could do. Nowhere to go. He was a coward, frozen. But the beast's trajectory changed. It was headed not directly for him but for the window next to him.

It plunged through the pane, shattering the glass, but its back haunches caught the wall and kicked out, thrashing wildly. A claw, long as a boot knife and sharper than honed steel, caught Orrin, slashing his shoulder. It ran a hot, red line from collarbone to forearm. With a second kick, the other leg splayed out, the barbed claw caught him in the face.

It was in that moment, for the first time in his life, Orrin knew he was hurt. Not the hurt of childhood bump or a bruise. This was the adult kind of pain. The kind people died from.

It was Orrin's turn to scream and bleed.

The pain somehow woke him from his terror, and he ran, leaping over the bloody piles on the parlor floor, out the back door, out of the house. Out into whipping storm billowing over the sky above the shadowy dunes of Yellow Hill. Orrin plunged into the onslaught of unnatural cold and cutting wind.

His feet were swift, and they carried him for a long time. He plunged himself against the dunes, away from the screams and gunfire and howling terror. Away from the carnage and the bodies.

Under a white sun, up and down the rolling hills, he scrambled, keening like a maniac. Half-crawling up their sheer faces, fingers clawing the sand. He came to a dune top, where he tumbled over his feet. The grit of the desert filled his wounds, and when he tried to wipe it away from his face, he realized that he could only see out of one eye. But still, he ran.

After a while, all the sounds were his. The wounded groans and the wheezing, the ragged breathing that vented vapor from his lungs. Then something built up inside of him, something terrified and loud. Orrin began to scream. Screamed and screamed, ran and ran, until his throat was raw and tired, and his legs could carry him no more.

How far had he gone?

Stumbling to the top of what he knew would be the final hill he would ever climb, Orrin looked around and saw nothing but the cold and desolate landscape of the Texas desert. His shirt and trousers were drenched in blood. Red and wet, caked with sand. The whole world was bathed crimson, everywhere except the place he tried not to look.

But Orrin did look. Finally.

It was only a sideways glance, but he saw the bone. The yellow line of bone peeping out between the split drapery of flesh down his arm.

He shut his eyes, overwhelmed. He wailed. He cried as only a child can announce a wound in hopes that parent will hear and come to heal. But there was no one to hear his cries. There would never be anyone again.

Never again would his mother calm him with a gentle stroke on his brow. Nor would he ever feel the soft, strong hand of his father cup his neck and pull him close, wrapping him into that safe familiar place where he could hear the steady paternal heartbeat.

A Red Winter in the West

Orrin was going to die among the mesquites and skeletal remains of rolling tumbleweeds. He shivered, clutching his ruined arm in agony, and fell to his knees. He was so tired, more tired than he could ever remember being. And sleepy. He wasn't sure why, but he wanted nothing more than to lay down to rest. But the cold was coming in with the falling night, and there was a deeper, more painful chill throbbing from where the creature had hurt him.

He realized he would never see Annie again. That pain, not the wound running down the length of his arm, hurt him the most.

Orrin faced the sunset, and he could hear the beasts coming up behind him. He could hear their thudding footfalls coming up the dune. They would tear him wide and bloody, stuffing their snouts in his guts.

They would eat him.

And he would face them, he told himself. He would, with his dying action, fall with courage enough to look upon the tremendous jaws and predatory eyes. He would face them as his father had faced them.

Orrin clenched the fist of his left hand and closed his eyes, but he rose and turned nonetheless. He heard their panting and their impossible speed chewing up the side of the dune on their way to rip him apart.

And as with every night in his dreams, he opened his eyes to see the wide open mouth that would swallow him whole.

Orrin flew up out of the nightmare, his consciousness shot out of a cannon. His shirt was damp with sweat. His cheeks burned from crying.

He slowed his breathing. Allowed reality to cradle him. He looked down at the itchy void where his right arm should have been. There was nothing but the pale stump where the bone saw had removed rotted flesh. Orrin wiped his brow and pulled his knees up to his chest. His eyes adjusted to the dusky lamplight spilling over his bed from across the room.

There, a scarecrow of a man leaned over the desk, well-lit in golden lamplight. His long stringy hair hung over his face like moss draped over an old sagging tree limb. The man dipped his pen into an inkwell, then slid the nib against its rim. He spoke without looking up. "I have often wondered at the utility of nightmares and dreams. What purpose they must serve the human brain. If they might be harnessed for our improvement. It remains a mystery." Professor Bass's voice was like a summer rainstorm: warm and persistent. He continued scribbling into a large leather volume. "I surmise it was the same this time as before?"

"Yes, sir."

"No changes?"

Orrin rubbed his tired face. "Don't think so."

"My accounting shows this is the third time this week. By that, we can take some small encouragement in the measure of change. They are becoming less frequent." Again, the golden nib of the quill went into the ink, scraped the side of the well, and then returned to the page with practiced rapidity.

"I should have done something," Orrin said.

"Hmm."

Orrin looked out the window. The moon's bright, reaching light comforted him. "There was another shell in the gun. When the beast turned its back—"

"Will you again punish yourself with the useless hypothetical?"

A Red Winter in the West

"I'm only saying that I could have done…done *something*."

"You did."

"I ran."

The grinding of the Professor's pen suddenly ceased. "No." He turned to face Orrin. His bright blue-green eyes shone like polished dimes through the golden rims of his spectacles. "You *survived*. Survived where many did not."

"If—"

"Not if," the Professor said, shaking his head slowly, speaking with a voice that always seemed to illuminate some dark corner of the world. "You are here, in the now, able to carry on. Move forward. The 'if' is the interrogative tool of the heart, not the mind. *Our* interrogatives are the what, the why, the how. And in this way, we are the lucky ones. Lucky that we might continue the greatest of all human endeavors."

Orrin's lip trembled. "To question."

The professor's lips pressed into a grin. "To find the answers in the service of all humankind. And so, my boy…"

"We persist," said Orrin.

The mantra was one of Professor Bass's favorites. During his time as the Professor's assistant, Orrin had adopted this saying, among many others. It had become a favorite of Orrin's too.

The professor shifted his weight in his chair, the angles of his figure cutting a hard line against the light. He clasped his hands in his lap, leaned forward. "In asking these questions, we quiet the loud ignorant thoughts that only distract," he said emphatically. "I do not know why your nightmares continue these three years gone, my boy. But, I believe, very firmly, that in embracing the questions with measurable answers, you can navigate their extreme disquiet. The only questions that go unanswered are the ones we refuse to ask."

The professor's long fingers coiled around one another like battling serpents. "So, let us continue to ask the questions we can answer. Solve the problems that, at present, seem unsolvable." He relaxed against the chair.

Orrin searched the spaces of the Professor's words in his mind. "What are you writing?" he asked.

The professor smiled and gave him a wink. "An answer."

"What's the question?"

"Ever the apt pupil. But this answer is for Judge Ellison and his agents, and not for tonight. We will confirm the research tomorrow, then post our letter before the mail leaves the station. Now, rest. Tomorrow is filled with many questions that need our attention."

"Yes, sir." Orrin peeled off the damp sleeping shirt, daring the unnatural July chill. He pulled the blanket up over his shoulder. It did not take long for him to fall asleep.

Before he did, he hoped to dream this time of Annie Miller.

Chapter Two

NEAR FORT STOCKTON, TEXAS

IT WAS THE middle of the afternoon, but there was little light. The howling blizzard stole the sun, unfurling a blanket of white that swallowed the horizon and the sky and all in between. Annie Miller tried to sink deeper into her coat. Not to be put off, the winter chill slid its thin fingers into every slender gap of her clothes. Just ahead of the snow-powdered remuda, a passel of twenty-five chuffing horses, Annie spied the outline of Boss Quinn. Tall and unwavering in the saddle, the drive boss rode at the front of the herd. Quinn, stubborn as the unchanging weather, trudged forward. He never wavered in direction or the certainty of his navigation.

The storm cut in from the east, relentless. Only a few days ago, they had passed through the Cap Rock. Had the winter storm come pounding then, they would have sought refuge among the narrow passages of sun-bleached caliche. Here, near Fort Stockton, there were no trees to protect them from the icy blow. No valleys to trundle into for protection. The wind was a razor, and the cold it carried bit down like a ravenous wolf. Only Boss Quinn's steadfastness and his irrepressible will shoved them onward.

The mass of cows crunched along the frost-tipped grasses. Annie watched as, on the far side of them, Percy Walker rode over from the point position toward Boss Quinn.

Annie swiveled in the saddle, looking back at the other ranch hands riding in the swing and flank. Most of the other riders were vague outlines. At the rear, however, she could clearly make out the wide, lumpy outline of Dutch. The big German was pounding along on his dark brown drafting horse. The wind toppled his tattered, black bowler from his head. Dutch, fast for a man his size, was quick enough to catch the hat before the storm claimed it.

Annie shook her head at the absurdity of the situation. This kind of storm made sense for January, maybe February. But it was July.

July in Texas.

Things weren't supposed to be this way.

For three years, winter had taken root in Texas, spreading out like a plague that was slowly crept into the surrounding territories.

Folks around the country had their guess as to why the cold remained. Annie was one of only four living souls who knew exactly where the winter came from. One of the few people alive who, if someone got her drunk enough, could have told them about the storm that formed over Yellow Hill. The unnatural cloud that brought the cold and the shadow, a tempest that carried in its wide, gray span something more than frozen rain and blinding snow.

Annie reached deep into the saddlebag draped across the mare. The horse moved forward but turned its head to spy on her rider with one eye.

"No," said Annie. The cold made the word a ghost. "The apples are probably hard as a rock anyway. You wanna break a tooth out here, girl?"

A Red Winter in the West

Vanilla shook her head and let out a chuff of dissatisfaction. The long mane trailing down the Appaloosa's neck whipped at Annie's gloved hands. Steam vented from the horse's nose in two vaporous clouds.

"You're so dang spoiled," Annie teased.

The prancing clatter of Percy Walker's brown American gelding came into earshot before Annie looked up to see them. Over his shoulder, the swirling snow stampeding toward them. The storm was getting worse.

Percy hollered over the howling wind, a red bandanna covering his mouth fluttered about his chin.. His green, almond-shaped eyes looked like lichen-covered stones shining up from the bottom of a clear riverbed.

"Boss wants you to loose the remuda to me. Needs you to ride ahead to the fort with the German kid and tell the Lieutenant Colonel to have hands ready at the barn. If this cold dips any further, we're gonna have to run 'em the rest of the way."

Annie squinted hard against the edge of the wind as she looked back at Dutch. His bowler was gone. The creases of his thick forehead already turning red as if he'd taken lashes from a whip. The hat was lost, and he did not look pleased traveling without it.

"I don't figure his horse is gonna be able to keep up with mine," said Annie.

Percy made a fist and jabbed a thumb behind him toward the figure of Boss Quinn. "Boss reckons you're one of the few who won't get lost on the way, but we ain't sending you alone. Dutch ain't got so much experience working the drive that we can't afford to send him with you."

Annie rolled her eyes. "That's bullshit and you know it. He's sending me with Dutch because I'm a girl and because Dutch is big."

Percy's eyes crinkled. His mouth was hidden behind the bandanna, but she could tell he was smiling. "Boss considered that too.. He also said he wants you to open the bidding for the beef. Believes you to be a shrewd trader."

"I think—"

"Annie." Percy's tone lost its friendliness. "You're the best person for the task. Now, we need you to kick for the fort and in a damn hurry. If you spot any force or situation hostile, turn back to us. If you have an opinion to be voiced with Boss about how you feel you're being treated, you'll get your chance after the cows are settled. When none of us are at peril of freezing to death."

She hated being cut off. If it weren't for the blizzard, she'd have taken the issue up with Quinn right then and there. Percy made a valid point, though, so she nodded.

"I'll get Dutch," she said.

"Annie." Percy reached over and stroked Vanilla's mane. "Be careful, huh?"

"What do I have to be afraid of," said Annie as she reined Vanilla out of Percy's reach. "I'll have a big strong man to take care of me."

"Now godda—"

Annie squeezed Vanilla with her thighs and trotted away from him.

She brought herself alongside the sulking, hatless German. Without stopping, she popped Dutch on the shoulder as she circled him.

"Come on," said Annie. "You're with me."

"Where to?" Dutch's voice was a low sound that droned out of his nose.

"To the place where fortunes are made and all dreams come true."

Dutch gave her a puzzled look as she circled him again. "San Francisco?"

A Red Winter in the West

"No, my friend. To the great enterprising metropolis known as Fort Stockton!"

"What about the flank? I don't want Boss yelling at me again for leaving the flank."

"Percy's got it." She slowed Vanilla a bit. "Now, come on. Time is a factor!" She was ready to give Vanilla a squeeze, to open her up and let the veteran Appaloosa thunder past Boss Quinn.

"Hold on, now," Dutch furrowed his brow.

Annie huffed, pulling back. "Dutch—"

"They told me, they said, 'Dutch, don't you leave this flank like you did near Odessa,' and I didn't forget it."

Annie rolled her eyes and let out a deep sigh. She pulled Vanilla to a walk. "It's Percy and Boss that told me, Dutch! The flank will be fine with Percy watching it. Now come—"

"Percy's with the horses. How's he gonna watch both at the same time?"

"Dadburnit, Dutch. Can you please just come on with me? Now, please!"

Dutch slowly took in the scene, his big blue eyes scanning the white expanse all around them, the herd, and Mr. Percy with the remuda. He leaned a squinting eye at Annie, mockingly curious. "Where we goin' again?"

"Are you *serious*?"

Dutch's mouth curled into a big, horse-toothed grin.

He was teasing her.

Dutch gave his big horse a kick and playfully slapped Annie on the shoulder. She was sure he didn't mean for it to hurt as much as it did, but the German's hands were thick with muscle and hard as mule bone.

They trotted together side-by-side. Their ponies cut through the powder.

"I got your goat," he said, his smile unwavering.

"You know," said Annie, "it'd be a shame if some tragedy befell you on our way to the fort."

"Is that a threat?"

"All I'm saying, Dutchy"—he hated when she called him that—"it's dangerous country. Perilous even. Accidents happen all the time."

Dutch looked over at her, his cold, reddened face mashed to a squint. "Whatever happened to make you so dang mean?"

"Lots of things," she said. "And meeting you was the worst of it."

They laughed despite the cold and shared a wave back at Boss Quinn as they pushed into the blanket of white, heading southwest toward the fort.

Chapter Three

NEW MEXICO

CARSON PTOLEMY SAT astride his gelding Abraham, looking at the long skinny hand of the pocket watch. How quickly such a small mechanism made the past a measurable thing. So long as he watched that little hand move, he was living in the present. Second by second. He didn't have to think of what had happened or what was to come. Only the moment mattered. This moment especially.

He looked up from the watch, over the edge of the cliff. His eyes traced down to the parallel iron rails bisected by timbers reaching as far east as there was an east, and westward, too.

Abraham stamped impatiently.

"It's coming, boy. Should be along any minute."

He checked the shells in his converted LeMat.

Far away, a shrieking whistle cut the air.

Carson holstered the revolver and looked west to the canyon valley where two great walls of limestone rose high above the rail line. A tendril of smoke climbed above the gap.

The timing would have to be perfect. There wouldn't be another chance. He and Abraham had practiced the descent down the embankment for the last two days. Now it was time to put practice to use.

Another steamy blast, another mechanical howl. Both closer this time. The train would come roaring out of the canyon but would have to let off steam before reaching the wide arc of the bridge. Carson needed to be on board before the ground gave way to the dark, rushing torrent of the Rio Grande.

The locomotive roared out of the canyon. Painted black as night, screaming like a behemoth straight out of Hell.

He gave Abraham a squeeze, and the gelding perilously bounded down rocky soil. He leaned back, trusting the horse to do the navigating. They hit the ground at the bottom of the embankment at a full gallop.

Abraham half-stumbled, stuttering his gait.

With one false step, the train threatened to thunder past them.

There was no need to kick or spur. Abraham opened up full speed. The horse raced against the power of the infernal machine, not needing to win, just to keep the contest close.

The shades were drawn over the car windows to protect from the prying light of the July winter sun. The wheels rolled over and over with a loud, undeniable momentum. But the horse and his rider leaned in close, close enough so the man could reach for the railing of the caboose.

Carson reached out, took hold of the rail.

His gloved hand slipped on the rail's slick surface, sliding along the frost-rimmed brass. Almost tumbling out of the saddle, he pulled himself back up to full height and posted high.

"Come on now! Come on, boy!"

A Red Winter in the West

The clopping percussion underneath them intensified as the gelding stormed forward. Carson threw a leg over to ride sidesaddle, where he struggled to balance amid the jostling pace. He groped again, this time throwing both hands at the rail in an all-or-nothing maneuver. The brass railing rebuffed his right hand, but the left found purchase.

Carson jumped.

The cold metal, slippery as an eel, threatened to send him down to the skull-splitting wheels thundering along the track. He threw his right arm between the vertical rungs of the caboose-terrace balustrade. The tips of his boots skipped and scraped against the hard ground, but he managed to pull himself over the rail.

Abraham tried hard to keep up. But even he, as resolute and faithful a mount as there ever was, could not keep pace. The horse flagging shook its head, charged full speed, still striving to win that impossible race. Carson tipped his hat to the horse, grateful. And once again, as had happened so many times in their years before, hoped it would not be their final goodbye. Abraham knew the way back to Silver City, and Carson, when he was done with his work aboard the train, would find him there.

On the door of the caboose, masterfully scrolled in silver, was a flower of flame resting at the center of a perfect circle. To the rest of the world it was nothing more than an extravagant adornment. To Carson it was assurance. A confirmation that Judge Ellison's telegram was right. This train, carrying an artifact of occult power, belonged to the Baroness, one of the head members of the Society of Prometheus.

For three years now, ever since the death of his adopted father Gilbert Ptolemy in Yellow Hill, Carson had focused the whole of his mind on destroying the members of the Society. They were willful harbingers, hopeful participants of sinister occult rituals meant to usher forth a new dark age. They worshiped beings of unknowable power, monstrosities whose sheer force of presence was enough to drive the human mind to lunacy. Carson had witnessed the lunacy for himself in the mines of Yellow Hill.

And before that, he'd witnessed it at the hands of his own father, who, unknown to Carson or to his freed slave Gilbert, had been working for the Society to bring about that terrible blight from beyond. Gilbert had saved Carson's life, and together they had joined up with Judge Ellison's Peregrine Estate, where they roamed and hunted creatures who preyed upon the natural world. But even then, the Society of Prometheus was ever on Carson's mind.

Jeremiah Hart, an insane prospector in Yellow Hill, had almost succeeded in bringing forth one of the Society's creatures. But Gilbert Ptolemy, who Carson had come to see as true father, had sacrificed his life to see Carson, and the whole world, saved from that terrible fate.

Carson slowed his breathing, despite the cold rush of wind invading his lungs. And, thinking upon everything the Society had taken from him, he drew the revolver.

His father's revolver.

Now, his own.

The Baroness would have a small contingent of armed followers. The other Prometheus members had been the same. It hadn't saved them. It wouldn't save the Baroness.

Carson put his back to the railing and kicked.

The door splintered off its latch under the weight of his boot, and he aimed his gun into the darkness. Where the light poured in, he could make out many crates lashed together. Stacked from floor to ceiling, they gave way to a narrow path. There was no one inside. At least, no one he could see.

A Red Winter in the West

He crept among the wooden crates, examining their bills of cargo, but none of them openly declared their contents. Whatever the artifact on this train was, Carson did not know. Any one of the crates might hold it. Only the Baroness knew, and that singular piece of knowledge would be the only reason he wouldn't kill her outright. There was even the possibility that she might have offloaded the cargo already.

There was only one way to find out.

He moved forward, as quietly as he could, only the ring of his spurs jingling over the hushed roar of the train's engine.

He exited the cargo car and stepped over the gap where the track raced below. There was a curtain draped over the window of the door leading to the next car.

Stupid, he thought. If the curtain had been lifted, they would have spotted him for sure. Luck prevailed this time, however, and he put his ear against the window. Over the sound of the train, he heard voices.

A few men, maybe two or three.

Then came the rising lilt a feminine voice.

Carefully. Slowly. He twisted the knob on the door.

Locked.

Carson removed his riding gloves and tucked them into his belt. He blew onto the naked flesh of his fingers to keep them warm. Each inhalation was slow, purposeful. Relaxing. In his mind, he found the eye of the storm, the calm place amid the hurricane of his anger born of his hatred for these people. The people who had stolen not one parent from him, but two. The men and women who had orchestrated death and horror on the world in the service of nightmare gods. Their agent, Jeremiah Hart, had opened a wound in the world, a tear in the fabric of reality that covered so much of the country in a pestilential cold.

Carson, feeling the heat of his breath on his skin, told himself that he would burn the Society and all its members to ash. They had wronged too many and sought to wrong more with their dark rituals and Black Manuscript. His heart slowed and slowed further still. At the center of the raging storm inside himself, he made promises to his near future self.

He would be fast.

He would be accurate.

This door, same as the caboose's, splintered under the weight of his heel. Revolver in hand, pulled so quick, so smooth from the holster. The car was illuminated by lamplight, the pale color of a moldering map, revealing a pair of guards standing at the end of the car. One man at the far end held a rifle. The gleaming brass and steel weapon slanted against his chest.

The soldier's head slapped against the wall behind him as Carson's bullet took him in the skull. The rifle in his hands went off, firing a round into the ceiling.

A woman screamed.

Before the other guard could turn his shotgun toward the broken door where Carson stood, the gunslinger shot him in the throat. His hands released the shotgun and groped desperately at the gushing wound.

On pure instinct Carson spun, putting his back against the outside wall of the rail car. A flurry of bullets splintered the doorframe. Needles of wood and the flash of lead on iron peppered all around him. Gun smoke billowed out of the aperture.

"Get to cover," a shrieking woman cried.

Carson replaced the spent cartridges.

"Who the hell was that?" A man's voice.

"Who cares, just shoot him," the woman commanded.

A Red Winter in the West

"Jesus! He shot Bill." The man's voice shook. "He's killed Pete, too!"

"And you're next," Carson said, though none could hear him. He took his hat by the back of the brim and let the lip of the cap peep just past the edge of the door.

A fresh salvo of gunfire cut the air.

Carson let the hat fly from his hand, rolled on his hip, and came up on one knee in the doorway. The man behind the diner car's bar was now visible, rifle in his hands but aimed too high to be a danger.

Carson fired again. He took no time to watch the aftermath of his aim and rolled back to safety against the doorframe.

"Ah, God," the man bellowed, wounded.

"Stop!" The woman threw her voice at Carson, commanding. She turned back to the wounded guard. "Get up, you coward."

"I..." the man grunted. "I-I think I'm dying. That son of a bitch has killed me."

"Pathetic," the woman said, malice dripping from her words. A small caliber shot spat out from within the car.

Carson replaced the spent shell as the train barreled over the wooden bridge overlooking the dark waters of the Rio Grande.

"He's dead," the woman said over the rumbling torrent of the train's engine. "I surrender."

"You the one they call the Baroness?"

"I am."

"Any other gunhands?"

"You killed two of them. I've mercifully dispatched the other."

"Answer the question."

"No! Damn you, no!"

His back planted firmly against the exterior wall of the car, Carson called to her. "Toss the guns out the window. All of 'em."

She did as he said.

"Have a seat in one of those chairs. Hands up where I can see them."

A moment passed.

"Well?" Carson asked.

"It's done."

Carson leaned his head ever so slightly into the gap, then pulled it back quickly.

No one fired at him.

He repeated the gesture, this time spying inside a little further before pulling back. He saw a woman sitting in the chair, her hands wrapped in navy satin gloves, upraised like pillars on the arms of the chair.

"I am unarmed," she said.

Carson stepped in, keeping his gun trained on her.

"We now count only ourselves among the living," she said. With a pair of navy-clad fingers, she gave a little wave, as if saying hello. "Holster your weapon, young tiger. As I said, I am unarmed."

She was a woman of severe features with dark brown hair cropped close to her skull, a boy's summer haircut. There was a suggestion of beauty to her face. A dark grace dancing in the almond brown eyes and high cheekbones.

"And now," she said, her voice cool, more relaxed. "We see if I am beset upon by thief or assassin."

Carson kept his pistol aimed at her. "Anyone else?"

"Just the two of us." She rolled her eyes over to the door. "And unless this is a runaway train, the engineer."

"Keep your hands where I can see them."

"Young, but seasoned." Her lips widened across her face, a confident smile.

"I know you, Baroness."

A Red Winter in the West

She nodded. "I know you, too, Carson Watts."

"Ptolemy," he corrected her. "Carson Ptolemy."

That seemed to amuse her. "Took the slave's name, did you?"

Carson pulled the hammer back on the revolver. "Took my *father's* name. How do you know me? We've never met before."

"Oh, now that's not true. Though I suspect you were too young to remember. You were such a little child then. Ezra's little boy. How we smiled at you in your infancy. Your father was so proud, even in his grief at the death of your mother." She wrinkled her brow at him, dismissing the memory. "Shouldn't you be off on one of Judge Ellison's errands?"

Carson grit his teeth. "Who are you? I mean really."

"My colleagues and enemies know me as Baroness. Friends and lovers know me by another name." The woman's eyes fluttered, only for the briefest of moments, slashing over to the floor behind the bar.

Carson ducked. A bullet whistled past him, blasting a hole in the roof. He whirled.

The man whom the Baroness had pretended to kill in 'mercy' lay on his belly next to the bar. He struggled to thumb back the hammer of his revolver.

Carson aimed, then fired. The bullet punched through the man's skull, snapping his head back like a mule kicking him in the face.

Something slender and sharp buried itself in Carson's shoulder. The hand holding the revolver involuntarily went slack, and pain streaked down to his fingers. The gun clattered onto the carpet.

The Baroness was on him, twisting a stiletto knife into the meat of his shoulder.

Carson grabbed her wrist, trying to pry her grip from the knife's handle. She was stronger than she looked, though. The muscles in her arms taut as piano wire.

"I'll bathe in your blood, you little welp," she promised, her breath hot on his ear.

Carson leaned his head forward then swiftly threw it back. The crown of his head smashed into the Baroness's face. He ignored the flash of pain and heard a satisfying *crunch*. The bridge of the Baroness's nose shattered on impact.

She howled, falling to her knees, but not in defeat. She scrambled for Carson's fallen LeMat.

It was clear she wasn't a seasoned fighter. Giving up the weapon in hand and the dominant position, only to reach for the gun was a crucial mistake. A mistake that Carson delighted in making her pay for. He shot his knee up from the hip. The ball of the kneecap smashed into the side of her head.

The Baroness went slack, all the fight knocked out of her.

Carson winced, looking at the knife jutting out of his shoulder. The tip of the knife was poking through his duster. He felt the warm blood pooling underneath, soaking into his shirt.

Carson wiggled his fingers. It hurt badly but he could do it. That was a good sign.

Carson took a deep breath and grabbed the knife by the simple, silver handle and pulled. It came free, sliding out wet and sharp. Wincing, he went over and grabbed a bottle of bourbon from the diner car's bar.

Carson looked at the unconscious Baroness on the ground and lifted the bottle at her in a toast. The brown liquor swirled within the glass, catching a shaft of light beaming down from the bullet hole in the roof.

"Here's to you," he said. "To you, and all of the secrets you're going to tell me."

Chapter Four

FORT STOCKTON, TEXAS

IT WAS A hard trail Annie and Dutch cut through the howling wind and blinding snow. The unforgiving weather deceived them twice over, forcing them to double back. The cold white light slipping through the storm clouds washed out the color of everything. The snowdrifts ran knee-deep, blanketing all but the thorny tops of short bestilled mesquite trees.

They rediscovered the path a second time and traveled some way. Ahead, the flickering blossoms of fire dancing in tripods outside the fort emerged from the whiteout. Annie called out over the wind, pointing, so that Dutch could see the gate too.

They kicked hard, their horses chewing up the distance. She was ready to be out of the cold and eager to prove herself a shrewd trader. Boss Quinn and Percy had made a decision in choosing her, she thought. It was a big deal to be promoted from remuda wrangler to negotiator. The older, more seasoned hands wouldn't like a woman bartering on their behalf, but Annie didn't give a tinker's damn about their feelings on the subject. Judge Ellison had hired her, and Quinn ran the show. One day she might be boss. Hell, she might even break off from the Judge, set up her own company. That's where the real money was, and the real freedom. Today would be a step in that very direction.

Riding up to the gate, Annie knew immediately that something was wrong. The flames of the tripods, whipping in the gale, showed the doors open wide. A bank of snow almost two feet high ran across the opening. It was dark inside.

She pulled Vanilla to a halt. Dutch stopped alongside her.

Annie looked up at the single guard tower of the high adobe walls, hoping to signal their arrival. The tower was vacant.

"Where is everybody?" Dutch asked.

"I don't know."

Annie scanned the area, looking for the livery stable, but the blowing white blizzard washed everything out. If it hadn't been for the flaming tripods, they might even have missed the fort itself.

"What I do know," said Annie, "is that I don't like the look of this."

"You think they abandoned it?"

Annie shook her head. "They lettered for beef two weeks ago, and I highly doubt they decided to ride out in this weather."

"Hello!" Dutch's voice boomed.

The wind stole the words.

"Aye, damn it's cold, Annie. We've got to get inside."

They made their way to the gate and dismounted their horses. As Annie led Vanilla inside, her foot hit something hard buried in the drift of snow at the entrance, tripping her. She fell into the snow, and the icy cold swallowed her up to the shoulder.

She placed her hands on the stones, pushing herself up. "Who the hell puts a bunch of rocks—"

A Red Winter in the West

Her breath caught in her throat. A pair of glassy eyes stared blankly up at her from the ground. The man's mouth was frozen open, a deep gash running from the dark, peeled-open skin of his cheek down to the open channel of his throat. The wound was so deep Annie could see his backbone.

She jerked away, cursing, and tumbled back in the snow, barking against Dutch's shins.

"Aw shit," said Dutch.

Annie scrambled to her feet and jerked her pistol free. With the tip of her boot, she began to scrape away the snow.

"Aw shit," Dutch said again.

There were six of them piled atop each other, their rifles and pistols and knives splayed out among them to reveal the aftermath of a final stand.

They were, all of them, Negro men wearing navy-blue uniforms. Their bodies were splayed open, and what was left of their innards had been ravaged. Organs torn away.

At the sight of them, Dutch turned away from Annie. The big man retched.

Annie continued pushing away the white powder until the virgin snow gave way to pink, then red. She holstered her gun and picked up one of the Henry rifles. It had been fully spent, never again to be reloaded.

Dutch ran a handkerchief across his lips. "What could have done this?"

Annie's mind flooded back to the stories of what had happened in her hometown of Yellow Hill the night she and her family escaped. The storm that ravaged the town clouded her mind. Her heartbeat climbed into her ears. They were a hundred miles from there.

"Annie?"

"I don't know, Dutch." She looked into the dark interior of the fort. There the wavy light from the tripods cast long shadows down the hallway. The wind howled through the fort's forward embrasures, only to die among the hall, leaving Dutch and Annie in heavy airless silence. Again it screamed, again it died, as if the fort itself were a wailing beast bellowing its death throes. Annie tore a sleeve from a soldier's tattered uniform, wrapped it around the stock of the rifle, and touched it to the fire on one of the tripods. The fabric caught.

"Get the horses inside," said Annie. "I'll get the doors."

Dutch pulled one of the tripods into the foyer with him, bringing in the light and the heat. Then he followed suit and made a torch for himself while Annie pulled the doors shut.

Inside now with the wind finally off their faces, Annie peered around the room. Dutch tied the horses to the huge timber beam that would have been used to brace the door.

The warmth of the torch melted the ache in Annie's face. The gun in her other hand gave her another kind of warmth.

But what the torchlight revealed stole away that confidence. There were dozens of men scattered along the hallway entrance. Their rigid bodies mapped out the landscape of a massacre.

"Hello!" Dutch called out again.

Annie jumped at the sound. She turned and booted the big man on the leg. "What are you doing?" She kept her voice low.

Dutch didn't like being kicked. "Trying to see if anyone is alive," he said, his voice a harsh whisper that echoed against the adobe.

"Yeah? And what if whatever killed these people is still here!"

"Well," he said, frustrated, "I didn't think of that! But don't be kicking me!"

A Red Winter in the West

She let out a rough sigh and angrily stabbed her chin at him. "Shh! Quinn and the herd are only a few hours behind us. We need to scout it out," she said, lowering her voice. "But real, real quiet."

Dutch shook his head. "I don't think I'd like to go poking around in all that dark."

"What if someone's still alive, huh? Wouldn't you want someone to come look for you if you were hurt and alone? Also, the herd is only a few hours behind us, we've got to make sure the fort is safe for them."

"I hollered twice a hello. Ain't no one hollered back."

"Of course not, why would they?" Annie swung an arm toward the bodies on the ground. "These men were Buffalo Soldiers, Dutch."

The big German gave her his familiar confused look.

"The war changed a lot of things, but it didn't do much to change the Texas attitude toward Black folks. Might be that one of these soldiers is hiding, worried that whoever showed up might be just as likely to finish them off as to help them."

Dutch took in a big breath, puffing his chest up to yell again.

Annie slapped a hand over his mouth. "Don't you dare do that again."

"Ow!"

"I'm going to look, Dutch. It ain't a good idea for us to split up, neither." She moved her hand away from his mouth.

His shoulders sagged in resignation. "Damn you if I get shot or stabbed or maimed in any fashion, Annie Miller."

She gave him a reassuring smile. "Big guy like you? Hell, if something is in here, it's more likely to run from you than attack. I sure as shit would."

They made their way into the dark, clutching their makeshift torches in one hand and their sidearms in the other. Making their way through the fort, they lit lamps and braziers along their path, refreshing their torches as needed. There was plenty of fabric to be shorn from the dead and a multitude of rifles that would never fire again. It took them almost an hour to trace out the fort on foot, searching the rooms and pantries. All they found were more dead soldiers. At the southern end of the fort were the officer's quarters where they discovered the Lieutenant Colonel splayed in a chair, his head leaning and his arms hanging limply at the hips.

Annie approached the body cautiously.

"Is he…like the others?" asked Dutch.

She examined the officer, finding herself gazing into his pale dead eyes flaked with snow. Looking away from the man's death mask, she spied little round hole, matted with frozen blood and singed hair, puckered at the man's temple. "Looks to be a suicide," she said. "Or an execution. Hard to tell which."

She searched the room, looking for the officer's gun while trying not to look at the pulpy mass of brains splattered on the floor.. Then she looked him over more closely. A sound of dissatisfaction escaped her throat.

"No gun," said Annie.

"So?"

"Thought maybe he came in here when the killing started, lost his nerve and—" She turned to look at Dutch and froze.

In the doorway stood a man so thin he looked half-starved, dressed in blue fatigues. His dark brown eyes, wide as boiled eggs, stared down the sight of the revolver in his hand. The gun was pointed at the back of Dutch's head.

"If you move," he said, his voice trembling, "I'll kill him."

Annie didn't hesitate. "Wait—"

He pulled back the hammer of the revolver. "Ain't a bluff. I'll do it."

A Red Winter in the West

Dutch's eyes went wide at the sound, then squished shut with the certainty he was about to die.

"Mister," said Annie, "we're a part of the company herding beef to the fort, as requested to Judge Hezekiah Ellison of Abilene. Our Boss, Mister Quinn, sent us ahead to—"

"Drop your pistols. Both of you."

Annie could see the man's revolver trembling; it was slight, but it was there. "We aren't going to hurt you. Like I said, we are—"

"Three."

"We're just—"

"Two."

Dutch's pistol clattered to the floor.

"One."

"Annie!" Dutch was terrified.

Gritting her teeth, she opened her hand. The revolver clattered to the ground.

The man, satisfied, shoved Dutch in the back, pushing him toward Annie. When the man's arm extended, an iron manacle peeked out from the navy cloth of his coat.

Dutch lumbered over to Annie, then turned and confronted his assailant. "We were looking for people to help. Not get stuck-up at gunpoint." His anger and fear mixed his tone into a strange, quaking sound. "See," he said to Annie. "This is why we should have stayed with the horses!"

"Horses," the man said. "How many horses you got?"

Annie closed her eyes and let out a deep sigh. "Two. But don't think about taking them and riding out in this mess. Mine doesn't shine to riders that aren't me, and Dutch's horse alone won't get you to the next town seeing as it's already rode down." She gave the man a considering look. "Who are you?"

The man's eyes slanted around the room. "Name is Private Amadeus Boone. I've got a way with horses." He smiled, gesturing with the gun in a waving motion. "Give me five minutes with your filly and she and I will be best friends."

Annie smiled back at him. "You're welcome to try, as far as I'm concerned. I feel obligated to tell you that the last person who tried to ride her that wasn't me got stomped to death outside a saloon. She and I are a lot alike."

"Yeah? How's that?"

"She's real sweet," Annie said, eyeing the man hard. "Right up until she ain't."

Dutch lowered his hands. "Point the gun away, huh, Boone? We aren't armed, and we won't rush. We came inside to help anyone that might be…" A thought passed over Dutch's face, like a ray of sunlight breaking through a normally overcast mind. "Wait, you know what happened here"

Boone kept the gun on them, his eyes scanning the room again. His thin jaw bulged, the lamplight glinting off his dark skin. He was searching for something to say.

"He doesn't know," said Annie. "He doesn't know because he was locked up in the stockade."

Dutch grunted a question.

"That's why he's got those manacles on his wrists." Annie nodded toward Boone.

"Shut up!" Boone jutted the gun at them again.

"Look," said Annie. "Whatever you did before all this happened, that's all gone. We don't want to hurt you, and we don't wanna get hurt. We just want to make sure that when our people arrive that they aren't gonna freeze to death like we're getting close to doing right now. So can you—"

A Red Winter in the West

"I could hear it," Boone blurted out. "But I didn't do none of this. I didn't kill anybody."

Annie nodded, listening. She kept her eyes on Boone's eyes, never letting them fall to the gun. If Boone caught her looking at that, he might assume she was about to reach for it or go for her own pistol. "No one said you did any of this. Like we said, we're just beef traders."

Boone's hand trembled harder, the gleaming cylinder of the gun barrel shaking with it. "I didn't know what the sound was at first, but I could hear the men calling out. I could hear them start scream-ing. Their guns started going off, and then—" Boone lowered the gun. He bent his head into his empty hand like a man resting after a hard day of labor. His breathing began to flutter, and, though it was terribly cold, his skin was slick with sweat.

"I heard the sound, kinda like the scream of a mountain lion and the howl of a wolf, but too big of a noise to come from either. And I could hear men shooting and dying. The horses were scream-ing too. I was in one of the cells when one of the guards came in to let me out to help with the fighting. A-a-and…" The hand holding Boone's face shook with a furious palsy, his mouth opened and he frowned as if ready to weep. "A-and, as the guard was coming to let me out, one of them came in the room…it was so, so unreal. So big."

Annie's left eye began to twitch. It couldn't be.

"It came at the guard. Just jumped on him. With one claw, it just—" Boone shook his head back and forth in the terror of remem-bering. His breath fogged in front of his face.

Annie spoke up. "What did it look like?"

Sweat dripped from his chin and the lowered gun wobbled at his side like an angry snake snatched up by the tail. "W-what?" He looked up. Fatigue masked his face. It was a mask that Annie knew. She had seen it on the face of her mother after she had confronted

Jeremiah Hart. She had seen it on Carson after Yellow Hill, when he arrived in Abilene with Vanilla at his side but without Mr. Ptolemy.

"Amadeus," she said, "what did they look like?"

He seemed to relax at the comfort of his name. "There is nothing like them on the earth, I swear. They were tall as a man and they had—you'll have to believe me on this; I know it's gonna sound—"

"Six legs." Annie's voice was flat.

Boone's eyes widened.

"Big curved claws. Mouths like this." Annie drew a circle with her finger around her head. "Teeth like fishhooks."

He looked at Annie sideways, his bottom lip trembling. He lifted the pistol and pointed it at her. "How-how do you know that?"

Dutch, confused, looked at his friend. "Annie?"

Annie's head fell.

"I know what attacked the fort," she said. "And they'll kill all of us if we stay here."

Chapter Five

ABOARD THE STEAM TRAIN *HEPHAESTUS*, RIO GRANDE

CARSON TOOK A drink. The warm, earthy burn of the bourbon delighted him. He tipped the bottle again, this time pouring the whiskey into the bloody hole in his shoulder. The grunt that left his throat was loud and angry. The storm of pain took its damn time in subsiding. To show the whiskey his displeasure, Carson threw the bottle against the mirror behind the bar. The whole of the car reflected in that glass shattered at the impact, the world inside broken into a thousand pieces.

The Baroness shot awake, her eyes blasting open from deep slumber. Her left eye was a fat black mess with a center purple as a plum. She scanned the room in a panic.

"Relax," said Carson. "This isn't the train that leads to Hell. You're not dead yet."

She pulled at the ropes knotted around her wrists and the arms of the chair. "Really? You tied me up?" she had the audacity to ask.

Carson plucked a fresh whiskey bottle and glass from behind the bar. He poured himself a drink. "You lied to me, then stabbed me in the back." He lifted the glass to her and gave her a wink. "To new friendships."

"You killed my men."

Carson took the whiskey in full, one hard swallow. He let out a deep satisfied sigh. "They shot at me. I shot back. It was self-defense."

"You shot first."

"Call it…premeditated self-defense, then." He poured again.

He kept his eyes on the whiskey, focusing on the tiny caramel-colored waterfall filling the glass.

The Baroness resigned herself, slouching back in the chair. "So what now?"

"Right now, I drink." He sipped, savoring it this time.

"And then?" she asked impatiently.

"Trust me," he said, leaning against the bar. "You don't wanna rush your way to the end of this story. Enjoy the moment, because it only gets worse from here. Relax. Have some of my bourbon."

"That's *my* bourbon." She frowned at him.

Carson took another sip, then raised the glass in a feigned toast. "You have excellent taste in whiskey. Many thanks." Tilting his head back, he finished what was left. He wiped his mouth with his sleeve, eyeing her. "Your taste in guards, however, leaves something to be desired."

She smiled. "When it comes to whiskey, I prefer quality. Hired guns"—she cocked an eyebrow—"those I buy by the barrel."

"I would say you should get your money back, but I doubt whoever brought these men into your employ would take back damaged goods."

"Look at you," she said, a whisper of marvel in her voice. "Look how tall you are now. You've got your father's build, but your time with the slave put a little meat on you. You look just like Ezra. Sound like him, too."

Carson's grip tightened on the whiskey glass. "While you were napping, I instructed your engineer to keep us headed for Chicago. That will give us plenty of time to chat. Plenty of time for you to answer the questions I've been wanting to ask one of you Prometheus members for a long, long time."

The Baroness tilted her chin upward in regal defiance. "And if I refuse?"

Carson reached into the breast pocket of his coat and produced a leather bindle rolled into a cylinder. Two leather straps, knotted at the center, bound it shut. "That would force me to use what's in here." He set the bindle on the bar in clear sight.

"Torture, is it? I don't think Judge Ellison would approve. I'm intrigued, though."

The storm of anger inside him began to swell again. But he only shook his head. "We're days from Chicago. I can make it last that long. Longer even. By the end of it, I'm going to get what I want, either from you or from your friends at the end of the line. Now," he said, pushing away from the bar, "I'm gonna tidy up the dead. You just sit there and remember all the things a person can lose and still have the faculties to talk."

The Baroness lifted one dark eyebrow at him. "You're right," she said confidently. "It's a long way to Chicago, and no matter what happens from here to there, it will certainly be the end of the line for one of us."

Carson turned and let her see the burning anger ensconced in his eyes. His was not the anger of a child stewing in the morass of sorrow. No, over the last three years since he'd killed Jeremiah Hart, Carson's rage, like the bourbon he'd drank, had aged. Matured.

"You don't scare me, boy," the Baroness said. "Not you, your bullets or your little billfold. I am a member of a courageous people. An unyielding people who will see the world changed the whole over. And not you or your traitor Judge or his many agents can stop that. A gate is open; Hart saw to that. And though you buried it in that mine, even now the cold is seeping into the world. With it comes an unfathomable multitude of glories older than Earth or time. Torturing me won't stop that."

Carson's expression did not change. "That's what Tanzer said." He smiled. "And Barron. And the Martin brothers. The more little pieces I took, the bigger the truths they let go of, leading me right to you. To your *Hephaestus*."

Some of the Baroness's confidence seemed to wilt. Her tall shoulders sagged.

Carson went over to one of the dead guards and hoisted the man's body onto his shoulder. He carried it back toward the cargo car, halting for a moment in front of the Baroness. "But you go on and make your speeches. They did too. And it seemed to comfort them... before I got started." Then he walked on into the cargo car.

He shut the door behind him and threw the dead man's body down. It slapped the ground like a wet flour sack, cold and lifeless.

Breathe. He just needed to breathe. The whiskey was meant to dull his senses, not bring them rushing to the forefront. But the Baroness had gotten to him with the talk of his father. What had she meant by saying the 'traitorous judge'?

He took a deep breath. Held it in.

The exhalation was long and slow.

He looked at the dead man at his feet. The man's head was bent at a sharp uncomfortable angle. Part of Carson wanted to adjust it, see the man laid in a more accommodating position; the other part

A Red Winter in the West

of him, the part vying for dominion inside him, told him to do something else.

And so, without making a sound with his lips, Carson screamed inside his mind and lifted his boot. He stomped the man's head, over and over, gritting his teeth in the quiet dark of the rocking crates. Carson stamped with the rage built up by having lost two fathers to the Society of Prometheus. Lost his chance at a normal childhood. Lost a portion of himself to the reading of the Black Manuscript. He had lost and lost and lost. And there is only so much a young, innocent heart can endure before the righteous want for justice becomes a furious want for wrath.

Carson stopped and looked at what remained. He shook his head and thought of what his father would have said at the sight. Then he cradled his head in his hands, his face hot on his clammy palms. "What am I doing?"

No one answered.

The back of his neck was boiling, and he was exhausted. It was the whiskey, he told himself. The drink and the wild exchange of gunfire. That, along with the Baroness's words, that's what had gotten to him, made him act the way that he did. He tried to believe it but he knew it wasn't true.

What had happened with Tanzer and Barron, those had been mistakes. This was the idea he comforted himself with anyway. Tanzer had pulled a derringer, so that was at least self-defense, but Barron…Barron had tried to surrender.

But the Martin brothers… Carson couldn't deny, that was a straight ambush. He never gave them a chance to say anything. The shotgun he brought into their room while they slept did all the talking: a booming volley of two barrels punching through the dead of night.

And now he was here, rolling in a long black train on the way to Chicago, where he would finally discover the beating heart of the Society of Prometheus. This would be his chance to rip their influence out of the Americas. Make them pay for all the wrong they'd thrust upon his life.

He took in another deep, calming breath. He brought the pocket square up to wipe his brow, and he saw that the white linen was covered in blood. He dropped it, letting it flutter to the ground like a wounded dove. it landed tenderly on the mashed ruin of the dead man's face. He stepped over the body and went into the diner car where the Baroness sat, displeased.

She had obviously been thinking over his words.

"Why are you doing this?" she asked. "Don't you see we're just trying to make the world as it should be? To restore the natural hierarchy?"

Carson walked past her, wordless.

He picked up one of the last two dead guards and carried him past her into the cargo car. Then, as the Baroness asked him more questions that he did not answer, he retrieved the final guard and stacked the body on top of the other two. He shut the cargo car door and went back to the bar. His hands were steady, his nerves turgid.

"I could tell you. The truth of all of it," she said. "Ezra taught you to read the symbols. You've seen but a glimpse of what I have seen, Carson. In the pages of the manuscript, I've seen a world restored. A globe unified under one banner. All things wasteful laid asunder and all useful works promoted in the worship of the timeless and undying. The gate of Alitranz was just the beginning. There is so much more waiting behind the veil, so much more for the cold to cleanse."

A Red Winter in the West

Carson tilted his head toward her, keeping his expression flat. He nodded. "Okay, Baroness," he said. "Tell me."

The woman's coy, confident smile returned. A woman holding a secret. "A truth for a truth. I'll tell you our story. But I'll hear yours first."

Chapter Six

ABILENE, TEXAS

TABITHA MILLER WALKED down the main street of Abilene on a cold, bright day, hand in hand with Judge Hezekiah Ellison. Their courtship was all the hushed talk of the growing cow town. The judgmental whispers, spoken backhanded behind closed parlor doors, didn't matter to her. To Tabitha, gossips were just groups of bored, cowardly people wanting the rush of an open secret to share. The wide, burly man at her side felt the same way.

From the moment she'd stepped off the train from Sweetwater to Abilene three years ago, Hezekiah was there. Without thought of repayment, he had put the Millers up in a little house in the city, given Annie a job as a hand on his ranch, and seen to all their needs, all at the behest of the late Gilbert Ptolemy. Judge Ellison had said that Ptolemy was 'a friend of whom the world was unworthy, but lucky to have for so long as it did.'

Tabitha knew that to be a truth. Mr. Ptolemy's money, and his telegram to Judge Ellison, had proved to be the hinge on which the Millers' fortune had swung out of destitution. Hezekiah's

71

hospitality was what had started the rumors. At first, they were just rumors, but the more time she spent with him, the more her admiration became affection. So rumor became, as it oftentimes does, reality. It was a new kind of happiness. A happiness she desperately needed, especially on a day like today.

Hezekiah had shown up early to her home that morning dressed in a fine black suit. A gray paisley puff tie accentuated his bright gray eyes in the morning's pink light. His head was freshly shaved and his big black beard trimmed. On the back of Hezekiah's gelding was a picnic basket. Next to his horse was her own horse, already saddled, a strong American bay she had named Starchild, for the little white spot between her eyes.

No words passed between Tabitha and her well-dressed gentleman as she stepped out of the house or as they rode into town. They dismounted in front of a coppice of winter roses growing outside the white-washed church on the town's main street. Hezekiah had helped pay for the church's establishment, as he'd done for the Episcopalians and a small community of Dunkards. If there was anyone who could claim a dozen winter roses from the church on this day, it was him. They clipped the roses and rolled their stems together in a sheet of butcher's paper. Hezekiah wordlessly gave her a section of red twine that she used to bind the flowers together.

Tabitha looked at the bundle of roses in her hands, considering them.

"Thank you for this." Her first words came quietly.

"It's important," he said.

She nodded, saying nothing else for fear of losing her composure in front of the stream of townspeople populating the street. They mounted again and rode silently into the green fields stretching out into the gold and pink horizon of the Texas plain. There was no true trail, but both of them knew the way. In the last two years they had traveled it together many, many times.

They came to a hill overlooking a dark creek, lonely save for a sprawling oak tree whose thick roots tunneled in and out of the earth. But Tabitha could only focus on what lay in the shadow of the massive limbs reaching over the water.

They cantered down the hill. Her eyes remained on the shadow. Time was supposed to heal all wounds, but Tabitha had lived long enough to know that was a lie to give hope to the grieving. The wounds of loss remain forever fresh. It was only two years gone since Tabitha had learned the most terrible of all earthly truths. Love, no matter how tremendous, cannot shield a child from death. Sickness and pain do not yield to it. Against death, nothing, not even love can find victory.

And so, Tabitha grieved. In her own quiet way with Hezekiah at her side, she remembered a loss too great to measure. In the shadow of the tree, there was a mound.

A little grave marked by a little cross.

Tabitha dismounted and gave Starchild's reins over to Hezekiah. She walked over to the cross and crouched down to brush away a few fallen leaves clinging to the name. She said nothing for a long time. Leaning the bright blue roses against the base of the cross gave her the strength to speak.

"Hi, Georgie."

Tears formed in her eyes. They fell.

"Annie says hello and that she misses—" The word caught in her throat. "We miss you. Very, very much."

Hezekiah loosed their horses off their halter ropes and let them wander among the golden shoots of alfalfa sprayed over the field. He went to Tabitha's side.

"Good morning, Outlaw," said Hezekiah. He'd given the little boy the nickname on the first day they met. Georgie had liked it and the Judge immediately.

In the brief seven months Tabitha's son grew to know the Judge, the two of them had formed a special connection. Hezekiah never forced the idea of playing surrogate father to the boy, but Tabitha knew from the moment Georgie felt important to the Judge, he'd unknowingly played that role anyway.

The boy had survived the killing field of Yellow Hill, the long, hard trip to Sweetwater, and the loss of his father. Even for such a boy with such an enduring strength, the flu proved too great a test.

Hezekiah folded back the cloth covering the picnic basket and reached inside. "Now," he said, "I know I can trust you to keep this just between the three of us. You know how your sister is, she would have a fit if she found out I'd given these to you without her." He brought his hand out of the basket and opened his fingers to reveal a handful of lemon drop candies. "But today's your day and I thought you'd like them."

Tabitha let out a little laugh, but it quickly tumbled down the staircase of her emotions. Her shoulders shook as she quietly wept.

Hezekiah wrapped one arm around her and set the lemon drops among the leaves of grass growing up from the mound. "There," he said. "Remember, it's just between us. Not a word to anyone else."

"Thank you," Tabitha said again.

"It's important."

"He would have been nine today."

"He's still nine today, Tabby."

"I'll never forget," she said. "The look on his face when he saw the rows of streetlamps the first night we took a walk in the Abilene evening. He just stood there, glowing in the light, astonished. They shined, and he shined with them, with Annie and me."

She clutched that memory, thinking of how Georgie had stopped in the warmly lighted place, marveling at its simple power. She remembered him turning back to them, his eyes sparkling with wonder. Then, he embraced both his mother and sister, his small arms pulling them close. Smiling, he pointed to the place where their silhouettes waved in a pool of light.

"'Look, Momma,' he had said. 'It's the shadow of our happiness.'"

Tabitha placed a quivering hand on her lips, trying to restrain the onset of a sorrow only a mother dares to know.

"He was so glad to just be with us. To have us with him in this new place, a brighter place than Yellow Hill could ever have been."

Hezekiah squeezed her gently. "And now, I believe that he gets to have that same kind of happiness with his father. I truly believe that, Tabby. Though we miss Georgie here, the two of them are someplace else, together among golden fields, enjoying the one final reunion that awaits us all."

"I just wish I could have had more time with him."

"So do I."

"He was so happy, even when he got sick."

"And that sickness no longer gets to have him. He has escaped the weight of all earthly sorrow." He placed his hand on her cheek and brought her gaze to his. "We will see him again."

She wrapped her arms around Hezekiah and squeezed him tightly. "Thank you," she said. "Thank you, thank you. I don't think I could have done this without you."

"You would have. You're the strongest person I know."

She choked back more tears. "It never feels that way."

C.S. Humble

"A star never sees its own light, Tabby, but it shines on nevertheless." He gently pulled back and lifted his hand up in front of her. In his palm were two bright lemon drops.

"Now, let's share a little sweetness with him, huh?"

Tabitha laughed.

Hezekiah smiled.

Their brows met, leaning on one another, wrinkles kissing.

She took one of the candies from his hand.

"That smile," he said, staring into her eyes. "That's my favorite thing in all living creation. I don't think I could be without it ever again."

"I know," she said. "It's important."

They sat together in the shadow of the oak tree, talking with one another and with Georgie. They lunched there beside the creek where the babbling waters trickled over stones thousands of years older than any human care. It wasn't until they got into Hezekiah's apple pie that Tabitha brought up the cattle drive and asked if there was any word as to their progress.

"It's a short trip. But I haven't gotten any indication that things aren't as right as rain. Quinn is good at his job. He wouldn't do anything to jeopardize the hands, including Annie."

"I know." She gently patted his arm, then traced his knuckles with her fingers, running down the veins to his fingertips. "It's just that Fort Stockton is so close to…well, you know."

"I wouldn't exactly use the word close; it's over eighty miles from the fort to Yellow Hill. But yes, I know your meaning."

"I've lost one child and a husband to the world, Hezekiah. I don't think I could stand to lose what I have left."

The man's gray eyes, having a brightness in the early afternoon light, sparkled like beryl stones. "Annie is your daughter—forever.

76

A Red Winter in the West

And she is quickly becoming a woman of her own mind. She has aims. You and I both know that. When she came to me asking to learn how to be a cattleman, I tried to tell that there was no way for a lady to make a living…" He chuckled. "Well, you know the look she gave me."

"I do." Tabitha laughed with him. "I know it all too well."

"The mind wonders at where on earth she might have learned it."

She playfully shoved him but kept her palm on his chest. "Be nice."

His own hand rose to meet hers. They moved in unison, lacing their fingers together with the measure of an old practiced ritual.

"Don't take my words for an insult. It was that look that made me a believer. That girl has her eye on staking her claim on a piece of Texas, and if she continues to prove herself to be like her mother, she might just claim the whole state."

Tabitha raised an eyebrow. "Just Texas?"

"Texas is plenty big for any one person's ambition, I figure."

She shook her head, her smile widening. "Maybe you don't know that girl as well as you think you do."

"Certainly not as well as I should like, Tabby." His eyes drifted from hers for a moment, looking over her shoulder back toward the grazing ponies. "Listen, there's something I've been meaning to tell you. Something that has to do with my work."

A snake of worry coiled in her stomach. "Okay."

"I've invited a few of my friends from Lubbock to dinner this weekend. By that time, Annie will be back from the drive, and I'd like for you and her to join us."

"I'm confused. You said that dealings with your…other business was something that you'd need to be discreet about. That you need-ed your privacy. And though I decried it then, I've come to accept it. Now you've changed your mind again?"

He nodded. "I did…" He fumbled his words. "I do. But some-one is going to be there who I think you and Annie will want to see. Deserve to see."

The snake in her belly coiled tighter. "Carson? But I thought you said you hadn't spoken to him in months—"

"Not Carson." His eyes wandered from hers. "You've been a saint about understanding and being patient, but I've thought about it a lot. I don't think I can keep this from you any longer. It certainly wouldn't be fair if he showed up and the two of you didn't have some kind of forewarning."

Her hand slipped away from his. "Who?"

Hezekiah let out a deep sigh. "When Carson was on his way out of Yellow Hill, he came upon a wounded boy. He took that boy back with him to Big Spring, where he wired me about the child's condition."

Tabitha shook her head, still confused.

"As I've said before, there are certain side-effects that can come about with direct interaction with the supernatural. And because of my lack of knowledge with the creatures who attacked Yellow Hill, I couldn't be certain that this child wouldn't…change because of it. So I asked my agent, Professor Robert Bass of Lubbock, to take the boy in."

"I don't understand why it would be such a…" A wave of reali-zation came over her. "Orrin Adolphus," she said.

Hezekiah nodded. "He was gravely wounded, and if not for Carson's timely aid, he would have perished. The boy was disfig-ured, Tabby. Lost an arm to stave off blood poisoning. An eye due to his injuries. He's been in the Professor's care, even took up as his apprentice when enough time had passed to prove he would not be-come like the beasts that maimed him."

A Red Winter in the West

She was shocked. "Orrin. Alive. A-And you didn't tell us."

"I had to be certain—"

"Three years, and you didn't tell Annie that her best friend was alive?" she said, her anger rising. "You could have at least let us write him. Do you have any idea how angry Annie is going to be?"

"Hence me telling you now, Tabby."

"Don't think to use that defense with my daughter. You will not enjoy the outcome, Hezekiah Ellison." She took a breath, trying to understand his reasoning. "Why tell me now?"

His eyes fell, then rose to meet hers again. "Troubling news is starting to come in from some of my people. News that I'd hoped was rumor but has been confirmed several times over. Before Carson and Gilbert found you in Yellow Hill, they encountered a very powerful vampire. They met him in battle, and, for what they did to him, he promised there would come a reckoning. I believe that time is coming, and right soon. So, I have need to bring my friends together to plan accordingly. I count you and your daughter among those friends. You are not like the rest of the world, those who have not seen the things you have seen. Those who do not know, as you know."

"My Lord," Tabitha said, shaking her head. "Orrin is alive."

"Not only alive, Tabby. He's pledged himself to me and, like Carson, to our mission."

"But he's just a boy."

"He's no more a boy than Annie is still a little girl. Pain and loss salt the fields of youth, forcing children to become adults long before they're truly ready. Robert says he's a voracious study and wholly dedicated to the cause. He's asked many, many times for a chance to write Annie. I allowed it but never gave the letters to her."

"Why not?"

A look of solemn honesty fell over Hezekiah's face. "The first time I met your children I saw a piece of innocence that had not yet been stained by this hidden conflict: the war of humans against in-humanities—dark gods and monsters. I believed that if Annie knew about what happened to Orrin, she would have tried to enlist herself in the fight. She has that righteous anger inside her. I couldn't do that to you, certainly not after what happened to Georgie."

She looked away from him, furious. "So you lied to me and my daughter because you thought we were too infirm to bear the truth."

"I didn't—"

"Annie and I don't need to be protected from the truth. And we certainly don't need it apportioned to us by *men*. All of you so self-certain that you know what's best for us…for the *delicate and mercurial* female mind."

"I don't think that at all. I don't believe I'm that kind of man."

"That's the problem—you, like every other goddamn man in the world, seem to think that you are what you believe you are. Well," she said as she stood up, "you are not what you *believe* you are. You are what you *do*. And what you did, Hezekiah Ellison, was lie. And that makes you a liar."

"Tabby, please. You can't see it that way."

"I can. And I do." She dusted her skirt in frustration. "Thank you for the picnic today and for being with me, but I think I'll spend the rest of today in my own company, thank you."

He tried to plead with her, but she was having none of it. She walked away from Hezekiah, Georgie's grave, and the sentinel oak tree beside the creek. She slipped the bridle back on Starchild and mounted her.

Hezekiah approached her, the picnic basket in his hand. "Won't you please let me ride back with you?"

A Red Winter in the West

"I believe I'll do just fine on my own. Oh," she said, giving him a glare, "when Annie gets back, you make sure to tell her the truth of what you did before you send her home. I won't be the one to announce to my daughter that a man she deeply admires lied to her because he didn't think she was strong enough to handle the truth."

He opened his mouth to speak.

Tabitha kicked Starchild and left Hezekiah and his excuses underneath the shadow of the oak tree.

Chapter Seven

FORT STOCKTON

———

ANNIE DID NOT have time to tell Dutch and Boone the whole story of Yellow Hill, but she did eventually convince Boone that the two cattle workers had no intention of disarming or harming him. Annie made a promise. Dutch swore to God. And Private Boone lowered the gun.

"We have to get back to the foyer," said Annie. "We'll bring in the other tripod and barricade ourselves there."

Boone rebuffed her. "No way I'm staying here. We should ride out immediately."

"He's right, Annie," Dutch said. "We gotta get back to Boss Quinn. Like you said, Percy told ya to come on riding back if there was any sign of trouble. And this here is trouble if I've ever heard it."

"The herd is the last place we want to be, Dutch." She walked out of the officer's quarters. The two men trailed after her.

"How do you figure that?"

"The blizzard shows no signs of relief, we're blind out there. We're safer inside."

"But Percy—"

She whirled on him. "Percy isn't here, Dutch. Nor is Boss Quinn. They're out there in the storm, along with the wolves that killed an entire regiment of well-armed, well-trained soldiers like him." She jabbed a finger at Boone. "Worse, the company is trailing cattle. Those wolves are gonna smell the stock."

Dutch's eyes went wide. "You think…you think those beasts got Quinn and the rest."

"I don't know, but what I do know is that here we have provisions. We have fire and protection. Out there, God only knows what would happen to us."

"I told you," said Boone. "I ain't staying here."

"No one is going to make you stay," said Annie. "But your ass will be walking if you decide to leave."

Boone's eyes narrowed at her. "Is that a fact, missy?"

Annie glared back. "Damn right it is."

"Let's not start pointing guns at each other again," Dutch pleaded.

It wasn't resolve that Annie saw in Boone's eyes but fear. The kind of fear that made people irrational. Made them dangerous. She looked at him unwavering. "You got the drop on me last time, private. You go to skin that pistol and it'll be touch and go which one of us gets killed."

"Stop it, Annie," said Dutch. "You're only making it worse!"

"You should listen to your friend." Boone's voice was calm, flat.

"You saw what those things can do," said Annie. "How do you think you'll fare out there in the open, half-blind, with your hands shaking like a rattler's tail in the cold?"

Boone's eyes wavered, his lids heavy with exhaustion.

"When was the last time you slept, huh? Had a decent meal? You're in no condition to go out into that mess, much less give orders to me."

A Red Winter in the West

"This is a fortification of the United States government, and I am the highest-ranking officer. That puts me in command." He flung his hands out in exasperation.

That was all the distraction Annie needed. Her gun was in her hand in a heartbeat, pointed at Boone.

"No, wait," Dutch cried out.

Boone's eyes went wide, then slacked when Annie didn't fire. "I suppose this makes me your prisoner?"

"No," Annie holstered her gun. "It makes us even. You're not taking our horses, which are rode down anyway, and you aren't leaving. If those beasts come back, the more people we have, the better our chances are at surviving."

"They killed my entire regiment. What chance do you think the three of us have?"

"I didn't say they were good chances, only better. Now, we're going to hold up in the foyer, give the horses a good feed and some rest. We'll brace the door and hope for the best. If the herd doesn't show up by morning, then we ride out of here fast as a hummingbird with the wind at its back."

Dutch looked at Boone. "Sounds reasonable to me."

"More than fair," she said. "Stay with us, help us, and we'll carry you out of here. And when you hook up with a superior officer at Fort Phantom in Abilene, we won't mention that you were locked up in here for what I'm guessing was a court-martial."

Boone shook his head. "I don't think I like you very much."

"I have that effect on people," she said. Then turned and walked back toward the foyer.

They did not speak again on their way back to the horses. Once Boone dragged the second tripod inside, they headed out together into the blinding snow. The soldier led them to the livery stable to grab a bale of hay for the horses.

Inside, they came upon the mutilated corpses of horses ravaged in their stalls, their lithe, powerful figures shorn open at now hollow bellies. Annie and Boone began to argue about who would carry the hay back through the snow, until Dutch wordlessly walked between them among the carrion, picked up the bale with one hand, and left them behind.

"You know," Annie said to Boone, "it'll go a long way if you'll just listen to me. I know what I'm doing."

Boone shook his head, his shoulders jumping as if restraining laughter. "I think you sound like you know what you're doing, which makes me think you're used to getting your way. You've got a buffalo personality, that's for sure. But ain't no one alive that knows what to do if those things show up.."

Annie fumed, knowing Boone was right. She said nothing though and followed after Dutch.

Back inside the foyer, it was Dutch again who, with considerable effort, lifted the cross timber and braced the doors.

The last, and most gruesome, part of Annie's plan was for the three of them to move the dead Buffalo Soldiers, stacking them six bodies high to form a wall between themselves and the open hallway.

They sat in the wavering warmth of the tripods, eating strips of jerky from Dutch's saddlebag. Vanilla and Little Dutch, the German's drafting horse, chewed hay. The cold wind howled, and snow blew through the narrowrifle gaps of the fort's adobe wall, dusting the ground.

"They should have been here by now," said Dutch, breaking the silence.

Annie didn't respond.

"Could be the storm held them up," said Boone through his chewing. "Maybe they made camp."

A Red Winter in the West

"No chance Quinn made camp," said Annie. She stood up and stretched her legs. Then went over to the embrasure looking out into the white curtain of snow. She thought of the stormy night her mother had bundled her and Georgie into that stolen stagecoach. The rolling thunder of the massive storm twisting over the mine boomed in her mind. "My guess is they got caught out in the open. Nothing survives these things."

"I did," said Boone.

Dutch nodded at Annie. "So did you."

Annie turned and looked at Boone. He was sitting in front of the pile of Buffalo Soldiers barricading the hall. "How'd you get free of your cell, Boone?"

"Better question," said Dutch. "How'd you get *in* that cell?"

Boone sneered at him. "Same way you got to be so ugly. Circumstances outside my control."

"You are not a nice person," said Dutch, more hurt than angry.

"Like I said before, one of the guards came to get me out to help with the fighting. One of those things came in behind him while he was fumbling with the keys to the cell." Boone looked into the fire, reliving the memory. "It pinned him down, then started eating while he was still alive. It took him a long time to die."

"I'm sorry, Boone," said Annie. "You were friends?"

"More than that; we soldier together. He was trying to save me."

"What was his name?" asked Dutch.

"Doesn't matter now much, does it? He's dead."

Dutch furrowed his brow and pulled another hunk of jerky into his mouth.

"You're lucky," said Annie. "The cell kept it from getting at you."

Boone nodded. "Didn't stop it from trying though. It pawed at me for a bit, snarling with that big mouth. I just put my back against the wall and shut my eyes. Eventually it got bored with me and ran off with the others around the time the sun started to go down. I waited for a long, long time before I even considered grabbing the cell key from John's…"—Boone swallowed hard, his eyes wide and distant in the firelight, remembering—"f-from what was left of his body." He wiped his wetted eyes. Cleared his throat and composed himself. "I couldn't find the key to my manacles. Busted the chain in half with a hammer."

Vanilla lifted her head, her ears swiveling toward the door. She let out a nervous whinny. Little Dutch stamped in his corner of the room.

"Easy, girl," said Annie. She started to walk over to the mare.

A low, droning noise came moaning over the howling winds. It rolled on and on. Annie knew that sound. It was the painful bellowing of a wounded heifer. The pitch dipped low, lower than any normal bovine register, and then it sailed up into a human-like scream.

Heart racing, she bolted back over to the rifle gap in the wall and drew her pistol.

"Is it Quinn and the herd?" asked Dutch, scrambling to his feet.

The snow had let up a little, allowing her to see further out than before. Twenty, maybe twenty-five, feet from the walls of the fort, a large shadowy mass lay in the virgin snow. The center of the shadow rose and fell slowly. Rose, then fell again. Ghosts of heat vapor roiled off its corpulent frame.

The lonely heifer, stranded in a sea of white, let out another baleful moan.

"Just one heifer," she said. "I don't see the re—"

A great noise came rumbling over the wind, the sound of thunder coming up from the ground.

Annie spun, looking at the two tripods they'd brought inside, remembering those points of light being the only sign they'd seen of the fort upon their arrival.

A Red Winter in the West

The thunder grew louder, closer.

"They're blind," she said in terrified realization.

The sound, growing louder and louder, trampled over the rush of the storm, overtaking it completely.

"What is that?" Boone screamed to be heard, sitting with his back to the doors of the fort.

"Stampede!" Annie took hold of Boone and yanked on the soldier, pulling him away from the crosstimber.

With a bone-shattering *crack* the door buckled on its iron hinges. The massive timber set across the middle of the door bent but held. Another massive blow against the door splintered the beam, and through the timbers came a groaning heifer, blood pouring over its skull. It fell to the ground, howling on its side, broken legs kicking wildly in the air. With pain being all that remained for the heifer, Annie drew her revolver and cut short its suffering with a single shot through the head. Then, like cannonballs going off against the adobe walls, the cattle, blind in the dark and the blowing snow, slammed against the fortification.

Annie screamed for Dutch, who stood with his back against the wall, wide eyed.

Then over the slowing booms of the cattle colliding into adobe came a harrowing howl—a sound of absolute primacy.

"Ah, Christ!" Boone hollered. "Ah, Jesus Christ, they're back."

"Calm d—"

"Goddamn it, girl, if we don't ride out now we're dead. Do you understand? We are dead!"

Annie Miller shot a look at Dutch, then looked to Boone. She was not going to die. Not today and not in this place.

The sound of cattle being slaughtered under claw and fang flooded the falling reign of night.

Dutch panicked, looking from side to side, unsure of what to do.

"Dutch!" Annie screamed his name again.

Their eyes met. Annie captured his attention.

"Knock down the wall!" She turned to the soldier. "Boone, help him! I'll get the horses." She shoved the soldier toward the wall of corpses.

The two men went to work, shoving the bodies of dead men, pushing them into a cascade of ruined flesh that spilled over into the hallway. Just as they were about to climb over the bodies, another screaming heifer burst through the door, splintering one door and blowing the other off its hinge. The wind and the cold and the carnage from outside poured into the foyer. The heifer's hooves splayed beneath it, kicking over one of the tripods. The embers caught the beast on the flank, filling the foyer with the smell of burning hair and flesh. Annie reached over to the horses, pulling them away by the reins. Screaming and wounded, the smoking heifer scrambled to its feet, turned, and pushed back out into the storm.

Annie, hearing the triumph of predators and the lament of their prey, looked to Dutch. She handed the reins of the drafting horse to her friend. "Little Dutch is big enough to carry you and Boone. You go first. I'll follow behind, make sure nothing gets after you."

"But—"

"No buts. For once in your life just do as I goddamn well say!"

They mounted their horses and barreled down the halls toward the southern door, the horses' hooves clopping over the fort's stone floor.

At the door, Annie dismounted and pulled it open. The black of night and the sound of the dying herd surrounded them. Over the clamor came the howling terror of the beasts now returned to the killing ground.

A Red Winter in the West

She swung herself back into the saddle and pointed at Dutch. "You turn left out this door and you ride. You ride, and, by God, if I catch you looking back for me, my bullet will be the last thought that passes through your mind."

Dutch nodded and cantered out the door. He kicked Little Dutch hard, and they rushed out into the night.

Annie patted Vanilla on the neck. "Come on, girl. You've been here before."

They burst through the door, Annie posting in the saddle. The power underneath her, the sheer force of Vanilla's seasoned gait, was unlike any other feeling in the world. As they flew around the edge of the adobe fortifications, Annie saw the field of white aglow with moonlight. The rivulets of blood flowing from the innumerable corpses of heifers shone like obsidian streams.

A snarling beast exploded out of the powdery wash, running on six legs, not four. Before it could gather its weight to leap, Annie took aim.

The pistol barked in her hand.

The massive wolflike creature yipped, its front shoulder burst open like an overfilled waterskin. A ribbon of red splashed against the snow as the beast collapsed hard against the ground.

Vanilla never slowed. Never faltered.

"Come on, girl. That's it!"

As they moved away from the fort, the blanket of dead cattle thinned out, replaced with the bodies of horses. The remuda had been slaughtered. Then they approached an imperfect circle of what could only be the shapes of men. On the far side of the circle, a man was screaming desperately as a creature dug its face into his belly. He beat at its head with his fists, battering its muzzle.

Annie kicked Vanilla hard, then turned the massive bulk of her horse to broadside the creature. The impact sent the thing sprawling into the white.

Annie aimed, then shot it in the head.

It moved to rise.

"Die, you bastard!" She fired again, ensuring the beast would never rise again.

"Please," the man lying on the ground moaned. "Please, help me."

She knew that voice.

Percy writhed on his back, and in his hands he tried to cradle a dark, steaming pile of everything the beast had tried to claim. He wailed, begging for Annie to help him.

Annie turned back, looking at the field of death and blood. The creatures were scattered, still chasing the heifers who'd managed to evade them thus far.

"Annie?" asked Percy. "Is that you, girl?"

She shook her head, hating herself for what she was about to do. Vanilla chuffed unhappily as Annie dismounted and went to the man on the ground. "It's me, Percy."

"I—" he coughed. "God, I think I'm dying, Annie."

"You are," she said.

"Please," he said. "Please d-don't let them eat me."

She shook her head and took Percy's hand into her own. With her other hand, she grabbed the pistol lying next to him. She checked the cylinder and, seeing that all his shells were empty, she reloaded it with one of her own.

She put the gun in Percy's hand.

The elder cowboy shook his head. "I can't," he said. "I can't do it. I don't wanna go to Hell." He swallowed hard through a trembling sob. "Annie. Please. God will not forgive a suicide."

A Red Winter in the West

A fresh set of howls filled the night, announcing the triumph of another kill.

"Percy," she pleaded. "I can't."

He pushed his own gun back toward her. "You can…please. God will see it as a mercy."

Vanilla stamped, raking a trench into the snow impatiently.

"Tell my wife that I died fighting. And"—he hacked a bloody cough—"tell my boy I went down shooting. That I went bravely to God."

Annie nodded, thumbing back the hammer.

Percy's head tilted. His eyes looked beyond Annie, going wide.

The revolver bucked in her hand.

Something slammed into her, sending her tumbling into the snow with a snarling hiss. A hard, raking slash caught her forearm as she reached for her own pistol. The hot, stinking breath of the creature enveloped her as it reared its head back and opened its mouth wide.

An explosion of gunfire split the air. A red spray puffed out the back of the creature's skull, fluttering like a cloud of mosquitoes, only to vanish in the wind.

Annie turned around.

Dutch sat astride his horse, holding the reins.

Boone sat behind him, a smoking pistol in his hand. "No need to thank me. Turning back wasn't my idea," he said.

Annie, holding her bleeding arm close to her chest, managed to throw a leg over Vanilla. Back in the saddle, she looked to Dutch. "Thank you," she said.

The big German's face was blank. "You gonna live?"

"If I don't," she said, "it'll be because you took your sweet time disobeying me."

"You're welcome."

They spurred their horses for all they were worth, pounding northeast toward Abilene. Into the darkness. Annie hoped the horses had the legs to run what might be their final race.

Chapter Eight

DEEP CREEK TRADING POST, TEXAS

WITH A JINGLE and a clatter, the door to the trading post announced their arrival. Professor Bass went in first, Orrin behind him. The apprentice followed his teacher, fiddling at the mask buckled to his head. The prosthesis covered the scars and his ruined eye with a plate facsimile painted to match the unmarred side of his face. It was not perfect, but it was enough. Many soldiers who fought in the Slaver's Revolt, both gray and blue, wore similar masks to cover the wounds they incurred during the war. While the veterans of that conflict wore them as badges of honor, Orrin wore his to hide in plain sight.

His missing arm, however, he did not hide. He found that a missing limb encouraged sympathy, whereas the missing eye only unnerved people.

"Well, I'll be. If it isn't my good friend, Robert Bass." The man behind the counter was a stocky fellow of middling height. His glossy black hair, cropped into a high widow's peak, shone dapperly in the afternoon light.

"Pete," the Professor said, throwing back a fold of his dark cape coat. The two men shook hands over a glass counter filled with an assortment of pistols. "It's been too long."

"Mildred," Pete called over his shoulder toward the back of the post. His sun-kissed skin was bright red and wrinkled at the cheeks from what Orrin was sure were years of a practiced, professional smile. "Mildred, come on out here. You'll never guess who just walked in." He turned back to the Professor. "Look at you, and who's this tall drink of water you've brought with you?"

Professor Bass looked back at Orrin, gesturing for him to join him at the counter. "This is my apprentice, Orrin Adolphus. Orrin, this is Pete Snyder. Former frontier man, now the purveyor of goods and accouterments to the fine people of this region."

Orrin greeted the man with a shake of his left hand. "My pleasure."

Pete smiled at Orrin, hollering over his shoulder again: "Mildred, honey! Come on out here. It's Professor Bass, I said. Got a young apprentice with him."

"I ain't comin'," came a woman's voice from the back of the post.

Pete shook his head. "She's still sore about the follicle powder. I don't know why; her hair eventually went back to being its natural color." He turned back again, his consummate smile fading a bit. "Mildred, please." Again he looked back at the Professor. "She gets like this, I just— Mildred, sweetheart! Come on now."

Nothing.

"That woman," Pete said, shaking his head. "Best thing that ever happened to me, but damn if she doesn't hold a grudge."

"To be fair," said the Professor, "the powder *was* experimental. I made that clear, Pete."

A Red Winter in the West

"Honey!"

The trading post went silent as a tomb.

Pete waved his hand, as if shooing away a bothersome fly. "Aw, she'll get over it."

The professor smiled over at Orrin. "I'm sure."

"So what brings you estimable gentlemen our way? Headed to Abilene, I'll wager?"

"Our business is our own. So, too, our destination."

The trader's expression soured. His tongue ran over the jagged top row of his teeth, then sucked them. "Well, no need to be rough about it, Professor. I was just being polite. You forget who started this here post. I built this place with my own two hands and now here we are with a gin mill, two banks, and a *second newspaper* is due to start printing soon." He reached over the counter and gave the professor a playful backhanded pat on his cape coat. "I know the coach line and their manifest."

"No soreness to it, Pete. You know how I value privacy. It would do me well that should anyone come asking about—"

"I know," Pete interjected. "I know. Seeing as you are here, I'm guessing you'll want to buy me out of silver. But I'll warn you, I've collected quite a bit."

"I'll need at least eighty pounds."

"Eighty pounds!"

"Bare minimum. I've made a list of the other essentials I require, which I'm sure you can fulfill while Orrin and I lunch over at the White Buffalo." The Professor's nimble fingers slipped into the folds of his coat, from which he produced a folded slip of paper.

The trader took the slip, then put on a pair of spectacles. "Let's see here." He squinted against the list, mumbling as he read.

"All is in order then?"

Pete continued down the list. "Mmhmm, mmhmm. Wait, your chicken-scratch handwriting—What's this word here?" He showed the professor the list.

"Essence."

"Ah yes, essence of rose. Mmhmm. Yes, sir, I can fill the whole of it. Should have you loaded in an hour or so."

"Excellent. I'll tell our coachman."

Pete removed his glasses and extended his hand. There was a big smile on his face. "If I had more customers like you, I'd be able to build the kinda house Mildred has been asking for. One of the big ones you know? Victorian, they call it."

"Lovely, I'm sure."

Orrin and the professor made their way out of the trading post and headed across the dusty street toward a white-washed, three-story hotel. In swooping white calligraphy, matted onto a large, swinging sign was written, 'The White Buffalo.'

Professor Bass called over to the coachman, who stood next to the watering horses, telling him to be ready to depart in just over an hour.

The interior of the hotel was elegant in its simplicity. Honeycomb-colored pine wood floors soaked in the sunshine slanting through the hotel's big front windows. They passed the clerk's desk and turned left into the cafe. Lunch was being served to a few patrons dressed a bit more dapper than Orrin expected for nothing more than an outpost town.

They gave their order to the waiter and sat.

Orrin looked out the window, silent.

A Red Winter in the West

Professor Bass reached into his coat and produced a flask. He took a sip. "You've kept to yourself since we left Lubbock. What's troubling you?"

"This will be the first time I've seen Annie since…since what happened. I've written to her so many times. I'm worried as to why she never wrote back."

"Orrin, my friend, I've studied all the natural and unnatural sciences of the earthly plain. From the great colleges of London to the academies of Germany and even the Far East. And yet, even to me with all my worldly and otherworldly knowledge, the female mind remains ever a mystery."

It was a playful comment, but Orrin didn't smile. "She told me before she left that we would always be able to write one another. That she wouldn't forget about me. It is hard on me that she did."

"Who can say why a person chooses one way or the other in matters of the human animal's emotional spectrum? I find examining it infinitely frustrating. The work, however—*our* work—is wholly measurable, and our purposes are fruitfully defined. That is where the powers of your gifted mind should focus. As I've said, we are at the precipice of a great discovery."

The waiter returned to their table, bringing a pair of plates slathered with hot cuts of meat and roasted potatoes bathed in gravy. As he did with all things that caught his voracious interest, the Professor wolfed it down.

"The encouraging thing," he said, dabbing at the corners of his mouth with his napkin, "the encouraging thing is that in only a few days, you'll be able to inquire. Ask the great question why, directly."

"Maybe I will," said Orrin.

The professor's brow wrinkled. "You must. Could you live with such a troubling unknown? And why not ask it? Is it for fear of what the answer might be?"

Orrin lifted his palm to slow the Professor's hurried speech. "I don't know. I only know this: I wrote, as she said I should, and she never wrote back. Those are the known elements, and they trouble me. I told her in my first letter what happened…." Orrin passed a hand over his mask. "Maybe I was too graphic in the telling, too honest."

"You are not your infirmities, my boy. They are a part of you. In some ways, they limit you, but they do not define you. None of us are as we appear. We are as we are. And for the people who love us, that is enough."

Orrin nodded, though he did not believe. He decided to change the subject. "Do you think the eighty pounds of silver will be enough?"

The Professor leaned back in his chair, allowing the change in the conversation's direction. "Eighty from here, along with the eighty we already carry. Add in whatever stores Judge Ellison has, and I believe it will suffice."

"If we do manage to capture one of them," Orrin's voice slid to a whisper, "how will we examine it?"

Something in the Professor's bright visage darkened at the question. "Thoroughly. Precisely. And with the knowledge such a specimen might provide, we might find a cure to that damnable pestilence that plagues the entirety of their population."

"How can you be sure the elixir will work? You haven't tested it yet."

"I cannot be sure, yet. Which is why we need a test subject, Orrin. Hence our accumulation of silver. Judge Ellison takes a great risk to his network by bringing such a wealth of his resources together in one place, but I have convinced him, over many, many months of letters citing our research, that the potential outcome demands the risk. We've never been this close to having a cure-all for vampirism."

A Red Winter in the West

"What about creatures that attacked Yellow Hill?"

"What about them?"

"When will we go after them?"

"Their time is coming, my boy. I promise. But they are a localized problem, while the vampire remains a global threat. Especially if what Judge Ellison tells me is accurate."

This was the part of their relationship that frustrated Orrin the most. As an apprentice, he was allowed to ask any question, but the Professor was the gatekeeper holding all the keys. Sometimes the Professor spoke in generalizations that were clear obfuscations, open-ended statements designed to be roadblocks. It was as if Professor Bass refused to simply tell Orrin the truth of things outright. This forced Orrin to ask question after question, following a trail of breadcrumbs that might be avoided if the Professor would just spit the whole thing out.

Orrin rubbed his tired eye.

"You really are troubled about this girl, aren't you?" asked the Professor.

"Aside from my studies, she's all I think about. I miss her. I'm ashamed to admit it, but I miss her more than even my parents. I think it's because she's still alive. Still real. I wonder what she looks like now, though her face is still clear in my mind." He lowered his gaze, considering his own face in his mind. "A person changes a lot in three years. I know I have."

"Yes, you have," the Professor said, his enthusiasm raised to its height. "You've become the finest apprentice I've ever known. Your ability to recall the tiniest of details is astounding, and I use that word very carefully, Orrin. Very little truly astounds me these days, but your mind is a marvel, despite your strange obsession with the occult sciences. I would much prefer you to focus on that which can be measured, tested against established laws. Not the flimsy rules of unauthoritative folklore and superstition."

The professor's final statement angered Orrin. He snapped his eye up to meet his teacher. "Science didn't do this to me."

The Professor leaned back, a sign of retreat. Clearly he didn't want to escalate the conversation into an argument. "Quite." He looked at his pocket watch. "Ah, I see our time in Deep Creek draws close to its end. Our next stop is Abilene, where I think we shall first visit the tailor."

"A tailor?"

"You're my apprentice, Orrin. It's time we got you a suit proper for your position and a tool set of your own. A man's first suit is an event, a ritual, or perhaps a rite of passage, if you will. It would be my honor to buy your first."

Orrin looked down at his shirt and trousers. They were warm clothes and fine enough, but a suit, that was something else entirely.

"That's...that's very generous."

"You've earned it, my boy. Our time as master and apprentice is come to the end of its wick. I've given you wings. Now comes the time for you to fly on your own. One day, you too will have an apprentice, and I only ask that when their time comes to go out on their own, that you pass along the kindness. All humanity has—"

"Is each other." Orrin finished.

The Professor nodded with a wink. "Is each other."

Chapter Nine

ABOARD THE STEAM TRAIN *HEPHAESTUS* EL MORO, COLORADO

———

THE TRAIN RUMBLED forth again, restocked with provisions and fuel in El Moro. Carson had watched the engineer closely during his exchanges to ensure that no message could be delivered to the Society members before the train's arrival in Chicago. He gave the Baroness what she wanted. What she truly craved. He told his story, giving her every detail in the hope that when the time came for her to divulge her secrets, she would be equally detailed. He told her of his early life, of learning the language of the Black Manuscript, of Ezra's attempt on his life, and of Gilbert's sacrifice. Of Sigurd and the confrontation with Jeremiah Hart and the terror of Alitranz revealed in the mine of Yellow Hill. All of it, top to bottom, horror to triumph. Though he left out the Miller family, seeing no reason to let her know of them.

The Baroness sat, listening in the chair. Carson had untied her. The trip was too long to simply keep her lashed to the chair in the

C.S. Humble

diner car. Though he had tied her to the bed when he allowed her to retire to her quarters, which he searched before and after she slept.

"You saw the dark brother. The champion," the Baroness said, her eyes gleaming with intrigue.

"I did. I also saw my father prove himself a greater champion by destroying the gateway."

The baroness rolled her eyes. "Once the gate is open, it cannot be closed. From whence do you think the blistering cold comes, boy? It is seeping out from the ground even now, rising up out of the rubble. The bright, cleansing frost is slowly creeping over the States. When the other obelisks are found, they will open other doors. And then shall the final obelisk ignite in fullness of power. Alitranz's brothers and sisters will come, and with them bring the restoration." She clasped her hands together in her lap, confident.

There was an unspoken pact between them: she could live and go where she needed, but at the first sign of escape or struggle, Carson would kill her on the spot. The Baroness loved her own life too much to attempt either.

It was early afternoon when Carson finished telling his story. He made his way behind the bar to prepare lunch.

"I'm surprised at you," she said, moving to sit on one of the stools in front of the bar. "I've never known anyone to read the manuscript and remain so unchanged by its absolute truth."

"That book is a poison in the form of language. And it did change me, as any measure of torture would," he said, letting the iron skillet get hot on the stove. He threw a pair of steaks into the skillet. The sound of the searing, along with the scent of the smoke made Carson's mouth water.

104

A Red Winter in the West

"Truth is a painful salve," said the Baroness.

Carson flipped the sizzling meat. "I've been patient with you. Told you my story. It's your turn."

She placed her elbows on the bar, supporting her chin with her palms like a child enamored with a story. "I suppose it is. Oh, I'll take my steak more rare this time. You cook it too long."

Carson grit his teeth. "Fine."

"No carrots or potatoes? Perhaps a bottle of wine? You'll find them in that cabinet over there."

He threw the steak onto a plate and slid it over to her. "Eat. Talk."

She picked up a knife and fork. "Very well. Go ahead and ask the obvious one first."

Carson obliged her. "What's your name?"

"Gwendolyn."

"That's it? Just Gwendolyn?"

"I left my family name behind many years ago."

"I'm guessing you aren't actually a baroness, are you."

"Oh I am, just not of any principality you'd know. It is an honorific given to me by the highest of our order."

"And who is the highest of your order?"

"We do not say the name." She went to cut into the beef.

Carson grabbed the lip of her plate and pulled it away from her. "So it's death by starvation, is it?"

"Harder way to go than a bullet, but I'm patient enough if you are."

"How little you understand of our ways, Carson Ptolemy. There is more in the manuscript than just the opening of gates. To say the name is to die. Even your Judge knows that. When one joins the Order of Prometheus, they seal a pact in blood, assuring the high priest's safety."

"You called the Judge a traitor. Why?"

"He never told you how he came to know of us, did he? Who would follow a man who was once one of our greatest members?"

"You're lying."

She reached over, gently pinching her plate between her fingers, and slid it back over to herself. "I have little use of deception. The truth, however…" She trailed off, slowly sawing the meat with her knife. "All you need is to look up at the night sky to see the truth of things. Once you throw off the lies of ancient desert cults or cast away proverb spewing wise men, only then can you see the cold brightness of it all. Only then can you see the truth."

"What truth?"

The shadow of her belief fell over her, veiling the woman in a kind of dark radiance given over to one who dares to truly believe. And in the baroness's eyes, Carson saw that belief. Absolute and indomitable.

"You don't matter, Carson, and neither do I. Not a one of us. We are a species infected with a gross overestimation of cosmic importance, and so humans wait, generation after generation. We subsist in a counterfeit advent, always hoping. There is no messiah who shall, upon the grand trumpet sounding, arrive from some celestial paradise to rescue the lot of us from universal malady. Humankind exists unto itself, for itself. The Society of Prometheus exists to upend the irrationality of hope and bring humanity into its higher state. A state of fear and trembling, for through that fear will we cling together as we once did, holding the fire of knowledge as the singular beacon of progress."

Carson gritted his teeth, hating every inch her logic, and yet he found himself trying not to be drawn into the woman's words. But a part of him was ashamed to feel a resonance in what she said. "And bringing these monstrosities into the world accomplishes that how?" he asked.

The Baroness slid a sliver of steak past her lips. Chewing it slowly, she kept her eyes on him. "In order for a species to rise, it must first be humbled. Shown its place on the cosmic food chain." She reached over, grabbed Carson's whiskey glass, and drank from it. "You are one of the truly lucky ones. You've borne witness. The witnessing of a thing removes the necessity of belief. Seeing changes you." Her thick brown eyebrows bounced. "I think your steak's done, Carson."

Only then did Carson hear the popping grease and sizzling beef. "Shit," he said, turning to pull the steak off the skillet.

The meat hit the plate, charred on one side as black as coal.

Her unbridled laughter came over his shoulder.

"Funny, is it?" He was angry. Not angry at her laughing at him, but furious that she knew how deeply her sermonizing had affected him. He felt very young and very foolish.

She continued in her riotous laughter, slapping the bar, her eyes closed.

Carson grabbed his whiskey glass and killed what remained. "All right, all right. That's enough, Gwendolyn."

She pointed at the whiskey glass in his hand. "That's certainly not going to help."

He let the anger pass over him. It was stupid of him to lose his head over such a small thing. "Laugh all you want. You're the one sitting here, a captive on your own train. I might burn steak, but I took your train all by myself. What do you call that?"

The Baroness's smile remained. Then it widened. "I'd call it a success, Carson."

"Damn right it was a suc—" His words ran together, his lips suddenly feeling numb. He blinked in confusion as his vision began to blur. His fingers tingled, and, out of sheer panic, he went for his revolver.

The gun flew out of his belt, and he heard—as if from some far-away place—the clatter as it hit the ground. "What di—"

He was too tired to talk. Every word was a labor. Heat flushed his face. He was sweating.

The Baroness spoke, but her voice was distant.

Carson pitched forward to go for his gun again, but by the time he was there, it was gone.

Then it appeared again, the barrel pressed against his upraised head.

The Baroness was still smiling. Now her voice was impossibly close, as if it had crawled into his brain. "Fight it. That's it, throw yourself against it. There is nothing I love to see more than a man take the long tumble down the staircase of his own capability."

Carson shot his hand out, grabbing the woman by the throat.

She slapped him away with ease. "Tumble, little tiger. Fall for me."

Chapter Ten

ABILENE, TEXAS

I**T WAS VERY** late and very dark when Annie recognized the shimmering expanse of Lake Fort Phantom. They were just outside the city limits of Abilene now. She should have felt jubilant at the successful return home—relieved that neither the cold nor the desperate flight from Fort Stockton had finished off what little remained of Boss Quinn's company. If there were any relief, it was only a trickling thing, rolling down a bedrock of gloom.

She would give the events no aggrandizement, nor a shelter of lies that would hide the truth from the Judge's circumspection. Annie would speak as she always did, plainly and truthfully. The fort, the attack, the loss of cattle, and the killing of Percy: all of it would come out of her slow and steady. She had a clear assumption in her mind on how the Judge would take the news, but even he, with his steadfast and unflappable behavior, was prone to fits of anger.

In her experience, Judge Ellison was a man who loved the general idea of human beings enough to hate its enemies with a burning absoluteness. He was a creature of justice. Not just in title, but in belief and in action. She wouldn't be surprised if he formed a raiding party and set out to kill, once and for all, the swarthy beasts roaming near and around what remained of derelict Yellow Hill.

Annie had already decided that, if he did, she would be the first to volunteer.

Boone slept in the saddle, leaning his head on Dutch's broad back, when Annie broke the silence.

"Wake up, soldier," she said. "We're near the fort."

The whites of Boone's eyes glowed in the starlight. "What's that?" he asked groggily.

"Dutch here can take you down the west fork, over to the fort. There you can check in. Let them know what happened."

"If it's all the same to you, I'd rather get a room in town tonight. Have myself a meal and a tub. I can report in the morning."

Annie nodded. "Have it your way." She nodded at the big, tired German leaning heavily in the saddle. "Dutch, take him over to the Windsor. When you're done, meet back up with me at Peregrine House."

Dutch gave her an affirmative groan.

"Boone, I don't want you to be talking to anyone in town about what happened. I get that you'll need to explain things to your superiors, but my employer would appreciate a tight lip on what happened in Fort Stockton."

The soldier just nodded. Clearly, he didn't have the energy to argue.

"Hey," Dutch droned, "after all this, I want to see my mother. She's over in Merkel. Tell Judge Ellison I'll be back in town in a week or so."

They were all exhausted. Annie could see it on their faces, and she heard it in the slow, plodding steps of their worn-out horses.

A Red Winter in the West

"Sure, Dutch," said Annie.

"Thanks."

With that, she said her goodbyes to both of them and took the easterly path toward Peregrine House.

Despite the newness of Abilene, Peregrine House seemed old, lived in for longer than it had known its foundation upon the earth. It stretched three stories high like a dark trio of flint arrows stacked atop one another. Trimmed in yellow paint that climbed the porch, shutters, and windowsills, the home bore a weather vane capped by a soaring falcon. Its wings always outstretched, forever flying east, to find, as the Judge often said, the eternal sunrise.

"That's where we are headed," the Judge had said while sitting on the porch with his egg-bowled pipe in his hand, the stem pointed in the same direction as the falcon's beak. "Toward the sunrise of an ever-brightening future."

The Judge was prone to sermonizing. Annie didn't mind, though; she found the measure of his voice, and the wisdom it often spoke, to be a comforting sound in a town where the conversations among the men in saloons and the livestock in pastures often sounded eerily alike. She liked his belief and the fervor with which he spoke it. The Judge's conviction made the world feel smaller and warmer somehow, shining in a way that helped her think past the death of her father.

Her brother also.

Annie gave Vanilla the slack of the reins. The veteran mare knew the way, and it gave Annie a few more minutes to think about the father she barely remembered and the brother she couldn't remember missing any more than she did at that moment.

Peregrine House came into view, the taper light shining out the window of the front parlor and casting a slanted rectangle of light against the porch. The Judge was there, Annie knew, likely working on his many correspondences to agents spread out over not just the United States but the world. He was kind, in his own way, but enigmatic also, and what was unknown about the man was the final barrier between him and Annie's mother. Judge Ellison and Tabitha were like two lonely doves wounded by grief, and each of them, having no more strength to fly amid the tumult, had come upon the same nest during a storm. Annie's family had lost Georgie, and Judge Ellison, only two months prior, had lost his sister, a woman of matchless intelligence, he said, though Annie never heard him say her name.

Annie dismounted and unsaddled Vanilla. She checked the mare for saddle sores, then let her take off into the tall, moonlight-blue grasses of the Peregrine Estate.

Exhausted, Annie stomped up the steps to ensure the Judge heard someone coming to the door.

The Judge answered her knock on the door wearing a red satin smoking jacket, the curve of his big pipe dangled at his chin. Wisps of smoke twisted about his surprised face.

"Annie? What on—" his face changed. "What happened?"

Annie, who had thought she'd tell the truth plain and simple as she always did, opened her mouth to speak. And began to cry.

She fell into the great bulk of the man in the doorway. There, in the light of the moon, with bloody grime still under the fingernails that dug into his jacket, she apologized over and over, unable to answer his simple question. The whole wealth of her emotional economy poured out, and with it she cried as she had refused to cry at her brother's funeral. She had not wept since the night she was attacked in Yellow Hill, when she killed the drunken miner. The night that set forth the events leading to the death of Charlie Gathers, who'd buried the truth in the hard caliche outside the city. Charlie was gone now, though.

Just like Percy.

Just like Georgie.

Just like her father.

And so, in the soft, strong arms of Judge Hezekiah Ellison, Annie found herself telling the story of what had happened in Fort Stockton by saying three words: "It happened again," she said, pulling back to look into his eyes.

The three words robbed the color from his face: his cheeks, usually reddened by whiskey and the sun, drained to pallid white. "What happened?" His voice was in full alarm. "Tell me what happened."

He pulled her at the shoulders, ushering her into the light of the parlor and guiding her over to a tufted leather loveseat.

Annie sat down and set her trembling hands between her knees. The Judge went over to a little marble bar cut into the parlor wall. There came the sound of glass clinking on glass, the soft rush of liquid filling a vessel. When came back over to her, he was holding a glass of whiskey in one hand, and a half-full decanter in the other. The decanter, though quite big, looked small in his large, weathered hand.

"Drink," he said. "All of it."

She cupped her fingers around the cut glass twinkling in the lamplight but stopped short of taking it. "I'm not supposed to—"

"I know your mother doesn't want you to drink, but seeing as she's already mad at me, I'll take the risk. It'll settle your nerves."

Annie threw her head back and swallowed. The heat burned her throat. She choked but kept the whiskey down. "God, that's terrible," she hacked.

"Now, this one you sip." The Judge tipped the decanter over her empty glass, pouring her another. "Do you want me to fetch your mother?"

Annie thought about involving her mother, but decided against it. She shook her head.

He pulled a wicker rocking chair over to sit in front of her. "Take a breath," he said, relighting his pipe. "Now, tell it, in your time."

Annie did, but the telling took no time at all. She did not aggrandize or speculate. She told it, as it happened. All of it.

The further she went into the story, the more red returned to the Judge's face. By the time she was finished, his cheeks and neck were as red as his smoking jacket.

Annie looked down into glass, somehow ashamed in the telling of the tale. She rotated the glass, watching a single bead of liquid trace the edge, roll down and pool over the bottom.

"I'm sorry," she said.

The Judge balked at that. "Sorry, for what? You saved the lives of two men and prevented the further suffering of another. Took a couple of those beasts with you, too. I can't think of any agent of mine who would have acted more bravely."

"Carson," she said. "He would have been able to do more."

The mention of Carson set a shadow over the Judge's face. "I don't reckon that to be true."

"You just want me to feel better, but there ain't any feeling better. Not now, maybe not ever. The cold is…growing, Judge. It's all the way up to the edge of the Cap Rock. Soon, I think it'll swallow up the whole of Texas, maybe everything."

The anger in his face drifted, subsiding into something softer, almost forlorn. "I don't believe that," he said, patting her on the shoulder. "You shouldn't either. The evil that's in the world wants us to think that, but we can't. This winter won't last forever, Annie. Me and my people are working very hard to ensure that it doesn't. The only way for evil to triumph is to slay every good and noble heart, and I firmly believe that to be an impossible task, even among the highest orders of evil. Satan was cast down, St. George pierced the heart of the dragon, and Tyr claimed the wolf Fenrir's pelt, just as Jael felled the great Sisera."

Annie looked at him, lips trembling. Her eyes glassy from the trauma of bloody conflict.

"My point is, Annie, evil has tested you many times over, and many times over you have proven, unequivocally, to be its martial equal. I have never known a braver or more capable person. I am very proud of you."

Annie just stared into her empty glass, her eyes getting heavier and heavier.

The Judge sighed. "This feels imprudent of me, but it's too essential not to say it now."

Annie looked at him.

"It is my hope you will take this as good news," he said. "I did not believe it best to tell you or your mother before. Something that was…perhaps an error on my part. But, your mother has the right of it when she said it was my responsibility to tell you."

"Tell me what?" asked Annie, the whiskey glass suddenly feeling slick and heavy in her hands.

"Orrin Adolphus is alive."

She blinked. She'd heard the words, but they sounded wrong. Far away and unknowable. The Judge watched her with appraising eyes, waiting. And then, slowly, the concept of what he said soared across the gap of impossibility, slowly transforming in its flight into reality. And when the words perched themselves upon her mind, there came a sudden rush of emotions. Surprise fluttered to elation, rising to joy.

He told her about Orrin, about his wounds, and his survival. There were other sections to the story that flew past her, over her, and around her.

he said.

The heavy mask of exhaustion she had felt for the last several days seemed to melt away. Fury, hot and fresh, seared her tired mind, giving her fresh clarity.

"I can see that you're angry," began the Judge, "but consider my posi—"

"Three years," she snapped. "Three years you've lied to me about this, kept it from me."

"We had to be sure—"

Annie's hand sliced through the space between them like a scythe, cutting him off. "Had to be sure. And is three years adequate time for your certainty? Orrin is my best friend, and we might have comforted each other through these years, but you left the both of us in the dark to suffer."

At that, the looked away.

Annie stood up, furious. "He must have tried to tell me he was okay. He must have written!"

The Judge, though he was unflappable, could not meet Annie's countenance. "Many times. But I destroyed the letters. To protect the both of you."

"Help me understand this, *Judge*. You thought it best to help Orrin by leading him to believe that not only did I *receive* these letters but that I refused to respond to them."

The Judge slowly turned his head to look back into Annie's eyes. There was no shame in that glare, only a cold brightness in his gray eyes. It was a look she had seen only a few times, and in those moments it had never been aimed at her. It was a hazardous gaze that wilted whoever stood against it. "I beg your pardon for how I have hurt your feelings." There was no sadness in his words, but there was a warning. "I make decisions based upon what I believe to be best, and those choices have come at a cost to those I love. The world is perched upon a delicate scale, Annie. A scale you cannot yet see, though you have been exposed to a small weight of it. So again, I beg your pardon for the lies I believed were best, but your approval is not something I require.

"As I said, Orrin and the Professor will arrive soon. Then the two of you can make right your relationship. It is my hope that this dinner will unveil to you and your mother the whole sum of what is going on. How desperate we are. But also how close we might be to achieving something unparalleled in history."

Annie shook her head at him, still angry. "And what do you hope to accomplish by revealing these things?"

The Judge stood up, his height allowing him to tower over her.

Unflinching, she did not move her eyes away from his.

"From your mother," the Judge said, "her full companionship."

"And from me?"

"Your assistance in the coming conflict."

Annie narrowed her eyes, saying nothing. Waiting.

"You've proven yourself a survivor time and time again. Capable. Unwavering. You're smart. Good with a gun." The big man took in a breath, then let it out in a long, considering sigh. "Though I've done my very best to stop it, there is a war coming. And I don't mean the one our friend Carson Ptolemy is fighting with the Society of Prometheus. There are many kinds of people I employ as agents for the Peregrine Estate, Annie Miller, and not a single one of them are anything like you."

She drew back, insulted at the notion. Her shoulders hit the cushion behind her.

The Judge smirked. "So quick to anger," he said. "My meaning is this: I have no one like you, and that is a deficit I can no longer afford. You rode for me as a cowhand, and now I'm asking, will you ride with me to war?"

Chapter Eleven

ABILENE, TEXAS

O**RRIN ADOLPHUS TOOK** in the whole measure of the man in the mirror of the tailor's shop. What looked back at him was little more than a one-armed skeleton dressed in a simple white shirt and brown trousers braced with matching brown suspenders. The dark, sunken sockets shadowed his remaining eye—an eye once part of a pair that his mother had often said reminded her of the waters just off the coast of Ireland. He had never seen the ocean but hoped to do just that one day, if only to understand what she had seen in him when he was whole. The Professor had attempted to match the shade when constructing Orrin's mask. He'd gotten close enough to the color for there to be a strange quality of two shades, so close that they might have been distant cousins but certainly not twins.

The short, pear-shaped tailor leaned next to him, his hooked mustache twitching as he stretched a measuring tape down Orrin's thigh. "With the pallor of your skin, I suggest a navy jacket and trousers," he said. "There are an assortment of vests for seasonal accents. I have plenty of cloth and many ladies tell me they enjoy the color." He spoke in a professional tone, though he still refused to look Orrin in the face a second time. Even with the mask covering up his wounds, Orrin understood people's compunction for avoiding his eye.

The tailor stepped over to the counter, where a register all trimmed in brass stood beside his notebook. Calling over his shoulder, he said, "To which angle do you lean?"

"Lean," said Orrin, confused.

The professor, sitting in a wicker chair, stared out past the swooping, golden letters painted on the glass. He chuckled. "Your manliness, Orrin. He wants to know which leg it runs." With a big smile, he looked over at the tailor. "First time."

The tailor smiled back. "Certainly."

Orrin looked down at the crotch of his pants. "Umm, left?"

"Very good, sir." The tailor stepped around the counter and brought out a flat section of wood upon which were several samples of cloth. Among the earthen greens and browns, lavender and deep blues, Orrin saw the color he wanted.

"Black," said Orrin.

The tailor let out a stifled cough. "Black is a fine color, indeed; nothing more formal. But here, sir, it is reserved for weddings and funerals. Now, as I said before, the navy you can see is quite—"

"Black, please, sir."

The tailor looked up at Orrin, then over at Professor Bass. "Will you have a secondary suit made then? For less ceremonial occasions."

"One suit," Professor Bass said. He was watching the bustling street, his mind mostly elsewhere it seemed. "The man wants black. Black is what we'll have."

The tailor nodded. "As you wish, gentlemen. Luckily, I have a jacket and trousers that should fit quite nicely. They can be

A Red Winter in the West

hemmed by tomorrow morning. Now, if you'd like to look among the vests?"

The Professor rose at this and wrapped a friendly arm around his apprentice's shoulders. At the far corner of the shop, a collection of inanimate torsos modeled several intricate fashions. He clapped Orrin on the back.

"Now, we have our base color. And since you shall be garbed in the shade of the midnight hour, picking the perfect accent should be relatively easy. As I'm sure you've observed, I prefer brown. It can easily hide tobacco or whiskey stains, and I find that red and yellow and chestnut work well in this pattern here." He pointed to one of the vests checkered with a set of dark squares offset with lighter ones. "These do the job for me. But I think this one would be perfect for you." He moved his finger to point at a bright gray brocade vest dotted with rows of white, hexagonal accents. "This," he said, "with a black cravat, will look quite fey."

Orrin imagined himself in a frock coat with the Professor's suggested accouterments. "You don't think I'll look silly?"

"Well, it's possible you might be mistaken for a preacher or fancy gambler, but otherwise I think the outfit will sing."

"It's the most expensive," said Orrin.

"An excellent observation, and one that will do you well when you are buying. Today, however, you are not."

Orrin nodded. Professor Bass had yet to lead him astray in all other matters of mathematics, alchemical theory, and philosophy, so it seemed reasonable that the man understood fashion as well. Turning back to the counter, Orrin said, "This one here."

The tailor looked up. His eyes brightened with the excitement of profit. "Excellent choice, sir."

"He'll need matching cuff links, and a few shirts as well. White, crimson, and a periwinkle if you have it."

"All that, Professor?" asked Orrin, beginning to wonder at the cost of all these fine things.

"Orrin, my boy, a suit is like the man who wears it: immaculately crafted and made to weather all seasons. The well-tailored suit is a divine invention, truly."

"How so?"

"Look at the form of it, a singular vision from toe to shoulder, save for the *V*." The professor brought his palms together to form the letter. "From the narrow point where the coat opens, the vest peeks out to the cravat, leading up to accentuate a man's face. A suit, my dear apprentice, is much like Samuel Colt's revolver. It is a device that renders all men into equality."

Orrin hated the notion that his clothes would draw the eyes of onlookers. He knew what they would see. Not the man, but the freak.

"Maybe a suit isn't the best idea for me then."

"Nonsense. This suit will lead people to see your face. Your kind and measured countenance. But it is what's behind the face that is the true treasure." He pressed the tip of his forefinger against Orrin's head. "The mind is the temple of the self, and yours is as grand as any I've ever seen."

Orrin swelled at those words. The Professor had taken him in and given him an unparalleled education, but what had sustained him on the trek from wounded orphan to disfigured man were these moments. Moments that gave value to what was, and might forever be, a broken vessel.

They paid the tailor his due. In return, he gave them the promise that all would be ready by noon the next day.

A Red Winter in the West

The streets of Abilene were bustling with activity. Dusty cowboys meandered among the saloons and gambling halls. Little boys wearing hand-me-down hats and girls wreathed in their bonnets bustled down the sidewalks, making mischief among each other as they walked behind their schoolmarm. The air was ripe with the smell of baking bread and ringing with the bright peal of blacksmith hammers and the percussion of horse hooves freshly shod. The sky was cold and bright.

It was a new day for Orrin. A new suit, new town, and new people. None of whom seemed to stare too long at him. Standing there filled him with a new birth of anticipation—mostly hope, but anxiety also, for there was the fear of what Annie would say when she saw him. Would she even recognize him beneath the wreckage of what the great wolf's claws left behind?

And if she did, what would she say?

He pondered this as they made their way back over to the Hotel Windsor, where they had procured themselves two rooms on the second story.

Professor Bass excused himself to his own room, saying he wanted a chance to go over a few personal notes he intended to present to Judge Ellison.

"You're sure I can't help?" Orrin asked.

"Certain. Now, do yourself a favor, walk the town. You can do me the favor of securing our cargo at the coach station. Instruct them to have all of our supplies taken to Peregrine House. We'll need them tomorrow night. After dinner, our work in Abilene will begin in earnest."

Orrin made his way down the main street, looking into the varying shops and saloons. The interior of one bar in particular caught his eye. It was mostly empty, which allowed him to see the massive oak bar; it was less a thing of function and more an extravagant couture of carpentry. He saw it first through the window and paused, thinking perhaps he would go inside. But, he kept walking, choosing to admire it from afar over the saloon's winged doorway. Curling threads of brass adorned an enormous pair of mirrors behind the bar itself. Bottle after bottle stood in line, a perfect row of soldiers waging their war on sobriety. Their commander, the bartender, polished the bar top with paternal care. He was smiling, conversing with a pair of leaning customers.

One of the customers called out: "I said to him, if a blacksmith wants to get his metal to droop, just have him ask my wife about her day."

They all laughed, and one of the customers, almost falling off his stool, slapped the bar in delight.

The bartender's laughter died and his face soured. "Goddamn it, Ambrose. What have I told you about whackin' the bar?"

Ambrose swallowed a chuckle and raised his hands as if at gunpoint, his chin curling into his neck.

"Christ, it's like talkin' to a haystack," the bartender said.

Ambrose's playfulness faded. "Aw now, I didn't hurt it, Ollie."

"Every damn day, hittin' the bar. Hell, you don't spend enough coin in here to do that."

Ambrose stuck his chin out at him. "Well, maybe I'll just take my business elsewhere."

Orrin shook his head, a smile on his lips, and carried on walking. The professor had advised him to get a drink, and he might, but he wanted to get the cargo settled first. He took a few steps, still looking into the bar windows, and strode shoulder-first into a woman passing by. They rebounded off one another. He caught her arm as she tottered, off balance, toward the nearby hitching post, but her feet twisted together, and her weight pulled them down onto the wooden planks.

The fall didn't hurt so much as it embarrassed him. "Oh, ma'am," he said. "I'm so sorry. Are you okay?"

She laughed politely as he helped her to her feet. "I'm fine." She turned to reveal her face.

Orrin's heart beat heavily. The hair on his neck bristled. Time thickened.

It was Tabitha Miller.

"I should be more careful about watching where I'm going," she said.

"No, ma'am," he said hurriedly. "It was my fault."

"Oh, never you mind whose fault it was." She looked at him. Her mouth drew up in reserved shock.

She knows it's me, he thought. At that, he felt a swell of excitement at the reunion. He opened his mouth to say her name.

"I beg your pardon, sir," she said, slapping at the dust on her skirt. Their eyes met again as she extended her hand. "I'm Tabitha."

"I…um." His excitement fluttered and died like a soaring hawk shot out of the sky. "I'm very sorry."

He looked away from her, unable to bear that a woman who had known him for so long could not see the familiar child in the young man now before her.

"Are you all right?" she asked.

He waved a dismissive hand at her. "I'm sorry, ma'am. I have pressing business."

She started to say something, but he was already pounding down the sidewalk in a rush. Again, she called after him, but he did not turn back. They had forgotten him. And why shouldn't they? He had been absent three years from their lives. They had moved on.

It had always been a fear of his, but now it was revealed as the truth, it made him sick to the bone. The only person he had left in the world was Professor Bass.

Chapter Twelve

ABOARD THE STEAM TRAIN *HEPHAESTUS,* ST. LOUIS, MISSOURI

WHEN CARSON WAS a young boy, a barber in Louisiana had told him that St. Louis was the most beautiful place in the world. Big Jim was a loud, happy man who told a lifetime of stories while providing what he advertised to be the "Best Dime Haircut in the World." As his large dark hands swooped and snipped at Carson's stringy black hair, he said, "Yes, sir. St. Louis. If there ever was a town made for a man, then that was the town for me."

Carson, now lashed to the crates inside the freezing cargo car like Christ crucified, dozed in and out of that memory. He remembered the smell of the leather chair. The swishing of the razor sliding along the strop. The smell of old blood. The sweetness of cedar on the man's breath while he carefully examined Carson's neckline. He remembered his father, Gilbert Ptolemy, who he could see in the great mirror before him, smoking his pipe and reading the New Orleans paper.

"Why'd didn't you stay there then?" Carson asked Big Jim.

"Aw, I had to give it up. Personal reasons, you understand."

Carson plowed on. "What personal reasons?"

"Son," Ptolemy extended the word into a warning.

Big Jim laughed. "I can't tell you all of it, my boy, but what I can tell you is that the white men of St. Louis didn't love me near as much as their wives did. Quit moving' your head, boy. Gonna lose an ear if you don't. The haircut costs a dime 'cause it's only fifteen minutes of my time, but me sewing an ear back on takes more of both. And I don't think you've got that kinda money for that kind of time." He poked the boy's shoulder playfully.

Carson could use a stitch at the moment, and he would have happily paid any price to mend the half-dozen cuts that Baroness Gwendolyn had made. Of the six, only one was deep. A hard, swift slash along the junction of his palm and thumb. He kept the thumb slack, trying not to move it. When it twitched involuntarily, he could feel the crusty scab pull open, sending a needle of pain into his hand. The other gashes on his chest and stomach were superficial. Little reminders she called them.

She gave him a ladle of water a day, but no food. His joints ached from disuse, and his feet and ankles begged for reprieve.

It was the call of the stationmaster that woke him this time. Carson could hear the man shouting over the multitude of whistling trains. "Last call for Chicago. Tickets for last call to Chicago!"

Carson tried to yell so that someone might hear him, but his throat was raw and no matter how he endured the pain of crying out, no one came.

He couldn't remember the last time the *Hephaestus had* moved; it must have been days. His only measure of time was when the sun would peek through the shuttered window set in the cargo door.

A Red Winter in the West

The acrid smell of decomposing corpses filled his nostrils. The men Carson killed were having their slow, putrid revenge.

A blast of sunlight filled the room, blinding him. He turned his head away and began to call for help. Someone might yet hear him.

"You hush now," the Baroness said over the sound of approaching boot heels. The door closed and darkness took the room again. "Lady," she said, "and gentlemen, this is Carson Ptolemy, the man I told you about."

There were three men and a woman, each of them armed. Their faces were streaked with grime and soot. The Baroness, dressed in an immaculate scarlet dress, sauntered over to him. "You will watch over him in pairs, in six-hour shifts."

"Listen to me," said Carson, his voice hoarse. "This woman is insane; she's going to hurt people. Lots of people. You have to stop—"

"How adorable," the Baroness smiled. "You think I would hire a few gunhands from a saloon? My dear Mr. Ptolemy, what you have before you are not ruffians pulled from the chattel masses of St. Louis but true believers." She turned back to the gunslingers. "Mr. Combs, if you would?"

The man stepped forward. Even in the dim light, Carson could see the man's droopy eyes set over a long, jagged scar on his chin. He pulled down his collar. On his exposed neck Carson saw a brand, the raised, puffy flesh of a flame burning inside a circle.

"Save your words, Mr. Ptolemy," said the Baroness. "These fine people are dedicated to the cause."

Combs brandished a smile, revealing a perfect set of teeth. He opened his coat, revealing Carson's gun belt around his waist. In the holster was his revolver.

His father's revolver.

"Thanks for the iron," said Combs.

Carson yanked against his bonds, furious. The pain returned, running a hot line through every aching joint. However, the rage kept him upright. The fury of such a theft kept his knees from buckling. He growled at Combs like a caged animal.

"Careful, Mr. Combs. This one has spirit still. Despite his ragged appearance, I'll ask that you treat him like a hungry tiger—remain close enough to observe but out of reach." The Baroness turned back to the other guards. "None of you are to harm him. As I said, the High Priest wants him alive." Her eyes met Carson's. "You are, after all, one of the few who is able to read the words of the Black Manuscript. Were that not the case," she said, approaching him, "we wouldn't have bothered with luring you onto this train with our falsified telegram."

She sniffed a laugh. "Oh, look at that murderous gaze of yours. Very scary, little tiger. Tell me, how does it make you feel when I tell you this: when your use is all spent, I'm going to butcher you alive, piece by tiny piece. Then I'll salt you over and ship you down to Abilene, where the Judge can have what remains."

"You'll have to wait a long time," said Carson. "I won't read a single word out of your damned book. I'll chew my tongue off first and spit it in your face."

"Oh," she said, shaking her head with a pitying expression. "This isn't some saloon filled with derelict drunkards that you can cow with threats of violence, Carson Ptolemy. This is not a hero's song. Nor is this a fantasy where somehow, someway, you will spring to action and destroy your enemies through sheer rage and power and righteousness. But you've warned me as to what you're willing to do. And I must respond..." She summoned Mr. Combs with a snap of her fingers. "Let me show you just how seriously I take threats."

A Red Winter in the West

Carson stared her down. He refused to give her any sign that her words bent his will.

"Mr. Combs, you and Mr. Reyes will do me the favor of taking a pair of pliers and removing all of Mr. Ptolemy's teeth."

Reyes looked at Combs, a long grin peeling his mouth open into a smile. Combs smirked backat Reyes, then he looked at Carson. They stepped toward him, slowly.

"Stay the fuck back," said Carson, warning. "I swear to God–"

In a flash, Reyes's right hand whipped out, smashing into Carson's face. His head snapped back, the world flashing white. Then Combs was somehow behind him, clamping a forearm around his throat and squeezing so hard against the windpipe that Carson gagged. Unable to breath, he thrashed wildly, but Combs was too strong and the bonds were too tight.

"What's that," said Reyes, turning on a hip to drive a crushing blow into Carson's solar plexus. "I can't hear you."

Just as his vision began to dim, an uppercut snapped Carson's head back, the force so powerful that he nearly bit his tongue in half. Combs released his grip.

"Go something to say now?" said Reyes, driving his shin up into Carson's groin.

The world became a heat-wave mirage, wavy and distant. Carson, captive to his enemies, felt his guts churn, and he vomited down the front of his shirt.

From someplace he could not see there came a sound of metal tinking. The teeth of a pair of pliers coming together lightly, quickly. Over and over.

"Come here you fucking little—" Reyes didn't finish with words, but with a deed. His strong hand twisted its fingers into Carson's hair, the other mashed his jaw, prying it open.

131

C.S. Humble

"No," screamed Carson, squirming and writhing. The word held no power. It was not a sound of rage but a pitiful noise. "N-no!"

Reyes held him fast. "Quit your fucking— I swear to God if you bite me, you little shit."

He then used a thick index finger to fishhook Carson's mouth, stretching the seam of lips so taut that if felt they might rip down the length of his cheek.

Carson stomped Reyes's feet, threw his knees up to try and catch him, but the Mexican slid around to his side, out of harms reach.

"That's it," said Combs, fish hooking the other side of Carson's mouth. "You fight, I'll take all that goddamn fight right out of ya."

The plier's pincers were suddenly in Carson's mouth, behind his front teeth. Their metal tips scraped his gums, rubbed raw the roof of his mouth.

He tried to move his head with the sudden yanking motion, but Combs didn't simply pull at the tooth, he wrenched it, twisting. There was a deep tearing sound as the tooth ripped from his gums. Blood and saliva and a wild sound of pain flowed from Carson's lips.

The Baroness watched every extraction, smiled through every bloody scream. Every time Carson tried to twist his face away, they would beat him until he no longer had the strength to deny the iron pincers they shoved into his mouth. Every tooth, pulled out by the root, was deposited at Carson's feet. He did not pass out from the pain, though many times he wished that he had.

Heart hammering, disbelieving that this was happening, he was rendered edentulous.

When it was over, his face dripping with sweat, his mouth drooling blood, Carson squinted through the slits of his swollen eyes. He looked at the Baroness and groaned at her.

A Red Winter in the West

She leaned her ear toward him, stepping only inches from his face. "Hmm? What was that? Something else to say, have you?"

The arc of blood that flew out of his mouth hit her across the eyes, flowing down the bridge of her nose in a crooked line.

Her eyes flashed wide in shock and she gasped. Carson spat again, a cloud of red mist that hit the woman in her open mouth.

Mr. Combs clubbed Carson behind the ear with the butt of his father's revolver. White flashed. Darkness closed in.

Just before he passed out, Carson heard the train whistle signaling their departure from St. Louis, and he found himself thinking of Big Jim. Big Jim would have been so disappointed that Carson Ptolemy never got the chance to see the beautiful city that the barber had loved best.

Chapter Thirteen

ABILENE, TEXAS

THE MORNING BEFORE the dinner, Annie and her mother sat at the breakfast table sipping coffee together. The words came easier this time in the telling of the events in Fort Stockton. Having all the trust in her mother's resolve, Annie told it as it had happened, sparing none of the details.

Tabitha took the story well, only listening. She didn't interrupt.

"Boone and Dutch went over to the Windsor," said Annie. "I went to Peregrine House and told the Judge everything you've heard."

Tabitha's eyes fell to the kitchen table where a plate of cold eggs went untouched. "God in Heaven," she said.

"We were very lucky."

Tabitha crushed the napkin in her hand. Her lips curled with anger. "You shouldn't have been there in the first place."

"I'm a wrangler for the Judge's company, Momma. I was doing my job."

"Still, you shouldn't be placed in that situation. You're just a child, you could have been…"

Annie placed her hand over her mother's. "I wasn't. I'm here, with you. Safe."

"And those…those beasts could have—"

"They didn't, Momma. Not even the Judge could have suspected—"

Tabitha snapped her eyes up to her daughter. In them, Annie saw the cold, slithering serpent of anger. "He knew what was out there. And damn it, so did I. I never should have allowed you to go in the first place."

"I don't want to have that argument again. Please." Annie squeezed her mother's hand gently.

"I don't understand this world anymore. The persistent cold or the things coming out of it. It was the cold that put the sickness in your brother, and now these…these *things* tried to take you, too."

"There is something else," said Annie. She took a deep breath. "Judge Ellison has asked something of me, something he knows you will be very displeased with."

Tabitha blinked, her brow furrowed.

Her eyes widened. With a whisper as sharp as the cold wind outside, she said, "No."

"Momma—"

"Absolutely not. Christ and all his holy angels, girl. I say no, and on this I will not relent."

Annie traced a thumb along her mother's thumb. "I love you," she said. "I love you very much."

Tabitha's jaw clenched.

Annie continued, "Tonight, at dinner, I plan to tell the Judge that I will accept his offer."

Her mother jerked her hand away, standing up so quickly that her chair slapped the floor. "Annie Joy Miller, I am your mother.

A Red Winter in the West

No matter how old you are, I am still that. You will abide me, and I say no!"

Annie looked away from her mother's hard rebuke. "Something is happening. Whatever started in Yellow Hill, whatever Carson thought his father destroyed, is seeping out. You and I, the Judge, Carson, all of us know what happened."

"You only know what that Ptolemy boy told you. Think of all the things Carson *didn't* tell you; didn't tell you about Orrin, didn't tell you when he was leaving or why."

"I know."

"Jesus, Annie, think about what you are saying. You were almost killed two days ago, and now you want to throw yourself slap bang into the fire all over again. Don't you care about our life here?"

"Our life here is—"

"Don't you care about me?"

Annie's own anger flashed. "It is *because* I care about you that I need to do this. That I have to do this. Can't you see that?"

"All I see is a girl, my daughter, throwing her life away. Everything we've worked to reclaim, the heartache of your brother dying. Don't you see that if you go, I'll have no one. Both of my children will be gone, one buried and the other digging her own grave!"

"Stop yelling at me, Mother."

"I will not! You will hear me, Annie. You will hear me on this, and you will heed me."

"People are dying, Momma. They are being torn apart out there, not only in the wilderness. Whatever came out of Yellow Hill is spreading into towns, flooding over trails that will eventually lead here. I will not wait for that rot to reach us. To reach you." Annie shook her head, struggling to keep the tears from falling down her cheeks. "A hundred men and more, Momma. A hundred

Buffalo Soldiers and almost a dozen friends who helped me learn to cowboy are gone. They're gone!" Annie slammed the flat of her palm against the table. The plates jumped at the impact, then rattled upon their landing.

"Judge Ellison, for all of his faults…for all the anger I bear toward him for lying to me about what happened to Orrin, on this thing he is right. People have to stand up and fight so that others can withstand the night. So they can see the sunrise. People deserve that. You deserve that. And I've seen too much of this cold coming darkness to let it reach this place, Momma. To let it reach you and tear us apart."

The tears that Annie had refused, her mother could not. Jewels of water fell down her face. She picked up the chair. "My life," she said, her voice quiet, wounded. "My family. It wasn't supposed to be this way." She sat in the chair, her nervous fingers pattering on the table. Her eyes frantic. "There was a time when our poverty was the only burden we were forced to bear. But now," she said, "look at us. You without a father or a brother. Me…all my strength feels used up."

Annie went to her mother. She knelt and wrapped her tired arms around her mother's waist. "It isn't, Momma. You're the strongest person I know."

Tabitha ran her fingers through Annie's hair. Tears fell. "All my grief, all this pain, it has robbed us both of the lives we were supposed to have."

Annie looked at her mother and, with a gentle stroke, brushed away a tear on the precipice of her eye. "Not your grief, Momma. It was the people who emboldened Jeremiah Hart. They are the ones who brought all this on us and so many others. All this death and frozen pestilence."

"I can't lose you."

A Red Winter in the West

Annie's smile lifted, the familiar preamble of heartfelt promise on the face of a loving child. "You won't ever lose me."

They embraced and for a long time. Huddled together, they conversed quietly in the muffled language of sorrow.

———

That afternoon, Annie soaked in a freshly drawn bath. Her nose and mouth were the only body parts that broke the placid surface of the water. The world muted in that warm place. She breathed slowly and deeply. The snarling face of the wolflike creature was ever present in her mind, the wide circle filled with what might have been a hundred sharp teeth. Her mouth lifted into a smile when she remembered its head snapping back as the bullet punched through its skull and the arc of blood that sprayed into the air. They, like any other animal or man, could be killed. That's all that mattered. Not their blood-chilling howls or their gleaming claws, only their mortality. Annie would take that from them. She would take and take until they were wiped clean of the earth.

But first, she had a dinner party to attend.

Drying her hair, she went to her room. A dress lay on her bed. It was a beautiful blue gown, gifted to her on her sixteenth birthday by her mother. More than a garment, it was a reminder. A reminder from mother to daughter that there were still gentle things in the world—gentle, beautiful things. She picked up the dress by its silky shoulders and, admiring it all the way, carried it over to her wardrobe and put it back on the rack. She pulled on her finest breeches, a white silk shirt, and a pair of freshly polished boots. Then came the dark brown jacket. A cavalry coat adorned with two rows of shining brass buttons. Her gun belt, its holster still streaked with dried blood, went around her waist. She pulled her dark hair back into a ponytail and tied it with a white ribbon.

Annie stepped out into the parlor and found her mother waiting.

Tabitha's shoulder's fell. "Honey, it's a dinner party. You're going dressed like that?"

"I love the dress, Momma. But I can't carry my pistol wearing it."

"One would think that attending the dinner party of a friend would preclude the need of it."

Her mother was the portrait of venerable beauty. Her dress was the shade of flowering jasmine, where rings of baby blue satin circled the skirt. "I'll tell you what," Annie said. "If we get there and I'm the only person wearing one, I'll take it off and buy you dinner with my own wages."

"And if you aren't?"

"Well, then, we'll go to dinner anyway. I'll still pay, *and* I'll wear the dress."

Tabitha tried not to smile, but her lips slanted to a smirk. She stood up. "I'll take that bet."

They walked out onto the glowing streets of Abilene, both of them bronzed in the light of the setting sun. Tabitha wrapped a navy shawl around her shoulders and mounted Starchild. Annie slid into Vanilla's saddle, and they were off, taking a meandering pace toward Peregrine House.

"Nervous?" asked Tabitha.

Annie pretended not to understand the intimation. "Nervous about what?"

"Don't act like you don't know."

A Red Winter in the West

"You mean Orrin?"

"Mmhmm."

"I don't know." That was a lie. She knew, and she sure as hell didn't want to talk about it. "Are you nervous?"

"Now why would I be nervous?"

Annie gave her mother a wry smile. "Oh, so you don't know yet."

"Know about what?"

Annie laughed. "I can't wait," she said. "I can't wait to see the look on your face."

Tabitha grew insistent. "About *what*?"

"You'll see."

Tabitha huffed and looked to the darkening path that led out of town toward the Judge's home. "You know it's cruel to tease your mother with ambiguity."

"Sure do."

"Vanilla," said Tabitha, looking over at Annie's horse, "why is she so mean to me?"

"You leave her outta this."

"Is it because she's so angry that you're no longer the fastest horse in the family?"

Annie looked at her mother, her mouth falling open.

Tabitha gave her a big toothy smile.

"Don't listen to her." Annie scrubbed her fingers through the mare's mane. "She just jealous."

"Oh, am I now?"

"You know it, and so do I."

Tabitha gripped her reins tightly. "Ready?"

"Ready for what?"

"Set…"

"Now just wait a—"

"Go!" And with a hard kick, Starchild reared and bolted down the path.

"Oh, the hell with that," Annie said and galloped after her.

Pounding down the trail outside of Abilene, Annie watched her mother's dress flutter against the wind like a victory banner.

With the head start, and Vanilla still fatigued from the long, hard flight from Fort Stockton, Annie didn't push her too hard. Starchild proved victorious, reaching first the hitching posts near the wraparound porch of the house.

Annie slowed to a trot, shaking her head in defeat, and smiled. Her mother began to dismount.

"What took you two so long?" said Tabitha, cocksure.

"You cheated."

"Oh, I don't think we cheated. Did we girl?" Tabitha scratched Starchild's chin.

Annie dismounted. "We'll try that again when we head home. We'll see who wins a fair contest."

When Annie saw the front door of Peregrine House, her anxiety grew as tall as the structure itself. Not only would she be making one of the biggest choices in her life, but she would also come face-to-face with a specter from her past.

What do you say to the resurrected? Oh, hi, Orrin. Remember when we were in school together? Nice to see that you didn't die with everyone else in town.

How do you approach a ghost made real?

With happiness, of course. That thought shrank the worry inside her heart, and it grew up in her a strong, familiar courage.

At the front door, Tabitha lifted the large iron knocker, then planted it hard against the door.

"Remember," said Annie. "What happened on the cattle drive wasn't his fault."

A Red Winter in the West

"The Judge and I will have our conversation, same as you will."

The door opened.

The Judge wore a dark navy suit, double-breasted, crisply lined. It slimmed even the great bulk of his stomach. His red cravat gave off a gossamer shine against the stark white of his shirt, and his gray eyes sparkled in deep sockets like warm coals slumbering in a fire.

He welcomed them inside and paused as Tabitha went by, waiting for Tabitha to extend her cheek to him, that he might greet her with a kiss, as he often did.

Tabitha strode past him, into the foyer.

Behind her mother, Annie gave the Judge a shrug.

He didn't shrug back. His eyes were set on her, as if to advise caution. Slowly, he turned his head toward the front parlor.

That confused her a bit. Her eyes followed his chin down the hall.

There was a tall, hauntingly gaunt man standing there. He wore a black suit that opened just above the navel to reveal a brocade vest. It was gray, like the moon veiled in an overcast sky. A broad, black cravat circled his throat. One of the arms of his jacket was folded at the elbow, the sleeve pinned to his shoulder. His face, half-shadowed in the overhead lamplight, tilted.

"Hello, Annie."

At those words, something sprang up in her—an ember of childhood kindled to life. Running to him, she said his name—half a question, half an exclamation. She hit him hard as a charging bull and wrapped her arms around his gaunt figure. Her face slammed into his chest, and she squeezed as hard as she could.

The boy she had known, now the man she would grow to know, said nothing.

Orrin set his cheek against the top of her head, wrapping his arm around her shoulders.

"I thought you were gone," she said. They didn't tell me."

"I know," he said.

She leaned back to look into his eyes.

What the shadows had obscured at a distance, the wavering lamplight and close proximity revealed. What she saw was half of the boy she remembered, the other half shielded by a painted mask, hiding what lay beneath.

His gaze fell to the floor. "I'm sorry," he said. "It's off-putting, I know."

Annie shook her head. Her smile never bigger, she lifted her hands and cupped his face. The expanse of his cool green eye widened.

Annie kissed the flesh of the cheek that remained.

Then, she kissed the mask.

"I am so glad you're here," she said.

Orrin, the boy who survived, cried a single lonely tear at their reunion.

Annie wiped away the falling droplet from his cheek and laughed, her own tears beginning to flow. "You're so tall!"

"You're taller, too."

She laughed again, hugged him again.

"I have a lot to say," he said.

The Judge and Tabitha approached.

"Oh my goodness," said Tabitha. "Oh Orrin, sweetheart, I can't believe I didn't see it yesterday!"

"Yesterday?" asked Judge Ellison.

"We ran into each other just yesterday while I was coming back from the market."

"Quite literally," said Orrin.

"I didn't recogniz—" she stopped herself.

Orrin nodded politely. "I know. Sometimes I don't even recognize myself."

A Red Winter in the West

From behind them, a man loudly cleared his throat. He was reclining in one of the wingback chairs. A slender man comprised of far too many angles, dressed in a brown suit, regarded the fellowship of Yellow Hill survivors by lifting a glass of whiskey at them. "Many happy returns to such a display of human hearts grown larger. *Quanta qualia, conventus gaudia erunt.*" He took a drink.

Tabitha wrinkled her face. "Do what now?"

The Judge placed a cautious hand on her shoulder. "Ladies, let me introduce Professor Robert Bass. Scientist, inventor, investigator of the supernatural and mundane realms. My oldest friend here has a love of all ancient things."

Professor Bass winked them. "My pleasure."

"What was that you just said?" Annie asked the Professor.

The professor smiled. "Orrin, would you kindly illuminate?"

Orrin looked at Annie, unashamed. "It's Latin. Translated, it means, how great and how wonderful the joys of our meeting will be."

"And how wonderful they are," said the Professor, just before he finished his drink.

"You'll forgive him his eccentricities," said the Judge.

Tabitha turned to give a questioning glance at the Judge's hand resting on her shoulder.

He lifted it away from her. "Ahem. If you all would, please, let's make our way into the dining room to continue our business? Dinner is ready."

They made their way into the dining room. Like the rest of Peregrine House, it was adorned with the finest furnishings. A great table capable of seating eight was bisected by a doily runner of white. The dark oak chairs, cushioned in white, bore embroidered crests of a falcon stretching out in mid-flight. The plates

were white as well, and the full measure of silver utensils shimmered under the lights of dozens of candles burning brightly
upon a chandelier. At the center of the table was a whole prime
rib, seared red to perfection. There were steaming potatoes piled
high in a serving bowl. Bright purple carrots slathered in thick
brown gravy and two loaves of freshly baked bread, their aroma
filling the room. Several black bottles of the Judge's favorite
Merlot stood tall near the head of the table, ready to be poured
into crystal goblets.

They ate and drank and laughed and told each other stories that
served as invitations to friendships new and re-kindled. With each
glass of wine, Tabitha warmed to the Judge again. On the his left
sat Professor Bass, who quipped from time to time, interrupting the
Judge when he went off on one topic or another, correcting his friend
with nuance or teasing him with old japes. And further to the left,
sitting in front of Annie, was Orrin. She found herself looking at
him. Studying the slim figure that had lengthened so much in such
a short measure of time. The dark hair brushed into wavey locks that
accentuated the soft quality of his eye. There was a bashfulness to
the man that had not resided within the boy, as if a long dark shadow had thrown itself over him to hide more than his painted mask
ever could. She smiled, watching him gracefully eat with a grown
man's hunger, using the delicate manners a boy can only inherit
from their mother. How had the silly, wonderful friend become such
a new thing and yet retain so much of what had drawn her too him
in the beginning?

Annie didn't know, and to tell the truth, she didn't care. She
only felt a strange kind of triumph at Orrin's return. She had promised they would be friends forever. And now, life had afforded a
chance to make full use of that promise.

A Red Winter in the West

The conversation among them sorrowed when Annie asked Orrin what had happened in Yellow Hill, but he told the story well. And when it came to all the letters he'd written Annie, she gave the Judge a hard, unforgiving stare.

"I see on your face the anger you have, Annie."

"Who could miss it," said the Professor, which got him an equally cutting look. "Don't shoot an observer, Ms. Miller. I mailed the letters. It was left to my friend here to decide whether you would receive them."

Annie looked back at the Judge, who was wiping the corners of his mouth. "Why?"

"The obvious reasons aside, I wasn't sure if Orrin would recover, or if he had somehow been…compromised. We know of certain creatures who can ensorcell the human mind or, worse, infect a person into becoming something like the creature itself."

"Three years," said Tabitha, disappointed.

"Yes," he said, almost exhasperated in his tone. "And for all the love I bear all of you, I do not apologize for the prudence I'm forced to engage in when dealing with powers and circumstances I do not wholly understand. Neither I, nor Robert, had ever encountered anything like what came out of that mine in Yellow Hill."

The mention of Yellow Hill brought a thought to Annie's mind. "Wait," she said. "Where is Carson? He should be here for this. Shouldn't he?"

The Judge gave the Professor a curious look.

"Don't look at me," the man said. "I'd have told them the moment it happened."

Annie's heart sank. "Tell me he isn't—"

"No." The Judge took a drink of his wine. "Carson is alive, so far as I am aware."

"Then what is it?" Tabitha was insistent.

The Judge's demeanor, normally placid and powerful, bent. "You recall the night he visited here? The conversations were delightful, but after you left…things were not so cordial. Gilbert Ptolemy was the second father that Carson lost to an occult order known as the Society of Prometheus. The Society represents one of two, maybe three, major threats that are, at present, actively working against all human life on earth. They worship beings that you might well enough call titans, maybe even gods. Their chief aim is to decipher the Black Manuscript. An ancient tome that reveals the location of certain obelisks that, should they be unlocked, become gateways for these titans to pass through. Jeremiah Hart was able to decipher one of these pages. This allowed him to open the gate buried in the mine of Yellow Hill."

The Judge took in a deep breath, as if his lungs were the bellows to some hidden fire within him. "I know all of this," he said, "because I was once one of them."

In that moment, at those words, Annie's vision distanced itself from the world. It was as if the table grew longer, and time drew taut. The words registered, but they made no sense.

The Judge continued. "Carson does not yet know this, but my sister and I were the people who hired his father, Ezra Watts. At the time, Ezra was a rising name among occult researchers. We hired him under the false pretense that I was working against the Society, when, in truth, I was their chief recruiter."

Her mother's chest swelled with a deep breath. She shifted in her chair, posture straightening. All the signs she was about to put a verbal waylay on the man. "You…," she began, but the Judge lifted a hand.

He tilted his head, eyes hardening on her. "Please, let me finish. Let me tell it all."

A Red Winter in the West

Tabitha shook her head but did not speak.

"My late sister coordinated their efforts," he continued. "I built a web of agents around the world, hiring the brightest minds. Linguists, philologists, anthropologists, alchemists: I hired one and all.

"Because the manuscript is everything to the Society. It is their Revelation. Their apocalypse song. Vast sums of money were spent bringing in experts, for generation upon generation, going back long before I became one of their number. Hundreds of years before, perhaps a thousand, the Society coerced, kidnapped, or employed countless men and women to throw themselves against those damanable words, and all of them failed. All their minds ultimately became riddled with madness. After my initiation, I was given the task of finding someone who could settle the language for all time. Someone who could provide a present key to the society's timeless lock. Ezra Watts, however, was a man with an uncommonly powerful mind. I truly believed that he would be the one to decipher the language…" The Judges his voice trailed off.

Annie had never heard his voice drift to such a sad, lonely place. It was shame. She had heard it in others. Never in him.

The Judge, penitent, looked deeply into Tabitha's eyes. His composure wavering. "The manuscript drove Ezra mad."

Tabitha slid away from the Judge, her mouth agape. "Hezekiah…, I—"

He acted as though he was going to reach for her hand, but thought better of it. And so, Judge Ellison leaned back and let his shoulders slouch against the chair. "Before I met Gilbert Ptolemy, Tabitha, I was a different man on a different path. A darker path. When I learned of what Ezra tried to do to Carson, what Gilbert did to save him, it changed me. In the actions of Gilbert Ptolemy, I fell in love with my humanity again. Gilbert had every reason to leave that child to his fate, every reason to run from the horror when he had the chance. Instead, after Ezra left him for dead, he tracked the two of them down, and he saved Carson's life. My sister and I saw the darkness that had swallowed us, and we recanted. I took Carson and Gilbert in, here at Peregrine House, and since that time I have dedicated my life to building not a web, but a shield. A shield of agents who work against the Society, and other threats as well. One of those other threats is why we are meeting tonight."

Annie looked at Orrin. The shock on his face clear; he was just learning of this, too. Then she leveled a hard gaze at the Judge.

"What. Happened. To. Carson." Her hands were wet, clammy.

The Judge nodded. "Rage," he said. "Ungovernable rage. You see, among a collection of Jeremiah Hart's notes, Carson found the location of several of the higher-ranked members of the Society. He insisted, as only he would, that the time to strike was at that very moment. He said we had to kill them—all of them. I tried to reason with him and told him that our numbers were too small, that I needed more time to recruit capable and trustworthy agents. If we struck too soon, while we were too fragile, the Society would crush us. I also told him, as Gilbert often said, that every person deserves a chance to change their path. I believe that, because I had rejected the Society's creed, though Carson didn't know it. I believe, very firmly, that every heart, no matter how infected with the disease of evil, can be cured."

"That's why Carson left," said Tabitha. "To take down the higher-ranking members."

The Judge took his wine-filled goblet in his hand and took a long, steadying drink. "Yes," he said, setting the goblet down. "And my agents report that he has been killing his way to the top for the last two years. He has communicated with me three times since then. He sends telegrams bearing only names. You can all guess what that means."

Outside, the horses whinnied, and the cold wind slashed through the night. Annie peered over Orrin's shoulder, down the length of the hall into the Judge's study. Through the window, she watched a heavy fog roll over the ground, misting up around the windows.

"That poor boy," said Tabitha. The meanness in the words gathered Annie's attention back to the table.

"My greatest strength is also my most unlovable trait," said the Judge. "I keep secrets and veil the truth so as to protect that which matters most, and on your faces I see the effect of that strength. The pain of betrayal in your eyes.. You have not seen what I have seen. None of you, except Robert, know how close humankind is to utter obliteration. If the world knew, they would fall over the precipice of insanity and tear one another apart trying to pick a side. Humanity's greatest power is our ability to come together for one another. However, that tribalism, turned on itself, is also the mechanism of our own destruction as a species."

Annie spoke up. "I was going to accept your offer to become one of your agents. But now, how can I do that? How am I supposed to trust you?"

The room seemed to darken, and the candles perched in the chandelier flickered. Outside, the wind howled harder.

"I have brought you all here to receive the truth. When I see Carson again—if I see Carson again—I intend to tell him the truth too, and to suffer those consequences. You three represent the final pieces of the force I believe we need to face what is coming."

"Why us?" Orrin asked.

The Judge's confidence seemed to return, the fire in his eyes inflamed. "Because you are survivors. You have seen the maddening horrors, and you refused to wilt under them. This gift, though it brings sorrow to the survivor, is rarer than you know."

He leveled his eyes at Tabitha. "My offer wasn't for Annie alone, Tabitha. I need you as well. Your strength and your wisdom. And with it, I need your daughter's ability to act under the most extreme pressure."

"Especially now, with what we know about the kingdom," said the Professor, and nonchalantly drained his wine glass.

The man was implacable, Annie thought. A placid lake of cold confidence.

"Carson is waging a war on the Society," the Professor continued, "and he has seen great success. But, because they struggle with translating the manuscript, they are not our most immediate threat."

"Who is?" asked Annie.

Professor Bass cocked a drunken eyebrow and leaned forward. "Vampires," he said. "Those who bear the banner of a very old and very powerful monarch. A king, undying, who presides over what is known to us as the Red Kingdom."

Part II

THE MOST FEARSOME HAND OF A FEROCIOUS ORDER

The light of civilization has pointed man upward, crawling out of the primal war between predator and prey. Civilization has smoothed his sharp edges, pampered him, and gifted him all he possesses. In his self-taming, man has rid himself of that ignoble and critical talent for true, unbridled ferocity. And what man has forgotten, the Nine remember.

Principe of the Society of Prometheus,
Lucio Gandolfi, *Illimitable Primacy*

Chapter Fourteen

ABILENE, TEXAS

THE CREATURE WHO was once known as Wesley Burrows followed his master. Of Sigurd's thirty thralls, Wesley was first among them. The vampire took many under his shadow, but it was Wesley he commanded. The others simply followed. The vampire horde was a knife unsheathed in the dark. Stealthily they crawled out of the cargo car at the empty train station. So silent, so quick, they ran a red line through the city of Abilene under a bright curl of moon. They took the homes first, bleeding out the women and the children, whose terrified shrieks were muffled by strong hands and sharp teeth.

It was a quiet slaughter of the homesteaders, whose husbands and fathers and brothers were out drinking and gambling among the town's saloons. Of the faithful, God-fearing men who were not given over to such vices, their throats were torn open. Their voices silenced.

Cowboys and quick-handed gunfighters, dancing girls and whores, drunken shopkeepers and the bartenders who had served them all, were swallowed up by the engine of death now fallen upon unknowing Abilene.

Sigurd, though weakened, was still more powerful than the whole of his horde combined. His potency revealed itself in the blanket of fog that issued from within his wings. A flood of mist rolled from out of his leathery expanse like a storm cloud borne out of a shadow deeper than the void of space. House by house, street by ever darkening street, Sigurd's brood ushered in a quiet red conquest. They slashed and reaved and drank greedily from wrist and shoulder, groin and thigh.

Sigurd, ever more vicious than the rest, killed and drank from his victims with a slakeless thirst. So many fell under his fang, and so deeply did he drink, that by the end, his moonbeam skin appeared as pink as living flesh.

The unconsumed blood, steaming in the bitter night, flowed in immeasurable volume over baseboards and bedsheets, saloons and straw-floored livery stalls. Nothing was spared. Not man, woman, child, pet, or chattel.

The mist swallowed the city of Abilene, and where the mist retreated there remained only the sign of a destroyed people.

By the time the moon climbed to its apex, there were only five living souls in Abilene.

Five people dining inside Peregrine House. The home of Judge Hezekiah Ellison. The man whom Sigurd referred to as "God's self-appointed falconer." "And for the falconer," he said to Wesley, "Peregrine House is the nest."

"The Judge will deliver unto me the names," he had told Wesley just after the young man's conversion. "Once I have those names—of the boy and his slave, who murdered my sweet Abelia—I will deliver Ellison to our king. Then, I will go out into the world and take my revenge on the little falcons he once commanded."

A Red Winter in the West

It was put upon the brood that they should remain hidden, to prowl under the misty veil of their master's shadow. It was Sigurd's right to take the Judge, and his right alone.

The darkened city of Abilene, annihilated of life, lay as quiet as a corpse on the prairie. The only light that remained was the flickering lamplight slanting out of the windows of Peregrine House. The fog intensified, so that even Wesley's vastly increased night-vision could only make out the vague outline of the three-story monolith.

A blur of shadow manifested next to Wesley.

Sigurd spoke.

"Should anyone escape me, take them alive."

"Yes, master," said Wesley.

"Those that remain shall fall under my fang and none other."

Wesley and his kin huddled together, and, under the dark light of Sigurd's indomitable power, they watched as their master approached the front door. His form dimmed against the moonlight. He himself became the smoke that flowed out from his wing, and he passed through the door—a vaporous calamity.

Chapter Fifteen

PEREGRINE HOUSE
ABILENE, TEXAS

AFTER PROFESSOR BASS named the Red Kingdom, it surprised Annie that it was Orrin, and not the Professor, who went on to explain vampires.

He spoke with measured authority. "They have existed for centuries, almost as long as humans, we believe. The origin of the vampire is shrouded but not a complete mystery. We have accounts from various cultures across the globe that speak of vampiric methods, abilities, and vulnerabilities. What the Professor and I recently discovered is an account from an Italian explorer from the late sixteenth century, which details the finding of a cave of such an unfathomable shape, so deep within the mountain, that it could not have been cut by the erosion of time, wind, or water."

"How was the cave made then?" asked Annie.

"Upon examining its walls, he found the signs that tools had been used to cut the stone away. After two days of exploration inside its vast depths, he discovered a gap so large, so wide, and so deep, that it had manifested its own ecosystem, and even its own weather. For miles and miles he went on, thinking that perhaps he'd found the entrance to Hell itself. At the edge of a precipice, he saw, to his horror, a great, subterranean valley where a city lay outstretched. A sprawling manorial estate bathed in the light of strange lanterns. The explorer named it *Il Regno di Luce Scarlatta.*"

"The Kingdom of Scarlet Light," said Professor Bass, translating.

Orrin nodded. "There in the valley, he saw humans wrangled about like chattel—used not only as slaves but as food. He observed them for a time, the vampires unaware of his presence. He observed the clearing of stone for further expansion, the ranching of humans, and a triumphant parade put on for a monarch: a king robed in scarlet. All bowed before him, the human cattle stretching out their necks in forced supplication. Seeing the horrors there, the explorer ran back to his patron and told him of all he had seen. His testimony was written down and sent by messenger to the Pope himself. We do not know how the manuscript ended up outside of the church, but we found it, nevertheless. It has given us great insight into the Red Kingdom. Where we once believed they hid in crypts and crumbling castles, we now have evidence that proves they have invaded the Americas. Specifically, the Astolat mountain range in Colorado."

"My lord," said Tabitha.

"Yes," said Judge Ellison. "Sven Erickson, a gunfighter and adventurer, one of my agents in Colorado, says has found evidence of a city deep, like the one described in the account, in the Astolat mountain range. We believe that out of fear of the Catholic Church's war against the vampire, the undead traveled west, where they can thrive unimpeded." He turned to Tabitha, his face grim. "The Red Kingdom is here, Tabitha, in America—"

A Red Winter in the West

"And so ever shall we be." The voice came cold and soft, from some hidden origin, and a rush of wind extinguished the chandelier's light. A sudden rush of acrid mist swallowed the room. Darkness.

Annie went for her gun— but her body did not obey her. She gave the mental command again, still she did not move. A great weight sat upon her mind and her chest, squeezing her lungs so hard that it became difficult to breathe.

At the foot of the table, a shadow manifested. A dark figure, tall, with skin like pink marble.

Annie's breathing quickened. Her diaphragm pulsed, trying to force air into her lungs.

The creature's eyes glowed like hot embers.

"I am Sir Sigurd of Antioch, the first among many, a king and Templar knight in my youth, reborn to serve an undying monarch greater than I. Made Ageless. As I told your little agent boy and his Negro three years ago, Judge Ellison, I am the most fearsome hand of a ferocious order."

A chill raked down Annie's spine, goosepimpling her flesh.

Out of the corner of her sight, she saw her mother and friends. All of them bestilled under the invisible oppression.

"I know you, Sigurd of Antioch. I am Judge Hezekiah Ellison," he said, his voice leaning into its deep basso resonance, confident. "It is my bad luck that my two agents did not finish you in that little saloon in Big Spring. For having so many valorous honorifics, you certainly ran as quickly as any coward I've ever known."

Sigurd, unfazed by the Judge's insult, did not walk but floated around the table, behind Annie and her mother, so that he stood over the Judge. "I know you, too, Ellison," he said. "Your little birds you've sent out of this *Peregrine House* have done much to injure my king's people." And with a simple gesture of his finger, Annie's head turned as if attached to that digit by an invisible string. But those days are over; the reign of man is soon coming to an end."

"We don't reign over the earth, beast." The Judge, showing his great resolve, turning his head to look up at the indomitable creature before him. "We are its good caretakers."

"All men are bad and in their badness reign. Your whole existence is rife with it," said the vampire. "I was once like you, Judge. I ruled once, too. But when King Kristian showed me the dreadful feast, I bent to his will. So, too, my good Judge, shall you. Firstly, by giving me the names and the location of the boy and his slave, those doomed men who killed my wife."

The Judge's gray eyes hardened at the thought, widening. "Never," he said.

Sigurd tilted his head, his eyes pinned to the Judge.

"Do you know that we can hear your heartbeat? Even as I stood outside your home, your desolated town behind me, I could feel each beat of every human heart fellowshipping in this very room. Yours, impressively, is still calm. Thump-thump, thump-thump." Sigurd made a metronome of his finger, ticking it back and forth. "The rhythm is a veteran's song. But, when I do this…" He stretched out fingers tipped with sharp black talons and pressed the tips against Tabitha's throat. The flesh dimpled at the touch, and a single bead of blood leaked out. Tabitha inhaled sharply.

Though she could not move, Annie could feel pearls of sweat wet her brow as she grit her teeth and battled with mind and body against the strange force pinning her to the chair.

The vampire took in a deep, satisfied breath. "Thump, thump. Thumpthump, thumpthump." His voice, filled with what Annie could only categorize as ecstasy, became a whisper. "There it is. Your fear, so easily compelled."

A Red Winter in the West

"Stop!" Annie cried out.

The Judge said nothing but only looked at the vampire, his eyes unwavering.

Her mother did not cow, she did not whimper, as Sigurd's razor-sharp talons pricked her skin again. "Annie," she said. "No matter what happens, I love you."

"Nothing is going to happen to you," the Judge said confidently. "He knows that if he kills you, I won't give him what he wants. He can't take it from me. He isn't strong enough. Are you, Sigurd."

Sigurd smiled.

It was a terrible thing.

"You mistake your arrogance for confidence, Judge." Sigurd's talons disappeared into Tabitha's throat. She opened her mouth to scream.

Blood arced onto the table, dark and wet.

The vampire, with what seemed to be the gentlest of efforts, pushed those talons out the back of her throat.

Annie screamed, still unable to move, as her mother's head flopped backward and slapped against the chair.

The table exploded with noise, the bellows of the Judge raging impotently, Orrin and the Professor crying out, but none able to take action.

"And so," Sigurd said, as he slowly slid his hand out of Tabitha's destroyed throat. Then, pressing his finger against her chin, he turned her flat dead eyes to face her daughter. "One heart is quieted by your defiant silence, Judge."

Annie was screaming. She couldn't stop screaming, couldn't take her eyes away from the face of her mother, could not wrap her mind around the totality of Sigurd's action. "I will kill you!" she raged, screamed so loud her throat strained against the effort. She grunted and writhed in her chair, trying to move, trying to reach for her gun. And if she could not reach the gun, she would take the vampire by the throat and tear his head off his shoulders.

"Look," said Sigurd, his voice smooth, unhurried. "Look at what your Judge has done. All for the sake of protecting two of his number."

"You goddamn monster," said Judge Ellison.

Sigurd whirled on him, snapping a bloody hand around the big man's throat. It took no effort at all for the vampire to lift the Judge out of his seat as if he weighed nothing. "Monster? How dare you? You, the lowest coward of a mongrel species. I'll tear out the heart of everyone you love and burn every human town from here unto the end of the world, lest you give me what I ask!"

Sigurd reached down and took hold of the Judge's wrist. With a violent jerk, the arm bent sharply at the middle of his forearm and a terrible sound, like a muffled gunshot, assaulted in the room.

The Judge howled in pain.

"Stop," commanded Professor Bass.

Sigurd ignored him. "Where is your silence now, O Judge? Where is your quiet? I underestimated your agents in Big Spring. A mistake that cost me my revenge. But their failure to kill me brings now an end to you and all your agents. To every little bird you've flown from this roost of yours." Sigurd's composure had vanished, his voice like a howling tornado. "Never again will you make a currency of my peoples' teeth." The cloak wrapped around his shoulders twitched. Its satin sheen spread to reveal that it was not a garment at all but leathery wings that stretched the great length of their span. The moonlight glowed inside their thin, almost translucent, flesh. "Never again will your mercenaries steal the immortality of my sisters."

The Judge yelled, "Stop. No more, please! I'll tell you!"

A Red Winter in the West

Sigurd's roiling power, which had so violently and completely taken hold of them, seemed to relax. Between deep, angry breaths, the vampire said, "Names. Locations."

"Hezekiah," the Professor cried out. "You can't!"

One wing swept across the table in a violent slash. The single talon jutting from its tip cut through the air like a plowman's scythe, slicing the Professor's head in half at the jaw. The top of his head rolled off his body. Blood fountained from the stump, spraying the fine table cloth dark and wet. What remained of Professor Bass fell, convulsing, in a violent spasm to the floor.

Orrin twisted his horrified face toward the body.

"No!" he screamed.

"Look away from that which is gone, boy" Sigurd said, shaking the hair from his eyes. "And look to what still might be saved." The wing that had so quickly claimed the Professor shot out toward Annie. Its bloody talon stopped less than an inch from her eye.

Frozen, she gasped

"Or lost."

"We don't know!" Orrin called out.

"No," said the Judge. "I do. And I will tell you." His voice was choked, barely audible through Sigurd's crushing grip.

"Weigh your speech carefully," Sigurd said. "I will know if you lie. Speak truth, Judge."

Staring past the needle-sharp tip of the vampire's wing, Annie's eyes fell on her mother's lifeless corpse, the great red hole punched through her neck. She wanted to look away, but she couldn't. Her eyes were transfixed on that bloody violation.

"The boy is Carson Ptolemy," said the Judge, hoarse. "The man you took to be his slave is dead. Killed in Yellow Hill."

Sigurd squeezed. The Judge's eyes bulged.

"Where is the boy?" Sigurd demanded

"I-I don't know."

Sigurd's wing twitched, and the talon dimpled Annie's neck. Her breath caught.

"I warned yo—"

"I swear," said the Judge, letting his hands fall away from the vampire's wrist. "I don't know where he is. What I do know is that if you do find him, you won't be facing the boy you met in Big Spring."

Sigurd laughed, the sound grating like the sliding of many stones. "Is that supposed to scare me, Judge?"

"Consider it a warning. One of my gifts to you."

"Gifts? And are these other two birds of yours also gifts to me?" Sigurd looked back at Annie and Orrin.

"No," the Judge said, his head lolling, the skin of his face was turning purple. His arms went slack.

"Pathetic," said Sigurd. "To think that our kind feared you. You, the terrible Judge Elli—"

The Judge's hand shot forward, a silver line flashing in the moonlight. Sigurd bent forward at the waist, bellowing a bestial roar that rattled the windows of the Peregrine Estate.

The Judge's hand drew back then again plunged the knife into the shadowy form of the vampire.

The invisible weight restraining her suddenly lifted. Fueled by rage and violent instinct, she stood up, knocking her chair over. The vampire's wing thrashed wildly at her, slicing through the air so close to her skull she felt the touch of wind tousle her hair.

Annie took one step back and drew her revolver from her hip. Clamping down the trigger, she fanned the hammer. Deafening gunfire filled the darkened dining room. The bullets punched into

A Red Winter in the West

Sigurd's back, then drilled through the flailing wing he brought up to shield himself.

Revealing a tremendous strength, Sigurd took hold of the Judge's skull. The man began to scream, then to wail, as blood welled in his eyes and streamed down his cheeks. With a smooth, easy gesture, the vampire twisted his wrists. There was a sickening, animalistic keening then a deep, hollow crunch as he twisted the Judge's head so violently it turned completely around on his spine.

Orrin howled, "No!"

Annie screamed.

Sigurd released the Judge, letting the body collapse to the floor. Then, snarling, the vampire spun to face Annie. "Harlot!"

"Annie, look out!" Orrin was suddenly airborne, tackling Annie to the ground as one of the vampire's wings lashed out. He fell on top of her, crying out as they hit the floor.

The vampire howled, his form bursting outward in a cloud of smoke that churned above them. The dark cloud, raining scarlet waters, rushed out of the dining room toward the front door.

"Are you okay?" Orrin's voice was hurried, filled with panic.

"I-I don't know," Annie said.

"Are you, gah—" Orrin winced as he pushed himself off Annie. Coming to rise, he turned. There was a wide, red line that ran the length of his suit jacket. The coat torn open, so too the fine vest and shirt, all parted to the riven flesh upon his back. Blood flowed from the wound, which ran from shoulder to hip, so deep Annie could see muscle and a portion of his shoulder blade.

"You're hurt!" she said, lifting her hands toward the injury. Then drew back, unsure as to help.

Orrin, flushed and bloody, turned to face her. Sweat poured off his pale skin. "I'll be—"

From outside Peregrine House came the voice of Sigurd, roaring.

"Inside," the vampire said, his voice filled with rage. "Kill all who remain. Then burn this damnable house to the ground!"

Who he addressed, Annie did not know. She ran to the parlor to look out through the window. What she saw on the lawn seized her heart. Dozens of pale skinned men and women, their eyes flashing like gold coins in the pale moonlight. Sigurd's cloak shivered, unfurling with a blast of wind. Then, with a smooth, practiced motion the wings flapped once, sending him soaring into the air.

"Orrin," Annie called. "He has…it's-it's an army!"

Suddenly, he was beside her, his hand wrapped around her elbow. "Come on! Hurry!"

"Where are we going?" Annie asked, rushing behind him through the house as the brood of vampires began to assault the windows and pound the front door.

Orrin led her to the staircase, leading to the upper floors of the house.

"We'll be trapped up there," said Annie.

"Not there," said Orrin. He placed his hands against the wainscot paneling. The panel shifted and slid aside, revealing a passage that descended down a hidden stairwell. "Down. Now!" he said, gesturing for her to go ahead of him.

Annie went down the staircase a few steps, probing the sides of the walls with her hands. "Will we be safe down here?"

"No," said Orrin, pulling the paneling shut just as they heard the front door splinter off its hinges.

The wavering light of oil lamps threw their golden incandescence against the near wall, which curved around a little corner to reveal a secret chamber underneath Peregrine House. Orrin leaned his elbow against the wall, every breath a shuddering effort.

A Red Winter in the West

"Come around me," he said, nodding his head. "I just need a minute."

Annie stepped around her wounded friend to see not some hidden study as she had suspected nor even a dry pantry, for there were no books or food stored here. Nor was it a clandestine laboratory, though there was some kind of mixing station in a corner. This room, hidden under the estate—under Annie's nose for all three years of her life in Abilene—was stocked floor to ceiling with weapons.

an armory.

Case after case, row after row, of rifles, shotguns, and an assortment of pistols lying dormant upon satin pillows in glass cases. Boxes upon boxes of shells and cartridge ammunition, both of the lead and silver-tipped variety, were stacked high. A circular white-sable carpet rested upon the floor, so large that it blanketed almost the entire room. On its plush, white expanse was embossed a black peregrine falcon, its wings folded in a killing dive, talons outstretched.

From above them came the sounds of breaking doors and shattering glass as the horde of vampires howled, screaming and thrashing about the house, searching in rage. It was the bellowing ravings of a bloodthirsty pack wishing only to fulfill their master's command: to find the survivors and end their meaningless lives

Annie sat on one of the munitions crates, her shoulders shaking violently. Her teeth chattered. She stared at Orrin, who took a deep breath, shoved off the wall, and removed a pistol from one of cabinets. Annie thought it so strange to see him hold a pistol. She could still somehow see the bookish child who had joined her years ago, running in pasture fields, wild and carefree. But the man before her now bore none of those things, none of his silliness. No measure of youth in the face those beasts of Yellow Hill had ravaged. Orrin stood sentinel at the bottom of the stairs, bleeding badly from the wound along his spine. Blood matted the tatters of his vest and the seat of his trousers.

Annie began, "How did you—"

Orrin spun around quickly and placed the pistol's barrel against his lips. Then, he tapped the gun against his ear.

Quiet. They can hear us. Was how Annie interpreted the gestures.

"Where are they?" a woman's voice screeched.

"Silence!" a man's voice boomed.

Every tramping foot and scouring hand suddenly stopped.

Annie held her breath. Sigurd had said that he could hear their very heartbeats. Could these others do that too?

A set of boots thumped down the steps immediately above them. The muffled voice of the man who had ordered silence began to speak.

No.

He was singing.

"All around the peregrine coop, the vampire chased the people. After them in double haste…"

A sudden burst of sound startled her. Annie covered her mouth.

"Pop goes the people!"

The footfalls terminated at the bottom of the stairs. "I know you're here," he said, taunting. "I can smell *you*. Come out, little people. Our master is gone. You don't have to worry. We won't hurt you."

The collective of vampires snickered at the lie. Their laughter muffled by the wall so thinly separating the hunters from the hunted.

"We. Just. Want. To. Talk."

"Wesley," another voice said, "look at these. They are still warm and delicious."

Annie imagined the lot of them circling the bodies like scavenger birds, then descending upon the carrion corpse of her mother.

A Red Winter in the West

Lapping at the precious blood of the person who had brought her into the world. Annie's vision flattened. She stood up and went to the crate holding the silver bullets. Paraffin light slanted off the silver-tipped cartridges just before they were encased in the shadowy hollow of the cylinder of her revolver. She then went to the glass case, where the cold steel of the pistols called to her like a siren's song. She lifted the case with trembling hands and took three of the pistols from their velvet cushions. She loaded them and tucked them into her gun belt. Then she took a fourth pistol, filled it, and clutched it in her off-hand.

Locked, loaded, and angry as hell, she went and stood next to Orrin. She leaned close to him, putting her lips to his ear, and with a quiet rage she whispered, "Kill them all."

Orrin regarded her warily, daring to whisper. "How many of them did you see?"

"Slim," she said, the word causing her lip to tremble in both fear and remembrance. She shook her head, overcome with bitter truth. "It doesn't matter how many."

Orrin understood. "We get them coming down the stairs, their numbers won't mean as much—"

"I hear voices!" a man howled above them, likely from the parlor. "Near the stairs!"

There came a great noise, the scurrying sound of many feet.

"Blood here!" another voice shouted. "One of them is wounded… gravely."

Their voices grew closer.

"See here. It stops at the stairs."

Annie grit her teeth and slowly pulled back the hammers of the guns in her hand.

"*Round and round the peregrine coop.*"

The vampire's sing-song chant no longer filled Annie with dread. There was only anger. A chaotic storm thundered in her mind. A red storm. Red as the blood Sigurd stole from her mother.

"*The vampire chased the peeeeoooople.*"

Against the paneled door came a scratching sound like the tip of a knife carving a line into wood.

"*After them in doooouble haste.*"

In a flat tone, Annie said, "Pop goes the people." The revolver jumped in her hand. The bullet drilled through the panel above, and there came a harrowing shriek. A woman's scream followed by what sounded like a bag of hammers hitting the floor.

"Silver!" the singing vampire called out. "They have silver!"

Annie fired again and again, spraying hot silver through the sloped stairway leading up into the hall.

An arm punched through the panel, pinned itself against the interior panel, and wrenched it off its hinges. The vampire revealed in the doorway, a big man wearing coveralls, looked down at them with absolute savagery. He leaped at them, claws outstretched.

The duo standing at the bottom of the stairs opened fire, taking him in the shoulder and chest. The vampire tumbled, punched through with holes, and hit the ground, only to burst into a pile of ash and bone.

The horde came streaming through the aperture, a flood of claws and fanged mouths. The relentless booms of the guns were deafening. Gun smoke filled the room. Coming in a rush the vampires charged through the narrow gap. Annie and Orrin fired over and over, a relentless battery of pistol shot. The silver within the rounds seared through vampiric flesh, transforming some to blue fire and ash and bones and the smell of death. Some of the vampires among them, shot in the head or heart, simply fell upon the sable carpet, never to move again.t

A Red Winter in the West

Annie's revolvers clicked empty. She dropped them to the floor and pulled the two larger pistols from her belt. The pair of pearl-handled .45s kicked like mules in her hands, sending limbs from their joints and bursting out the backs of the vampires in peach-sized holes.

Still they came, a writhing, tumbling mass. Out of each cloud of immolated vampire turned to dust came another screaming predator.

A woman wearing a yellow sundress stained with gore slashed at Annie, so close that her talon slapped the iron sights of Annie's revolver.

Annie's mind was too clear, too fierce, to consider retreat. She leaned into the vampire and shot her through the cheek, leaving a dark powderburn on her face. The bullet blew open the top of the woman's head open, spraying hot blood and brains upon the wall.

"Backup, Annie!" Orrin screamed.

No.

There would be no running. Not from these damnable vampires that killed her mother. Not from those creatures that claimed the life of her father or the lives of the Buffalo Soldiers in Fort Stockton. She would make a stand here and now, and if this basement was to be her tomb, she would make her end a song that every vampire survivor would, for their immortal lives, recount a triumph over the human terror they faced at the battle of the Peregrine Estate.

A man garbed in a preacher's frock grabbed her by the wrist with an impossible strength, pulling her into his chest. Annie went with the momentum, turning her back so that he could wrap his arms around her, then tucked the barrel of her gun under his chin and fired a shot that sent hot powder, fire, and ash into the air.

A claw raked her shoulder, bloodying her, but she swatted the hand away and fired again.

Click, click, click, click.

Annie's revolvers spent, she began to pistol-whip the bastards and bitches, who she swore would see the fullness of her anger spent on them.

Annie was suddenly pulled back. Orrin shoved a revolver in her hand.

"Three shots left. Keep them off us!"

Annie did just that. And with Orrin's pistol, Annie counted only four vampires remaining. Three coming down the stairs, one standing in the open doorway. His dark eyes, set in a scarred face, watched her intensely.

She fired another shot, but it sailed wide of all three of the oncoming vampires. Again the gun thundered, this time taking a boy, not much older than her late brother Georgie, in the chest. His bright green eyes went wide just as he became nothing. The two remaining vampires were big men, one of them larger than Judge Ellison. They scrambled along the basement floor on all fours like hungry dogs.

Annie hit one with her final shot, blowing his head open from brow to scalp. His head snapped back. and he tumbled across the carpet in a tangle limbs, splashing darker red upon the ever reddening carpet.

The final vampire tackled her at the waist. They spilled over each other, smashing into the floor. The vampire rolled on top of her and pinned her down with mouth open wide. He howled in victory, fangs flashing, ready to tear her throat open.

"Orrin," Annie screamed.

A spray of hot liquid splashed across Annie's face. The vampire's eyes went flat, his howl muted. Orrin stood over him, gripping the handle of a long skinning knife in a reverse grip. The blade was sunk hilt deep into the man's temple and protruded from the opposite side, sizzling and smoking in the vampire's blood. The creature became ash, and the flecks fell into Annie's eyes.

Wiping it away, coughing, she looked up to Orrin. Her elation transformed to fresh horror when she saw the last vampire above his head, crawling along the ceiling. The scarred vampire bared his fangs.

"Above—"

Before she could finish, the vampire threw himself from the ceiling and crashed into Orrin with a sickening thud. Annie scrambled to her feet, pointed the revolver at the back of the vampire's head as it vampire ripped at Orrin's chest and stomach, and pulled the trigger.

Click

Orrin screamed. Crimson ribbons painted the air with each looping slash. Orrin flailed with his knife, but the vampire slapped it away, howling in delight at his work.

Weaponless, Annie threw herself into the vampire, attempting to tackle him at the waist. Stiff as a brick wall, the vampire didn't budge. And then, taking her by the shirt collar, he threw her across the basement. She slammed into one the rifle case, shattering the glass door. Shards sliced open her back and rifles spilled out, battering her as she lay on the floor. Her ribs and spine felt broken. Every limb buzzed with pain.

She shook her head. She had to get up. She had to help—

Orrin's cries lost all semblance of human sound.

There was a sickening, wet *crunch*.

He stopped screaming.

The room was a swirling blur, but she could see the vampire rising, coming to stand erect and menacing, his hands and scarred face slathered with blood.

"You little wench," he said, stalking over to her.

Annie tried to rise, but her legs wobbled, and she fell back into the heap of rifles, their wooden stocks jabbing into her tender skin.

"Look, what you did."

Annie tried to say something, but before she knew what was happening, she had been lifted into the air as though she weighed nothing. Then she was flying. The air felt as thick as a river flowing over her. She smashed into the revolver cabinet this time. The glass shattered all around her. A box of bullets poured out onto the floor. She reached out, palming one in her hand. There was a pistol next to her, another Scofield, broken open and ready to be loaded.

She scrambled to reach it, but the vampire was too quick, snatching her up by the throat. He slapped her so hard that a red-white light flashed across her eyes. Her hand threatened to open, but she held tight the silver bullet.

"How could such a weak thing," said the vampire, his voice cruel and cold, "make such a ruckus."

Annie mumbled.

The vampire smiled, turning his ear to lean closer to her mouth. "What's that? I can't hear you over the sound of your dying."

She positioned the cartridge in her hand as though she were clutching a knife. "I—"

She positioned the cartridge in her hand as though she were clutching a knife and lashed upward, aiming the tip of the silver bullet at the vampire's eye.

A sizzling burst of smoke flashed. The vampire screamed and thrashed about, though he kept her in his grip.

A sudden burst of energy cleared her mind, giving her needle-sharp focus. Annie Miller reached over, and with all the strength in her hands, shoved the silver bullet deep into the vampire's eye socket. Something ruptured there, and the bullet sank into the creature's skull. With a terrible howl, he dropped Annie.

She landed upon the broken glass near the open Scofield on the ground. Bullets, scattered across the refuse of the case, found their way into her trembling fingers. She filled the cylinder and slapped the revolver together.

The vampire, screaming, was already clamoring up the stairs.

Annie fired.

The bullet sparked against the brick wall, missing the fleeing vampire by less than an inch. It disappeared into the main house.

She sat, aiming the revolver at the stairs, staring down the iron sights. Waiting. The vampire did not return.

Annie let the pistol fall away.

"Slim?" Her voice sounded far away.

She called for him quietly again, using the nickname she'd given him so many years ago. His body was hidden from her sight by the bulk of a crate. What she could see was the pool of blood expanding over the carpet, reddening the peregrine falcon.

Slowly, carefully, Annie slid herself away from the bullets and the broken glass. She crawled around the crate and looked to her friend.

None of Orrin's defining features remained. His head was obliterated. Only the mask that had hidden half his face remained intact.

"Orrin," she said again, an apology begun.

Her shoulders convulsed, and the tears began to fall, and so too did Annie Miller fall. She fell upon the tatters of Orrin's chest, not caring that he was soaked in warm blood. Wrapping her arms around him, she wept, clinging to the shell of what had been her best friend. Returned for only a time, only to be stolen away again. This time forever.

Annie Miller was alone. The only surviving soul amid the desolation of Abilene.

Chapter Sixteen

UNKNOWN LOCATION
CHICAGO, ILLINOIS

CARSON AWOKE FROM a deep, dreamless sleep to a metal door moaning on its hinges. He was curled up, facing the damp stone wall. A dull heat caressed him.

He opened his eyes.

Though there was the warmth of a fire on him, there was no light. Total darkness remained.

Impossible, he thought. How were they able to navigate the room without any light? No one could—

There were too many footfalls for Carson to discern how many had just entered. The door moaned again, then slammed shut. A bolt latched, the lock sliding deep into the wall.

In the fresh silence, he heard the squeaking of a small hinge like that of a lantern's handle.

He didn't move. He played opossum.

"Doctor, if you would, please." A gentle voice, belying an aristocratic authority.

"Of course." A woman's voice.

A pair of boots crossed the room, approaching Carson.

"Mr. Watts," the aristocrat said. "Or, excuse me, Mr. Ptolemy. If you are awake, I will ask that you allow the good Doctor Van Horn here to examine your injuries. She has nothing but your best interests at heart."

Again, Carson opened his eyes, but there was nothing. Only a flat wall of black before him. He sat up and put his back to the wall.

"I see that you've forgone the firewood and the bed. Seems you haven't touched your breakfast either. If you are of a mind for suicide, know that we have methods for keeping you alive."

Carson didn't speak.

Snap.

The sound so close to him jolted him upright.

Doctor Van Horn clicked her tongue. "He didn't forgo any of them, Walther. Did you, Mr. Ptolemy? Tell me, what do you see?"

Carson shook his head. "I can't see anything."

"Oh dear, the Baroness's brutes might have cost the boy his eyesight." The doctor's soft, cool hand flattened itself against Carson's brow.

He jerked away, his whole body tensing. His fists came up in a defensive posture. "Don't touch me."

"Fair enough," said Van Horn. "Tell me, do you have a headache? Feeling nauseated?"

"Yes."

"Oh dear."

"What is it?" asked Walther.

"My initial thought is swelling around the brain is putting pressure on Mr. Ptolemy's optical nerves, causing his blindness. I mean, look at him, Walther. Just look. We're lucky they didn't kill him.

A Red Winter in the West

And even if he'd been able to see the food, there's no way he could have eaten it."

"He threatened to bite off his tongue, doctor," said Walther.

"They could have sedated him."

"Not everyone has your methods and knowledge at their disposal, Doc—"

"She does," Van Horn snapped. "The Baroness did this not out of necessity but out of cruelty."

Silence passed between the two of them.

Van Horn clicked her tongue again. "Mr. Ptolemy, I'm afraid that if you ever want to regain your sight, I'll need to examine you more closely, perhaps even operate."

Carson shifted away from her, his aching spine sliding against the cold stones.

"Things will go much easier for you if you cooperate. I promise you that. I could make an impression of those gums, fit you with false teeth. Could even splint those fingers for you, if you—"

"Those are self-inflicted wounds, doctor. Had he not resisted, he would not have endured them. We only need him alive." Walther's voice was cool, sharp as a razor. "Anything else is outside our concern."

Carson struggled to speak, his lips feeling strange against the slickness of his gums. "W-where am I?"

"You are in a Hell of your own making, Mr. Ptolemy," said Walther. His heavy-footed approach echoed against the walls. "And so, like Dante himself, I urge you to abandon all hope of escape."

Carson slid away from the approaching sound, but there was nowhere to go.

A set of hands swallowed Carson's entire head, gripping his throbbing skull. There was tremendous strength in those hands, but control as well. "I could kill you now, you know. Barron and Tanzer. They were friends of mine. And some little shit like you—"

The hands became a vise, squeezing Carson's head so hard that he groaned.

"For months I heard of this gunfighter," Walther said. "Terrible and deadly. I am disappointed at this skinny, trembling sack of shit before me. That's all you are, you hear? Just a goddamn pile of shit."

"Walther!" Van Horn snapped again.

The pressure intensified, and Walther's nails sliced the skin beneath Carson's hair. Two huge digits wriggled themselves into his ears. Carson flailed against them, but his strength was gone. Though he gripped at the man's wrists and kicked at him, Walther regarded those dangers with little concern.

"Yes, that's it, squeal you pissant of a man." Walther's spit splashed against Carson's face, his hot breath smelling of tobacco and rotten meat. "Squeal until your brains come pouring out of your—"

Click-cl-click. It was the sound of a revolver's hammer drawn back.

"Control yourself, Walther."

The man laughed. "Or what, Clara? You'll kill me? I don't think so."

"Release him, unless you prefer to live out your days as a eunuch."

The grip, already a crushing thing, intensified, then relaxed. The fingers, thick as sausages, released Carson.

"Satisfied?"

"No," said Van Horn. "Go tell Olivia that I require my surgical tools to be cleaned and my operating theater prepared."

"Who are you to order me—"

"Your money has bought you much favor, my friend. But never forget that should harm befall you, it's me that'll be keeping you alive. You, and your daughter."

A Red Winter in the West

Walther's voice and stinking breath leaned into Carson's ear. "She has a bigger set of balls than you, eh?"

"Now," Van Horn commanded. "Time is a factor. The internal bleeding could kill him, and I would hate to be the one to tell the High Priest that his prize possession died because you have the deference of an ape."

Walther spat in Carson's face. "I'm going to enjoy crushing your little brain when your usefulness is all spent."

The fat wad of mucus crawled down the bridge of Carson's nose, but he was too tired to care. His head was swimming, swirling. The pressure, the all-over tension, turned his stomach over. His gut spasmed and he began to heave, but nothing came out.

"Now, Walther. Hurry! I don't know how much time he has." The hammer of the revolver relaxed. "If any at all."

Chapter Seventeen

PEREGRINE HOUSE
ABILENE, TEXAS

THE REMNANTS OF what was once the front door lay in splinters across the carpet and the stairs. The open frame looked like a portal to another world. A white spangled landscape, cold and bright, where a river of carnage snaked through the snow.

Annie scanned the front yard. What she saw ran a dagger through her heart.

Vanilla was there, her reins still tied to the hitching post. The beautiful mare lay on her side, as if sleeping. The blood-soaked grass, like a scarlet sheet thrown over the ground, glimmered oily and wet beneath her.

Annie ran to her, throwing her arms over the body. Her sobbing fell upon the ears of dead men and women, children and cattle.

The bitter wind blew snow about them, the girl and her horse. The world indifferent to her agony.

She slept during the afternoons but stayed awake from dusk till dawn. At night, she sat waiting for the vampire who killed Orrin to return. Annie, for the sake of her safety and want for revenge, had become a nocturnal creature.

During that lonely time, she buried the bodies of her mother, her best friend, his mentor, and the Judge out near the great oak tree on the Peregrine Estate. She dug graves for the men near the creek where gentle waters trickled over sand and shale. To the men, she said thankful words of praise and wept for them.

Annie buried her mother next to Georgie. Waters ran there too: tears on her cheek, sweat on her brow.

At the foot of the graves of her kin, Annie Miller made promises. She spoke those promises into a cold wind, where they became steam. A vaporous ghost that swirled among the shoots of alfalfa.

Back at Peregrine House, Annie sifted through the Judge's study. There among his effects she found a black leather-bound ledger with a seal of silver stamped on the front. Pressed into the seal was the bird for which the house was named. She ran her fingers over the smooth silver seal and opened the book. Inside was page after page of names, detailed notes of correspondences, profiles, skills, and plans for each Peregrine agent.

She read the ledger cover to cover while drinking too much coffee. She ate very little, slept even less. Smoked her pipe, bowl after bowl, until her tongue was bitten raw from the heat. The agents had to be warned as soon as possible, the gunfighter Sven Erikson especially. She needed to find him. She needed his help to find the home of the Red Kingdom…to find Sigurd.

Abilene had a telegraph she could use to warn the agents, but she didn't know how to operate it. On one of the Judge's detailed maps, she saw that there was one in a little town known as Eastland. That's where she would set out for first. Then, after sending out the telegrams, she would go to Fort Worth. Several of the Judge's agents were stationed there. Colorado would be next. There, she would find Sven Erikson and potentially other agents, and she would convince them to make war with the Red Kingdom such as they had never done before.

If Erikson and any others refused, Annie would go her own damn self. She'd kill Sigurd. Kill his king, too.

There were volumes of books she found in Orrin's things at the abandoned slaughterhouse of the Windsor Hotel. One was entitled *Known Origins and Study of the Vampire*. She had taken that, along with a few other leather-bound journals, both from Orrin and Professor Bass, though she hadn't yet read them.

Her ears perked up at the sound of rustling outside.

She had nothing to fear from vampires during the middle of the day, but she strapped on her gun belt all the same. She stepped out onto the porch and shook her head at the sight.

Starchild had her nose buried in the water trough next to the pile of dirt Annie had placed over Vanilla's body. When Annie's boots hit the porch, the wary horse looked up, saw the woman staring at her, then went back to drinking.

Annie went to her, calling her by name upon approach. Then, reaching into her mother's saddlebag, she removed a brush and slowly stroked the timid horse's mane.

"Good girl," said Annie. "What's say you and me take a trip together?"

Chapter Eighteen

CHICAGO, ILLINOIS

TIME RAN LIKE water poured through a muddy rag. Carson fell in and out of the world. Between the serial haze of waking and sleeping, he caught very little of what was going on around him. He could make out voices and blurry shapes of light. The pressure inside his skull was gone.

Carson sat up in the bed, every muscle groaning. He reached up and felt the damp strips of cloth bound tightly around his skull. Where the bandage did not cover, he felt smooth bald skin. At the ridge of the back of his skull, there was a tender place. He felt a thick, bumpy row of stitches.

His other hand throbbed angrily from knuckle to fingertip where Combs and Reyes had broken every digit.

The room was a hodgepodge of blurred shapes. Fire crackled in the hearth near the bed. There was an end table where something resembling a plate resided. Though he was starving and weak, the idea of trying to eat did not appeal to him. There was a steel carafe of water and a tin cup on the bedside table. He reached over slowly, aching, and took the carafe. He didn't bother with the cup. He tilted the carafe, and the water ran over his swollen gums right down his throat. Too much, too quickly: drinking the water was like swallowing a bag of nails. The carafe fell out of his hands and clattered onto the stone floor.

The room was a big blur of gray walled in stone. He was underground, that much he knew. It was safe to guess that he was in Chicago, but it was just as easy to think that the Baroness had taken him someplace else on the Hephaestus and deposited him there on her way to Illinois. Still, she had said that she was taking him to meet her High Priest—that likely meant Chicago.

The bolt shifted in the iron door.

In stepped a tall woman, her blonde curls glimmering in the lamplight like golden hooks around her face. She wore a long white coat cinched at the waist by a thick black belt looped through a buckle. "Welcome back," she said, smiling.

He recognized the voice of Doctor Van Horn. He didn't wholly remember how he'd pictured her in his head, but this certainly wasn't it. "Where am I?"

She picked the carafe up and set it back on the nightstand. "We will talk, but first…" She snapped her fingers and gestured for Carson to lean forward. "Your eyesight has returned, yes?"

"It's still blurry."

"Give it time. If you rest and give your body a chance, I am sure it will return to full clarity. Your hand?"

"Broken."

She gave him a look of faux surprise. "What a keen prognosis. Tell me, where did you get your medical degree?" She took his splinted hand into her own, carefully examining it. "Swelling is down. Good. Though I am sure it is quite painful."

A Red Winter in the West

"I've had worse."

"Unlike for your eyes, I cannot promise a full recovery for your hand. I am guessing this was your shooting hand?"

Carson let his eyes sink. "Yes," he lied. He could shoot equally well with both hands, but the less they knew, the better.

"You might one day venture to hold a pen again, but your days as a gunslinger are almost certainly over." She regarded him with a kindly appraisal of pity. "I'm afraid that much of what you once believed your life would be is gone."

"I've never been that ambitious." His tone was dry as his throat. "Where am I?"

"You are underground, in Chicago, Mr. Ptolemy. You've been here for six days, two of which were spent in my operating theater. You're welcome, by the way."

"I'm not going to help you translate the manuscript, so you might as well kill me now."

"Is that what the Baroness told you?" Van Horn shook her head, chuckling to herself. "That woman's predilection for lies is a mystery even unto me." Van Horn wagged a finger at him. "You aren't being kept alive to translate anything, Mr. Ptolemy. The book itself has been completely translated as of six months ago. Even now, there are many, many believers headed to locations of divine power. To the obelisks."

"You're lying. If you didn't need me, I'd be dead."

"I didn't say that the Society didn't need you, Mr. Ptolemy. I said that they do not need you to translate the text."

"Then why—"

"Ours is not question how and why, but to do and die, yes? I must admit to you that there are things secreted away from me, from many of us. For if too many know all the secrets, then no more

191

secrets shall there be. Only the High Priest has the full command of the whole manuscript. In time, you will meet him."

"When?"

"When you are ready." Her eyes glazed as they drifted away from Carson, as if her mind's eye took her some dreamy place inside her. "When the stars are aligned, and *he* is ready."

Carson shook his head at her. "You people are insane. How can you entertain this godforsaken madness."

"Madness?" Her eyes snapped back into focus, and again her kindly demeanor returned. "Can I call you Carson? I prefer first names. Mine is Clara."

Carson glared at her. "I know."

"Ah, from your little run-in with Walther. A brute of a man, but all creatures have their ways that meet their station, I suppose. You're something of a prize to him, you know. He is very angry that you killed his friends."

"Fair is fair," said Carson. "They brought about the death of my family, so death is what I offered in return.

"Quite." She sat on the bed next to him and began to examine his bandages. "Should you find yourself alone with him, I suggest you not make him angry. His temper is…mercurial at best. Hmm, you'll need fresh dressings." She leaned closer, sniffing loudly. "No sign of rot though, and the blood is nice and clean."

Carson thought of grabbing her with his good hand. He could strike her hard and fast, but then what? What if she got away from him? What if there were guards outside?

"I want you to know that you are captive here, but this place doesn't have to be a prison. Tell me," she said, her eyes widening, "do you like to read *fiction*?" She said the final word as if it were a quiet profanity.

A Red Winter in the West

"Never had much use for it."

"Well, with all of your earthly adventures over, I would greatly suggest that you visit my library. There is an excellent selection. The writers of our time are producing some truly marvelous things in those pages. I'll have a few selections brought to you with your lunch. We'll whet both appetites, yes?"

"I hope it's soup."

"Ah yes, your teeth. I took a mold of your gums while you were unconscious. A friend of mine is a dentist, and he is working up something that should fit quite nicely. At the very least, dentures will keep you from drooling so much."

There was a strange warmth to the woman, a gentle kindness that Carson would never have expected from someone working so hard to end the human race. She placed a soft hand on Carson's bruised cheek. "The world is so close to changing, Carson. We should enjoy the little things in it before they are lost for the sake of progress."

With that, she redressed his bandages.

The conversation had exhausted him. While he fell silent, she continued to speak on what she told him were her favorite stories: *The Count of Monte Cristo*, *Frankenstein*, and a newer publication entitled *The Eternal Husband*.

But while she was still talking, Carson's eyes became heavy, and he fell back asleep.

Chapter Nineteen

EASTLAND, TEXAS

ANNIE NEEDED TO get to the telegram station in Eastland, but her affection for Dutch pushed her west. On her way toward Merkel to check on him and his mother, she thought about going by Fort Phantom to check on Boone, but after a long deliberation with Starchild, she decided not to go. If anyone at the fort had survived, they would have come through Abilene to check for survivors.

She had visited Dutch and his mother only once before, but she remembered the way to the small shack that leaned among red cedars and pear trees now curtained in snow. Resilient, the trees' white blossoms remained open in the afternoon sun. She pulled Starchild to a full stop when she saw the front door of the house lying on the porch.

Revolver in hand, Annie dismounted and walked slowly toward the house. She called out for Dutch.

No one replied.

Inside, the dining table was flipped over. The kitchen windows had been shot out, and bullet casings were strewn about the ground.

She set one of the chairs upright and sat down. She looked over the place, quietly smoking her pipe.

There was a sign of a scuffle, but no bloodshed. Frustrated, she shook her head. "Goddamn it, Dutch. What the hell happened to you now."

Outside, she searched the snow, but it was undisturbed, save for her own tracks. She thought about leaving a note for Dutch, in case he came back, but that wouldn't do any good seeing as Dutch couldn't read. Instead, she drew a crude map that showed a line leading from Abilene to Eastland, Eastland to Fort Worth. She signed the map and hoped that if Dutch ever came back, he'd have an idea of where she'd gone. It wasn't much, but it was all she could think to do.

She rode away from the cabin, heading east.

Almost two days later, she found herself on the outskirts of the little town. Well, Eastland wasn't so much a town as it was a bank and sheriff's office set across from an old, white-washed Methodist church. A muddy road, all chopped up with horse tracks, served as the separation between church and state. The west end, where Annie rode in, was populated by a little saloon bearing a sign reading 'The Horny Toad.'

Annie, well provisioned from the resources she'd taken from Peregrine House, rode Starchild through the sloppy mess. The smoke from her pipe billowed from under the wide-brimmed hat set low on her face. She guided the mare to the saloon. Starchild pulled back from the bent hitching post, not liking the idea, but Annie tied her there anyway.

Annie gave Starchild a few carrots, then left the mare to water while she grabbed a meal. A duo of cowboys, their faces slathered with mud and fatigue, shared a bottle near the swinging doors. Each of them, pausing their conversation, gave her a hard look over.

A Red Winter in the West

"Howdy." she said, then shoved the doors open and gave them no more mind.

She could hear what they said, but she didn't listen. The idle chatter of idiots needing a whorehouse didn't concern her.

The Horny Toad was a run-of-the-mill place. A simple bar with low-set tables, and unvarnished cedar floorboards streaked with muddy boot prints. A boy, smooth-faced and smiling, hammered a banjo. His foot stomped up and down, steady as a metronome, keeping the rhythm to the tune. The song rolled off his fingers persistent as the turning of a wagon wheel.

Behind the bar, a woman polished the damp wood, the tasseled sleeves of her brown dress dancing. She looked up and smiled, her mussed hair falling in strands to hide half her face, though it did nothing to conceal the missing teeth. Unashamed, the smile was big and inviting.

"Rye? Or what'll it be, sweetheart?"

"Beer. Side of beef and potatoes if you've got some,' said Annie, setting her hat on the bar.

"Steak and potatoes we've got, but if it's beer you're after, I'm afraid that'll go an unanswered prayer. We serve whiskey."

"Bourbon?"

Her eyebrows arched, impressed. "It's twice as much as rye, big spender."

Annie nodded and took a seat.

"Name's Rosie. Welcome to the Toad." She turned her head, but not her eyes, to face a room at the back of the saloon. "Joey! Steak and taters!" She turned back, lowered her voice. "You got a name, big spender?"

"Funny you should ask," said Annie. "My name's Rosie, too."

197

Rosie reached behind the bar and pulled out a bottle with a fancy label slapped to the body. "They call that a coincidence," she said, filling a short glass with a long pour. "Or a lie. But a liar's money spends just the same as true gold here. Don't often see a lady traveling alone, but I can see you're a serious customer. I don't mind those guns, just so long as they stay in those holsters." The woman's mouth struggled with the last word. Flecks of spittle sprayed out of her mouth. She mopped it with the rag, giving it little thought.

"You talk this much to every person who comes through?"

Rosie leaned her elbows onto the bar and placed her chin in her hands. She looked up adoringly at Annie. Her eyes playfully rolled to the left. "Just the pretty ones."

That got a smile out of Annie.

"The conversation is free. Dollar fifty for the drink and the steak. I like you, so the taters are on the house." She winked.

Annie pulled the coinage out of her pocket and handed it to Rosie. "Lucky me. Say, last couple of nights, you wouldn't have happened to have seen a fella. Little taller than me, pale skin. Travels by night. Big puffy star of a scar on his cheek?"

"Afraid that's where your luck runs out, sweetie. Can't say I have. Let me guess, your husband run off?"

"Something like that." Annie took a swig of whiskey and slid the glass back over to Rosie for a refill. "Broke my heart," she said. "Hoping I can get him back."

Rosie laughed, looking down while she carefully refilled Annie's glass. "Well, damn him. You ought to find yourself a good person, not go running after the one that did you wrong. Though, you'll wanna push on from here." Rosie leaned closer, the scent of cinnamon wafting off her skin. She lowered her voice as if passing on a not-so-quiet secret. "Not many of the marrying type here in Eastland."

A Red Winter in the West

"The heart wants what the heart wants, Rosie," she said.

The woman straightened up, nodding hard once in staunch agreement. "I know exactly what you mean. A word to the wise: you go chasing the wrong man for the right reason, and you just might find yourself behind a bar in a horseshit town wishing a rich dentist with a drinking problem would come wandering through to solve all your worldly problems."

Annie lifted her glass to Rosie. "Here's to the men we want to find and those we hope to find us."

Annie sipped the drink, savoring it this time. "I hear you've got a telegraph in the town. Where might I find it?"

"Sheriff's office. Deputy Woodford is there now. A real dunce of a man, but from what one of my boys says, he's hung like a mule."

A voice called out from the back of the bar. "Steak and taters up!"

"Like I said," Annie winked back at Rosie, "I've got eyes for another."

"Yeah," said Rosie, sliding a gentle hand over Annie's shoulder. Then, even more slowly, the hand slid over the smooth leather of her jacket. "I'll get that order now. Don't you go anywhere, Rosie, or whatever your name is."

A ruckus of cowboys came piling into the Toad. They were slapping one another, half of them were drunk, and the other half, bawdily laughing, were well on their way there. One of them, a boy with red freckles that matched the tangled mop of hair on his head, stumbled over his boots when he looked up and saw Annie sitting at the bar. He playfully slapped one of his friends and stabbed his chin over where she was sitting.

The red-head approached her, pulling at the lapels of his tattered, brown vest. "Howdy there, ma'am." He couldn't be older than seventeen.

"Well, if it isn't Sean O'Malley," Rosie said, sashaying back behind the bar. She slid a steaming plate of food onto the bar, in front of Annie. A knife and fork were laid across the thick steak. The potatoes steamed hot giving an earthy aroma. It reminded Annie that she hadn't eaten a proper meal for days.

Sean smiled, wide and confident. "Name me true and—"

"I'll be yours forever," interjected Rosie. "Yes, yes. I know. And one day you'll cry if I hold you to it."

"They'll be tears of joy," said Sean, leaning his elbow on the bar much too close to Annie. "Tears as pure as me own mother's tears upon my birth."

Rosie set a few glasses on the bar for the group of cowboys. "I've got news for you, kiddo. Those weren't tears of joy."

Sean feigned being wounded. "How could you cut me so deeply, Rosie? My sweetheart of the bottle. And in front of our new friend here. Whatever made you so prickly?"

"Marrying an Irishman." Rosie began to fill the glasses.

Sean leaned closer to her, his big smile disarming. "Well, we ain't all the same you know."

Rosie leaned back into him, brandishing the gap between her teeth. "Maybe not all Irish, but all men, certainly. I've met plenty of your people whose company I enjoyed; they was all women though."

"Speaking of women," Sean said, turning to Annie, "who do we have here?"

The cowboys behind him started laughing. Without looking, he shoved a boy, even younger than him, in the chest, causing them to laugh even harder.

"A famished lady," said Rosie. "Busy eating with no time for the company of the town rake."

A Red Winter in the West

Annie shoved a wad of potatoes in her mouth, eating hungrily. Once the melted butter and salt hit her mouth, she stopped caring about the words of Sean or the snickering of his friends.

Sean stared at her all the same, his head tilting on his shoulders, waiting for Annie to say something.

"My name's Sean," he said.

Annie swallowed, then picked up her glass. She placed the lip of the glass to her lips, hesitated. "Heard that."

"Well," he laughed, a little more nervous than before. "What's yours?"

Annie sipped the whiskey. Wiped her mouth on her sleeve. "Rosie."

"And what brings you to this sparkling metropolis of ours?"

She ate, ravenous, keeping her eyes forward.

"You do know what metropolis means, don't yah?"

"Sure do."

"It's a joke. An irony. Seeing as Eastland is—"

"Oh, let the woman eat in peace," Rosie pleaded, tossing the white rag at Sean. But the young man caught it, and let it fall to the bar.

Annie finished the steak and scooped out the last of the butter-soaked potatoes.

"I'm done anyhow," she said. "I know it's a joke. Just wasn't funny." Annie set the fork down, but kept the knife in her hand, its horn handle smooth in her hand. She looked at Sean, her eyes flat. "I'm looking for my man. Maybe you've seen him. He likes to travel at night. Tall as you, bigger in the shoulders, though. Got a big scar on his cheek, looks like a star. Real noticeable. Handsome despite it."

What little color was in the pale Irishman's face drained. His smile fell, and his friends stopped chuckling. All three of their rough faces drew grim.

201

Sean's hands slid off the bar to hover at his hips, next to a big buck knife on his belt. "What's say we did?"

Rosie, sensing the newborn tension, let out a laugh. "Well, then tell the lady, Sean. So she can be after him."

Sean looked at Rosie, his boyish demeanor gone. The early meanness of manhood filled his eyes. "Two nights ago," Sean began, "me and Phil Tanner, with the boys here, we was all sitting around our campfire, waiting' on a pack of coyotes. They been harassing Mr. O'Day's sheep and goats. Well, we was out there having our fun, and from out of the pasture comes this fella. Walking quietly as you like. Doesn't announce himself to us, but Phil spotted him coming." Sean looked back at Annie. "A fella just like what you said. Same build, same big scar."

"Yeah?" It was a careful tone Annie gave to the question.

"Yeah. First he comes up to us, all nice-like, saying his horse took a tumble. Had to put it down. But we figure that ain't no truth because he weren't carrying no saddle nor tack. Just one man. Empty-handed, walking in the dark. Phil calls out to him, being hospitable and all, offering him a place by our fire. When he gets close enough, we see that his clothes is all torn up. Then Phil offers him a pull on our bottle, and this right fucker just grabs 'em, almost tears his arm off. All of us rush over, myself almost falling into the fire, but we get a hold of him. And he was strong, your man. Strong enough to put a waylay on Phil, but we put the boots to him. We put the boots to him hard."

"Did you kill him?" Annie asked, already knowing the answer. Was the vampire weakened by her assault? Did it have something to do with the silver? Annie didn't know.

"Said we put the boots to him. Little rat shit got away from us. Cut Phil across the face, probably cost him his eye. Mr. O'Day ain't

A Red Winter in the West

a doctor, but he was able to clean the wound. If we see him again…" Sean looked back at his friends. "Well, let's just say it'll be worse than what he got before. O'Day's hired on three more hands—gun-men—just in case the fella circles back to do something foolish."

"Before he attacked you, did he say where he was headed?"

"He didn't, but there's only one of two directions he was going' if civilization is something he cares for. He's either going east to Fort Worth or west toward Abilene."

Annie, wordless, slid off the stool and headed for the door.

"Say," said Sean, "I don't reckon you try to rescue your engagement with that fella. He's a crazy bastard. A crazy bastard who's gonna get his head broke if he comes 'round Mr. O'Day's place again."

Annie punched through the batwing doors, grabbed the Peregrine ledger from her saddlebag, and left Starchild at the Toad. She hurried past the darkened bank to the sheriff's office and knocked on the door.

From inside there came a voice. "It's open."

Annie entered.

The place was all dried-out pine with cedar walls and one big rack of iron bars closing of the single cell. Three oil lamps were stationed at the opposing corners, and one was placed on the desk where the deputy reclined. He was a middle-aged man, dark-haired, with a fat set of warts bubbling up on his pudgy face. He lifted the brim of his hat with a single finger. "Problem, ma'am?"

"You work the telegraph?" asked Annie.

"Sure do," he said. "Trained and certified. Where you sending a message?"

"Messages," said Annie. "Lots of them, all over the country. Need them fast and accurate."

"Well then," said the deputy, popping the two front legs of his chair onto the ground. "Let's be about your business."

Chapter Twenty

CHICAGO, ILLINOIS

THE DOOR OPENED with a clatter, startling Carson awake.

"I don't know what makes you so goddamn special," said Walther, carrying a tin plate toward the bed, "that I've gotta wait on you hand and foot." The man sulked over, the plate looking tiny in his big hands. He slapped the plate down onto the bedside table where an oil lamp was burning. "Here. Eat. And if you give me any of that 'I'll starve myself to death' bullshit, I'll stuff it down your throat 'til you swear you'll never miss another meal. We clear on that?"

Carson shook the cobwebs out of his mind, blinking hard against what little light filled the room. He was starving. "That a fact, Walther?" he asked.

"Damn right it is." He turned and stomped back toward the door.

"Wait."

Walther stopped with his hand on the open doorknob but refused to turn around. "What?"

Carson couldn't remember the question he intended to ask. His mind was still hazy. "I—" He struggled to find the words. "Your friends, Tanzer and Barron. They fought well, both of them. Right up until the end."

"Is that a fact," Walther said, but the big man didn't exit. He slowly pulled the door shut, cutting off the interloping light. His great bulk vanished in the swallowing dark.

"Yes," said Carson. "Tanzer especially. Almost ran me through with that sword of hers."

"Is that supposed to make me feel better?"

"No. It's just the truth. Everyone deserves that."

"Is that your grand philosophy? Everyone deserves the truth," said Walther mockingly.

"My father taught me that. I believe it."

Walther's massive frame and dark eyes seeped out of the shadows. Carson had not heard the man cross back over to him.

"And which father would that be? The traitor or the slave?"

"The free man," said Carson. "The one who was truly free."

"You two were lucky for a long time," said Walther. "After that little dust up in Mississippi, our High Priest was ready to send me down to find you. Hart's translation of the manuscript was the only reason I didn't." He smiled. "Lucky you."

"You'd have fallen," said Carson. "Like the rest."

"Oh, I disagree. It'd take a lot more than a boy and his property to keep me from doing what I do."

"And what is it that you do for the Prometheus Society, Walther?"

He stood there, silent against Carson's question, seething. His shoulders rose and fell slowly, his breathing audible. "I serve the High Priest, and he has empowered me to do great and terrible things according to his purpose. I am one of the many instruments called to play during this particular overture in human history. A trumpet on the lips of Gabriel, readying the song that will reshape the world."

"All that," said Carson, reaching over to pick up the plate off the nightstand. "And a waiter."

Walther's shoulders tensed. His hands balled into fists.

Carson looked around, feigning confusion. "Tell me, Mr. Trumpet of the Song that Reshapes the World, did you forget my spoon?"

Walther went to step forward, but caught himself and regained his composure. "I won't be your suicide, Ptolemy. When the time comes, and believe me, it's getting here right quick, I'm going to end you. And it won't be quick, or humane."

Carson blinked. "So I should just use my hands then?"

Walther's eyes widened, a killer's grin lifted from out of his frown. "I'll be using mine," he said. "When the time comes, but not before. You're going to get to see our work come to fruition first, Carson Ptolemy. You'll watch it come falling out of the sky like a righteous storm. A blizzard of truth that'll make what happened in Yellow Hill look like an autumn cold snap. It'll sweep across the whole face of the world, and humankind will finally see the ones who came before. I really can't wait for you to see it and to know, in that moment, that every person you know or love will be swallowed up."

He leaned down so that their eyes were an inch apart. "Eat."

Carson, keeping his eyes pinned to Walther's, flipped the plate. The tin lip clanged against the nightstand, twisted in the air, and clattered to the floor.

He could hear Walther's teeth grinding. The man's head trembled with rage. Through some trick of the light, Walther's face seemed to change, the angles of shadow bending his countenance.

Walther's big hand clamped itself around Carson's throat. The strength in that hand was absolute. This was a strength of a wholly different type, unnatural among the order of men. And it was with that unfair power that Walter lifted Carson out of the bed and threw him to the floor.

Carson hit the ground on his back, all the wind driven out of him. The world spun again, as it had spun so many times since the Baroness had drugged him.

"You *will* do as I say." Walther's voice was terribly quiet.

Carson swirled his tongue around in his mouth, scooping a thick wad of blood and mucus. He spat in Walther's face.

Walther's eyes shot wide open, his rage now unhinged. He began to scoop up handfuls of the splattered beans off the floor. His fat fingers pried Carson's mouth open and stuffed the gritty mass inside. Then the hand slapped down over Carson's lips.

Carson fired a knee up into Walther's groin. The big man bellowed and keeled over, clutching himself.

Carson blew out the beans and sucked air into his lungs. He reached for the big man, feeling his way up the man's bulk. His groans were music in Carson's ears. Hard as he could, Carson hit Walther in the throat. Then in the face, opening a gash over the man's eye.

Again. Blood sprayed out of the cut.

And again. The gash became a gaping wound.

He lifted his hand again, but nausea was filling up his stomach, and his fist loosened.

A big, looping punch caught Carson behind the ear, sending him sprawling against the stone floor. His chin barked against the stones.

Walther was over him again, turning Carson to face him.

Carson looked up at the deep red line on Walther's brow.

A Red Winter in the West

"You little shit," Walther screamed, cocking his fist at the shoulder.

He was going to die here. Carson knew that now. No matter what he did or how hard he fought, death would find him in this place. And for a reason Carson could not understand, that thought amused him. He began to laugh.

Laugh hysterically.

There was no strength in him anymore, only the violent laughter of a man who has lost and lost and lost, and no longer cared for what the future might bring.

Chapter Twenty-One

FORT WORTH, TEXAS

A NNIE CROSSCUT THE trail many times on her way to Fort Worth, but she was never able to pick up any sign of the fleeing vampire.

She had expected Fort Worth to be more than what it was. Where she'd hoped to find a bustling city, she found a dirty little outpost, simply built. It was one big courtyard boxed in by stores, saloons, and the like. Starchild, heavily laden with Annie's provisions, carried her rider along Chapman Street. The gray sky overhead painted the town in bleak desolation.

A group of sweaty workers, far too young to wield the tools in their hands, were toiling on the north end of the square, laboring to finish the stone walls of a courthouse. The Slaver's Revolt had swallowed up the men of working age, as it had done to so many others. The path around the court was all cut up with longhorn prints leading toward the Red River. The air was filled with the pungent stink of dried chips and puffs of fresh cow pies.

The ledger was in her off-hand, where Annie looked back to the Judge's swooping cursive.

It read: 'Larry Cornish, Postmaster.' After that, a small section of text was quoted: 'See that I am making all things new.' Every name in the ledger bore sayings like this one, code phrases, she surmised, to ensure that Peregrine agents, though they may have never met, might trust one another on the trail.

Annie asked directions to the post office from a group of ladies passing through the courtyard from a baker's stall, and quickly made her way where they pointed.

The post office was a one-story cube of weathered pine. A single door set between two large windows tinted brown and powdered with dust, stared at her from the center of the building. The sidewalk steps leading up out of the street were already bowed with moisture, the nails pulling up from their foundation. It was a sad building, she thought. A sad little building for a sad little town.

Annie hitched Starchild and went inside.

The counter, all barred in on the sides, had a small rectangle cut into the iron that bore a wooden sign reading 'Reception.' The gaunt, hawkish man behind the counter, glasses hanging on the perch of his nose, shuffled through a box of envelopes.

Annie approached him. "I'm looking for the postmaster. Mr. Cornish."

The man did not look up. "Present."

"Mr. Cornish," said Annie. "I'm here in regard to a telegram posted via Eastland a few days ago."

"Many telegrams come by Eastland's way."

She put her hands on the counter. "See that I am making all things new."

Cornish's fingers stopped flipping through the leaflets, but he did not look up. "More bad news?" he asked.

A Red Winter in the West

Annie furrowed her brow, looking around at the empty office. "Only details of the same news. I didn't want to say too much."

"Good. Smart," he said, then turned around and began to slide the letters into little wooden slots in the wall behind him. "The Falcon's Roost, east side of town. Meet at six. Will deliver the word to others. Not sure which players remain in the game."

Annie leaned forward, trying to understand the man's strange way of speaking. And it confused her to hear him use the word *game*. She took umbrage with it. "This isn't a game, Mr. Cornish."

"Only game worth playing. Our business is concluded at present. Falcon's Roost. Six. Upper room. Ask Desdemona."

Annie took Starchild over to the livery stable, where she had the stable master give the horse a good feed. While the horse ate, she took her time brushing her mother's mare.

No. Her mare now.

Knives buried themselves into her heart. She leaned her head against Starchild's shoulder, closed her eyes, and felt the animal's warmth. She leaned there for a long time.

She spent the late afternoon milling around town, which only further served to depress her, and then made her way to the Falcon's Roost.

It was a quiet place filled with thick smoke and the dull smell of booze, but no music and little conversation. In their tired faces was that hollow, desperate look she had grown familiar with among the men of Yellow Hill: the gaze of surrender in the eyes of the conquered.

Annie found Desdemona waiting tables in a black and red dress that looked as if it had, at one time, been a vibrant beautiful thing, but now the skirts were matted and much of the lustrous color had long been washed out.

213

The dark-haired Mexican girl led Annie up a single flight of stairs that leveled out to a balcony overlooking the place. Without a word, Desdemona slid a key into one of the doors and let Annie inside.

Annie turned to thank her, but Desdemona was already closing the door. The lock clicked back into place.

The room was circular, the whiteness of the wall interrupted at equal intervals by slats of mahogany wood. At the center was an oak pedestal table. The evening sun slanting through the windows flashed on the table's surface, setting the grain within its color on fire. Five chairs surrounded the table, their clawed feet standing on a large carpet that matched the one Annie had seen inside the Peregrine Estate.

Annie's eyes passed over a few paintings on the wall, but they seemed of cheap quality and their dull artistry failed to draw her into them. They seemed placed there an afterthought, a way to make this room's purpose seem mundane. But she could feel the weight of the room, its history. How many choices had been made here? How many people had walked through the same door and made decisions that changed them forever? Were these the kinds of places Carson spent his formative years? Had Gilbert and Carson ever stood in this very room?

Being an agent in a conspiracy must have been a terrible childhood, Annie thought. While Annie had been playing with Orrin and Georgie and buying candy at Pete's General Store, Carson had been in places like this. A little child always among adults. An unfortunate son drafted into war—one with no medals, no glory. Only blood and terror and inevitable loss.

She too knew that war now. She had been conscripted into it.

Not for the sake of saving the world, though. No. She didn't want to save the world. She didn't even really want to rid the earth of the vampiric horde the Judge had warned her about.

A Red Winter in the West

She just wanted Sigurd.

The lock behind her unlatched. The door opened.

Through the door came Larry Cornish, leading three others.

"Punctual. Good," he said, speaking in his strange fashion, his tone stripped of emotion. "Dinner shortly. Will be here a while."

A short boxy man behind him tipped his hat at Annie, his green eyes flashing. "Ma'am," he said, then went to sit at the table. Sunlight shined off his full, well-oiled beard.

"Julius! Get your sack of bones outta the way, would you?" asked a dusky, alto voice coming from the large man in the doorway.

Julius was the tallest man Annie had ever seen. So tall that in order to enter the room, he had to duck to keep from bumping the crown of his head on the door frame. He'd been staring at the ground, his mind in deep contemplation, but now he roused himself. "Keep your skirt on, darlin'."

His voice was deep water, churning.

"I swear," the woman said, squeezing around him, "you are as slow as Christmas."

"Damn it, woman," said Julius, struggling to get out of the way. "Just…Sarah, I'm trying to move."

Sarah was a Black woman with hazelnut eyes. Her plump cheeks lifted into an imperfect but arresting smile. "Now let me take a look at this glass of milk with all the bad news." Her smile widened, slanting in a way that both charmed Annie and revealed the woman's confidence. She and Annie were the same height, but Sarah was older, fuller—more a woman. Her black hair hung about a white silk shirt clung to well-muscled shoulders. Her gun belt hung heavily on her hips, and she moved with a purposeful stride.

Sarah cocked an eyebrow at Annie. "Sarah Lockhart," she announced. "You must be the prophet Jeremiah."

"I'm sorry?" asked Annie.

"What with your news of destruction, I mean. I hope you've got more to tell, and, whatever it is, there's some good to go along with it."

"I…" stammered Annie.

"Give the girl a chance to sit first," said the bearded man sitting at the table. "Or get a goddamn drink. Jesus, Lockhart."

"Don't you blaspheme, Ashley Sutliff. You know I won't have it."

He put his hands up in resignation. "Hallelujah and all that bullshit to ya."

"You are lucky my love for you is so great!" Sarah barked playfully. Then she looked back at Annie. "Have a seat," she said. "Let us see if you are more than a doomsayer, eh?"

When they were all seated, the door opened again. It was Desdemona, carrying a quartet of tall whiskey glasses and a bottle.

"Different bottle," Cornish said to her.

"Whisky nuevo, botella nueva. El que te gusta se agotó." She set the bottle and glasses down on the table. "Yo no lo compro, yo solo lo sirvo."

"Don't like surprises."

"Eso no me sorprende, señor Cornish."

He watched closely as the waitress filled each glass. When she set the bottle back down again and made to leave, he stopped her. "You first," he said.

Desdemona gave him a slanted, annoyed glance. She took the glass in front of Cornish and took the whiskey down in a single swallow. Then she cocked an eyebrow at him, as if to say, "Satisfied?"

Cornish nodded at her.

She refilled his glass, then exited the room and locked the door.

"If she was going to poison you, Larry, she would have done it a long time ago," said Ashley, as he lifted his glass to his lips.

A Red Winter in the West

Before he could drink, Corish cut in,"Toast." he said. "Julius."

Julius was a statue of consideration. His pale blue eyes were heavy, as if, Annie thought, they carried a secret sadness. The man nodded. "To the dead, we raise our sincere thanks. To the living," he paused, something catching in his throat, "and to those still unborn, we raise our own lives, for a safer creation."

"Amen," said Sarah.

Annie joined in with Cornish and Julius, repeating the word.

Sutliff rolled his eyes and drank.

"Ms. Miller," said Cornish. "What news do you bring us?"

Annie told them everything, interrupted halfway through by Desdemona serving dinner. Fried chicken, served with gravy, potatoes and honeyed carrots.

Sutliff ate loudly, while the others ate politely, listening as Annie spoke. She told them about Fort Stockton. The cattle drive, the Buffalo Soldiers, and the creatures slaughtering them all.

"My lord," said Julius, shaking his head, the deep waters of sorrow inside him drenching the words.

"Goddamn society," said Ashley and bit a hunk out of a drumstick. Then, chewing loudly, she said, "Those fucking people."

Annie went on, and when it came to the events of the dinner, she opened her mouth to tell. But only a croaking noise sounded from her throat. Lips trembling, she looked away from her food. Set down her fork and began to smooth the perfectly smooth napkin in her lap. "They…" she said, but the heartache stole all her sound. Robbed her of her voice.

"It's okay," said Sarah, whose confident smile brightened her face although her eyes moistened with tears, and her own lips trembled. An understanding passed between the two women in that moment amid the silence of all.

A tear dared to fall down Annie's cheek, but she swatted it away. Her grief, like a bellows, enflamed the fires of her want for revenge. And the voice that loss had stolen, and her rage, returned.

"I sent telegrams to most of the agents in the ledger," she said. "My intention is to take a train to Colorado and meet with Sven Erickson. And to see my mother's killer put in the ground."

"Distressing," said Cornish. "Judge Ellison was essential."

"His death raises many questions and considerations," said Julius, slicing into his chicken.

"Such as?" asked Sarah.

"He was careful, more careful than any of us," Julius said. "It was his organization that made what few of us there are into a viable instrument. Without his coordination, what will become of the Peregrine Estate?"

"We lost," Sutliff said, filling his glass for what Annie thought might have been the fourth time. "And they won. Simple as that."

Sarah dropped her fork. "You can't mean that."

"I can, and I do. Judge Ellison was the thread that kept the garment stitched together. Without him, it'll all come unraveled. I knew that the moment I read her telegram." He eyed Annie, then turned back to the other members of their huddled conspiracy. "The Society of Prometheus, the kingdom, the Werewolf Campaign out west in California, and let's not forget what's happening with that doctor out in Virginia. Those are just the big ones, which does not even begin to take into consideration what's happening here in Texas. The winter is expanding, and none of us know of a way to stop it."

"Maybe Carson does," Annie blurted.

Sutliff laughed at that. "Ptolemy's boy? Last word of him was that he went rogue after the society killed Gilbert. And that word was a good while back. He's probably dead."

A Red Winter in the West

Annie scowled. "You don't know that."

"True," Cornish agreed.

"Oh come off it, Larry. Look," said Sutliff stabbing his fork at her from across the table. "Ms. Miller, I'm sorry about your family. I truly am. But I will not lead you down a path we all know to be folly. If you go up to Colorado, you'll find the same thing we've all been finding since we started doing this."

"Which is?" asked Julius.

Sutliff's cold, green eyes hardened on her. "Death." He slid his empty plate forward, as if it now offended him. "She's better off leaving her anger behind. This Sigurd sounds more powerful than any vampire any of us have encountered, and he's not even the master of them all. And if she starts with Sigurd—let's say she kills him—we know where it'll end up. War. That means an assault on the Red Kingdom, which, let's all be honest, is like trying to bring down the gates of Hell with a fucking tack-hammer. It'll never be enough." A pall of sadness crept onto his face. "None of us are enough. Hell, *all* of us aren't enough."

"There were dozens of vampires at Peregrine House," Annie shot back. "And just two of us held them off."

Sutliff shook his head. "It was one, kiddo. All those others you managed to gun down in that basement, those were babies. Couldn't have been more than a week or two old. He raised a battalion with ease. And out of the five of you, only you survived. That, in and of itself, is a goddamn miracle. I don't think you quite understand, so let me make it clear: the Judge and Professor Bass, they were the most capable of us. Certainly the most knowledgeable. If the Professor had survived, maybe we'd have had some chance. But he's dead. So, we're *all* fucking dead."

"So, you're folding," said Sarah, her brow narrowing to a wrinkled, angry V.

Sutliff nodded. "Even gamblers like me know a losing hand when we see one. Bluffing only works when you know your enemy, when you know how they think and what their tells are."

"How did Sigurd know where to find the Peregrine Estate?" asked Julius. The question quieted the room.

"Betrayal," said Cornish.

"Or," Sutliff said, raising his hands in consternation, "he damn well deduced it. These things are hundreds of years old. Some of them even older. They know things we will never know and have lifetimes of experience surviving against greater enemies than we ever were or ever will be."

"I never thought I'd see the day that you'd quit on this," said Sarah, her countenance dark as a thunderhead.

"You won't be the first woman I've disappointed, beautiful. And if I play my cards right, and time permits, you won't be the last. I'm going someplace warm—some goddamn place with better goddamn whiskey than the goddamn Falcon's Roost."

"Sadly," Julius said, just before downing his whiskey, "I am convinced by Ashley."

Cornish let out a low, unhappy hum.

"I'm sorry, Larry. But Martha's given us a son. And I can't in good conscience continue to labor in such a fashion. I have family in Canada. I can keep them safe there." He looked at Annie. "You are welcome to come with me, Ms. Miller. You have cattle experience; I am certain I could help you get work. Have a real life for yourself."

Every eye fell on Annie, who looked down at her untouched food.

"The only reason I had a chance at a real life was because of Carson and Gilbert Ptolemy. If they hadn't come along and risked their lives, I wouldn't be here now."

A Red Winter in the West

"And look where that got you," said Sutliff.

Annie gave him a wilting stare.

"Think me cruel all you like, kiddo. But I'm not wrong."

"Thank you for your offer, sir," Annie said without taking her eyes off Sutliff. "But I am going to Colorado."

"And what if you get up to Colorado, go looking for Erickson and find him dead or, more likely, drunk in a tavern with no desire to help you at all. What then? You going to go after the kingdom yourself?"

"I will."

Sutliff slapped the table. "Hell, do whatever you want, but let me tell you something you might not have considered. What if you get up to Sigurd? Let's say you do," he said, lowering his voice and slowing his speech. You get right up to him, closer than I am to you, and he invades your mind. Freezes you in place just like he did at that bloody dinner. Then consider, little Miss Blood and Thunder, how you will feel when he makes you his own. Dominates you. Forcing you to live out the rest of the whole span of time as *his* puppet. You will be powerless. Helpless to refuse whatever command he gives. Him or his king."

"I won't allow it." Again, Annie was blurting out a response before thinking. He was getting under her skin, and she didn't like the doubt it poured into her mind.

Sutliff rolled his eyes. "Goddamn kids. And all of you here are gonna let her walk right into this. That makes you guilty. You hear that? *Guilty* and culpable in what happens to her when she's all alone in the Astolats."

"She won't be alone," said Sarah.

Those words inflated Annie's stomach and sent goosebumps down her arms.

Sarah Lockhart looked at Annie. She brandished her smile. "You'll have me."

"All that's gonna do is make a coffin maker in Colorado a little more money," said Sutliff.

"What do you care? You're quitting." Annie's tone was harsh.

Sutliff exploded up, his chair toppling to the ground behind him. He wobbled a bit, his face red from anger and booze. "Six years, you little pup. Six years of my life I gave to the Judge. I've lost two brothers. One to cholera by way of a living, breathing horseman of Plague, and the other I watched get ripped apart by a pack of werewolves right in front of me on the plains of Kansas. I've saved countless lives, including hers." He stabbed a finger at Sarah. "I've gambled with demons, fooled angels, and lived to stand here before you all for the sake of a world I love more than my own life, a world that never loved me back. No one here has sacrificed more than me, and I won't have my concern for your goddamn life turned against me. Damn you, and damn the rest of you."

Annie's eyes broke away from him and she hated herself for it. Despised letting Sutliff cut through her nerves.

"Leave then," said Cornish, his hawkish features devoid of any emotional direction.

"I am, Larry." Much of the anger went out of Sutliff's voice. "It isn't the honorable thing to do, I know, but I've never been an honorable man. Though much of me wishes I could be that very thing for you." He looked at the others around the table. "All of you."

He took a deep breath, and something more than just his shoulders sagged at the exhalation. "It's like the Judge used to say, 'The minute you start doubting why you came, it's time for you to go.' Well, my time is done. I don't have the sand to start this all over again. Even if it means the world will come to an end."

A Red Winter in the West

"The same goes for me too, friends," said Julius. "For the love I bear my wife and child, I cannot travel with you on this path. Should you reconsider, head north, find me, and I'll give you sanctuary."

Annie's heart broke at what she was witnessing. There was an undeniable bond between these people, and it was her telegram that brought the breaking of that bond. They were losing their friends and loved ones, albeit in a different and less bloody fashion than what she had experienced in Abilene. It was loss all the same.

Is that all this is, she thought. Is life just striving to collect people who matter, only to lose them when God has his say? Did she even still believe in God?

She shoved the question away.

"Wounds me to hear, Ashley," said Cornish.

"It wounds me to say it, my friend," he replied.

"We are, all of us, forever chasing those exhilarating moments that remind us that our gifts, when we share them well enough, have a lasting effect on those we love the most," said Cornish. "I consider myself luckiest to have shared yours over the years."

"I wish you both the best," said Sarah Lockhart. "But you'll pardon me if my forgiveness is slow to manifest. We are lesser now, because you are leaving when so much depends on our joined success."

Sutliff turned to her, his countenance sad. "There's too much darkness in the world for candles to light, Sarah. One day, hopefully not too late, you'll realize that. You too, Ms. Miller."

There were no more goodbyes. Julius and Ashley exited, and a gloom hung in the air, even over the already taciturn Cornish.

After a few moments in the quiet, he spoke up. "Gather supplies. Meet here early morning. Depart then."

Chapter Twenty-Two
CHICAGO, ILLINOIS

IT WAS THE old nightmare that found Carson in the darkness of sleep. He was a boy again, there in the dream, prone on his back. Helpless. His father, Ezra Watts, thundered the old proclamations, his voice blasting, hoping to wake the final destruction—the hoary blast that would split the firmament of the Earth and play the final song that would end the world. Ezra's form was a great, dark blur, but the bone-white skin of his face was clear. So too were the bulging eyes and the mania that infected them. Ezra screamed over the pestilential wind, his mouth growing wider and wider.

So very wide, wide as a striking snake.

The great stone obelisk, striking up from the earth, glowed, throbbing with an empty green light. A light the color of malice itself.

Carson awoke, slathered in sweat. His gums ached. He tasted fresh blood on his lips. With a grunt, he pushed himself to sit up in the bed, resting his back against the headboard.

"I am told you are set against me."

Carson's snapped his head over to the hearth. A man sat before the dancing fire. The light from the flames washed out his every feature, as if he were a void in the shape of human likeness.

"I am sad to hear it," the man said. "I have made many enemies in my life, Carson Watts Ptolemy. It is to my sorrow that my most tenacious foe should be the son of a man whom I loved as a brother."

"Who are you?"

"Our ways have stripped me of any name that I might claim as my own. To my people, I am a governor of sorts, but that honorific does not suit me. I am a servant. Nothing more."

"The High Priest," said Carson. It was a heart-fluttering revelation.

"I watched while you slept. Nightmares trouble you. It was a familiar one, I surmise."

Carson said nothing, dumbstruck. How could a man who had worked so hard to keep himself out of the range of Carson's gun now so brazenly sit before him?

The voice, soft, almost pastoral, spoke from the void. "I've wanted to meet you for a long time. I wish it were under better circumstances."

"I would have preferred different circumstances as well."

"No doubt you would. I am sure if you were armed, I'd already be dead."

"Damn right you would."

"There it is," the High Priest said. "There's that familiar fire. Your father had that too. An indomitable zeal. Were that he was alive…I could use his wisdom in these war-filled days."

Carson's anger flared. "He was a lunatic who tried to kill his own son. As I happen to be the particular son he was going to murder, I'm glad he's dead."

"Are you?"

The question cut deep.

A Red Winter in the West

"By all accounts, your father loved you with the magnitude of Abraham. And you, like Issac lashed to the stone, were spared." The shape moved, the darkness comprising him shifting. He produced a pipe from his jacket pocket. With the strike of a match, the man's face was dimly illuminated for only a moment, vanishing again in the dying of the match. Smoke swirled about his head. "Spared by Gilbert Ptolemy, and we are lucky that you were."

Carson shifted his legs under the blankets, testing their mobility. They felt strong, limber. Strong enough that if he decided to rush the High Priest, he might find a way to overtake the man. Perhaps tackle him into the roaring fire.

It would be a fitting end, he thought. Both of them burning unto the end.

Flexing the fingers of his right hand to test their strength, Carson kept the conversation going. "I've killed dozens of your people. Hunted you until this moment. How is it that you are lucky I am alive?"

"Ezra was a brilliant man, albeit rash and impetuous. His understanding of the manuscript dwarfed even my own. He was burdened with knowledge that the world was not yet ready to endure. Had he succeeded in killing you, we might have lost our chance."

"Chance at what?"

The man let out a long sigh. Smoke billowed into the twisting light. "At reclamation. Soon the protective obelisks will be destroyed, the stars will align, and at the last obelisk, your sacrifice, will make the world right again. The gate will open, and the world will welcome the light of a new revelation. The story of the Society of Prometheus is very old, Carson; the manuscript is a testament of that older age. Now, soon, shall we bear witness to the age of the new testament."

"I've seen a glimpse of what that looks like. I don't think you'll care much for it."

"Yes, I know," he said. "And you, like Mary at the empty tomb, are the first of many, many witnesses. Tell me"—his voice dipped to a whisper—"tell me of the glory of mighty Alitranz."

"You mean before or after Gilbert blew him to Hell?"

The man shook his head, quietly laughing. "Alitranz cannot be destroyed by any weapon of human or divine make, my boy."

"I'm not your boy. I'm the man who is going to kill you—kill all of you—and leave this Society you love dead in the ground. Forever."

"If there is anything I have learned in my life, Carson, it is that you cannot kill your way to a just world."

"A man can try."

The High Priest slapped his leg. "Oh," he laughed. "Believe me, in my youth, I tried. I aimed my brothers and sisters at the throat of humanity, and with them I tried to squeeze the weakness and fear out of every man and woman we could find. That humanity might see the better portion that awaits us all. Those efforts produced nothing but blood and sadness, Carson. The blood of my friends and the sadness of the spouses and children they left behind. When a man makes a war in hopes of increasing the world, all he leaves behind are the shattered lives. Has your experience differed in that? Two fathers taken. My spies tell me that you left the care of Judge Ellison. And so, you are alone on this crusade. Your own little war has brought you to me, helpless. Even now, I can see in your eyes that you think to murder me in this very room."

Carson set his feet on the ground, feeling the cold stones on his bare feet.. "Yes. In this very room." He stood up, naked save for the long-underwear they'd dressed him in. He stepped around the bed and faced the man sitting in the chair. The effort was exhausting, making him woozy.

"Neither of us are going to die in this room, Carson. It is not our fate to die today."

"On that," Carson said, clumsily stalking toward him, "we have differing opinions." He centralized all his anger and all his malice, long grown up inside him. He balled his hand into the oldest of all human weapons: one made of flesh and bone. A hand that trembled wearily but was as hard as the rock that slew Abel.

He raised his fists at the High Priest. Signaling for battle.

The priest did not move, inviting his own destruction.

Carson's swung wildly from the hip, but his feet twisted beneath him, tangling, and he lost his balance. The priest caught him in a tight bear-grip, capturing Carson in arms the color of darkness itself. There was a hideous strength in those arms. And where a child caught in such a way might have felt safe and protected, Carson felt an unparalleled fear. He was at the mercy of this man...no, this *thing* that carried itself as a man. A dark artifice.

The High Priest began to squeeze.

The pressure from the priest's embrace sent a shock wave of cold down Carson's spine. His hands trembled, then shook; his shoulders and his hips trembled, too. Carson began to sink. His feet slapped the ground in uncontrollable spasms.

"I see you, Carson," the man's voice was the cold whisper of death. "Your anger, your weakness. Your grief. All of it. I see it naked before me."

Carson felt his bladder release.

"You are the last leaf barely clinging to a dying tree in winter."

Carson's body writhed as if struck by lightning, but the priest held him. He wanted to scream, but it was refused him; Carson was abrogated of all self-command.

Helpless.

Helpless as the night his father took him before the obelisk. But there was no loving, protecting Gilbert to save him this time.

Carson's vision bounced, and when his eyes turned outward, when the power of his own vision came to him again, his gaze fell into the great abyssal pit of the High Priest. A great hollow of the yawning infinite swallowed the child of Ezra Watts, the son of Gilbert Ptolemy.

"Let go of earthly attachment, my boy. See here, yes! See here, that which was unknowable, now discerned in this transformed flesh. Witness the oncoming dusk, the approaching night. The all night forever."

Chapter Twenty-Three

ABOARD THE
YELLOW DOVE EXPRESS,
EN ROUTE FROM
FT. WORTH TO DENVER

FOR SIX DAYS aboard the *Yellow Dove*, Annie Miller mostly slept. She spent her waking hours in the opulent dinner car with Sarah Lockhart, growing more and more appreciative of the woman's no-nonsense demeanor. During one of their many conversations, Sarah told Annie of her former life as a slave on a Georgian Plantation, her flight from bondage, and how she met Judge Ellison while trying to kill her former master.

"Most white abolitionists would have told me to forget my former owner and move on to a better life." Sarah said, as she sipped her coffee in the golden light of the early sunrise. "A life without them in it."

"What did he tell you to do?" asked Annie. She listened, looking around the diner car, taking in the other diners and the car attendant moving among the little tables with his professional smile and dark brown eyes.

Sarah gave Annie a slanted look. "He avoided making the mistake of 'telling' me to do anything. Instead, he took me under his wing, taught me how to use a gun. And with that gun, that he himself purchased for me in a little Savannah shop, he set me loose on the world. He told me that if I wanted a life after my revenge, he would help me find it."

Annie, entranced, asked her, "So you did it?"

"Of course. And then I burned that plantation—and the quarters where I survived sickness and starvation under the lash of that white bastard—to the ground. Killed him and all his sons. He was a widower, so I was glad I didn't have to kill his woman too." She then looked up at the car attendant and said, "Can we get some more cream, please?"

With Sarah's confession so plainly stated, Annie said, "I killed a man three years ago when he tried to rape me behind a saloon in the town where I grew up." She looked intently at Sarah, waiting to see her response.

The woman sipped her coffee, then set the cup down. "Good."

"I've never told anyone that."

"Well, now you have. How does it make you feel to get it off your chest?"

"Not sure."

"Well," said Sarah, leaning forward as if to tell Annie a secret. She glanced at the table across from them, where two men were smoking cigars and enjoying their coffee and each others' company. "Look over there at that table. What do you see?"

"Umm, two men laughing?"

Sarah shook her head. "Certainty."

Annie wrinkled her brow, unsure what she meant.

A Red Winter in the West

"An absolute confidence that the treasures of the world are lined up for them. We're all playing 'the game,' as Cornish puts it, and those two fellas might not admit it outright, but the rules are built for their success, if not totally rigged in their favor. They're sitting at the table of life, ready for the feast to be served. All they have to do is sit and be patient. Sure maybe some of them have to wait longer than others for an invitation to that feast, but they all get one, eventually. The rest of us?" She leveled her hard brown eyes at Annie. "The rest of us have to break down the door just to try and get a mouthful before we're gunned down for having the audacity of wanting a taste."

The attendant returned to their table, a fresh carafe of cream in his hands. He set it down with a little bow. "Ma'am."

"Thanks, darlin'," said Sarah, sweet as a sugar cube.

"I don't know that I see them that way," said Annie.

"Obviously. You might have been poor once, Annie Miller, but you ain't ever been a Negro. Certainly not a slave. But you weren't born with anything dangling between your legs, either, and to them, that means you're something to be owned, either by golden ring or iron shackle. And to be honest, often times they're the same damn thing."

"What about the other men, the ones like the Judge?" She thought for a moment. "Like Carson Ptolemy?"

Sarah looked insulted. "*What about them*?"

"They aren't that way. Like you said, the Judge helped you, put a gun in your hand and taught you how to use it."

"I don't reward a man just because he meets the bare minimum of human virtue. Neither should you. Demand their decency. Their goodness."

Annie wasn't sure what to say at that. As she watched the Texas landscape roll by, looking so big and wild and untouched, she was unsure about so many things. "There's so much space in the world," she said. "I don't know why anyone would think it was made just for them and not for everyone."

"It's greed. Plain and simple. Greed is the greatest affliction of the American character; it rots the heart and impoverishes the soul. What's worse is that no greedy person can ever have joy. Not real unassailable joy."

"I don't know about that," said Annie. "The greediest man I ever knew looked about as happy as he could be."

"And therein is the lie." Sarah smiled. "Happiness is the child of joy, but they are not the same thing. Because they are so closely related, they can be mistaken for one another. Joy is older though. She's mature. She knows things that happiness will never grow to learn."

Later, lying in her bunk as the *Yellow Dove* bumped its way along the long track between Texas and Colorado, Annie thought about that for a long time. She liked the way Sarah spoke. Liked her confidence. Liked her.

The world hadn't offered Annie too much in the way of kindness, and most of what it had given to her, it quickly took back. Sarah felt different. Something about the woman seemed lasting, reliable. The woman had so quickly offered to help Annie.

Why?

Annie dared to believe that it was because Sarah liked her. It would be nice to have a friend and an experienced gunfighter.

Larry Cornish, on the other hand, had proved less amiable, though he was friendly in his own quiet, reserved way. Much of the time, he kept to himself, taking his meals late at night. When he requested the Peregrine ledger, without giving much reason as to why, Annie had given it to him.

On the third morning, she found him sitting alone at a table, nursing a cigarette and a cup of tea.

A Red Winter in the West

"Mind some company?" she asked, removing her hat and placing it in the seat next to the one across from him.

"Naturally," he said without looking up from the ledger. "Plans to make."

Annie sat down.

"Erickson is the key to understanding the kingdom. He has hunted them. Knows them," he said. "Will advise us on locations, logistics, weaknesses. All essential. Much depends on him being alive."

The waiter brought over a fresh cup of coffee for Annie. She ordered breakfast. When the waiter stepped away, she asked, "Why wouldn't he be alive?"

"Guild member. Life always in peril. Prefers it that way."

"Guild?"

"Gunfighter's Guild."

Annie shook her head. "You say that like I'm supposed to know what that is."

"Association of pistoleers all aiming to be number one. Twenty-five members across the globe. Membership comes by invitation only. Each one begins at the bottom, challenges preceding member, one at a time. Each contest of the gun follows structured rules of engagement, never to be broken. Members climb the ladder to be named first among their number. This is the badge of highest acclaim."

"Sounds like a dangerous life. What's the reward for being number one?"

"Being number one."

"They don't win anything?"

He flipped a page in the ledger, eyes scanning the page, never looking up. "Erickson, like other members, is compelled by competitive sickness. Acclaim among peers is all the reward such people require." Cornish took a long, hard drag from his cigarette. The look of relief that washed over him was the first sign of feeling to reveal itself. "Erickson, number seven, is much sought after by number eight, Stephen Walker. Professional rivalry there goes back to Slaver's Revolt."

"I can't imagine living that kind of life," said Annie. "Always looking over your shoulder, wondering when the next challenger came calling."

"On topic: Erickson, if alive, is the fulcrum on which plan can be leveraged. Without him, our plan will adjust."

"Just as long as we find Sigurd."

"Tertiary concern."

"Mr. Cornish…sometimes it's very difficult to have a conversation with you?"

"Not main priority. Not second priority."

It was the way he said it, coupled with the way he kept his head buried in the ledger, that frustrated Annie. "He's the only priority for me," she said, almost a warning.

"Change priorities."

"He murdered my mother and my best—"

"Failing to grasp problem. Grab bull by the horns. See, they meet in the middle. Two are one. Crush the kingdom, crush Sigurd. Personal feelings are tertiary."

Annie's face flushed with anger, but before she could unload on him, the waiter arrived with her breakfast.

She took a deep breath while unrolling her silverware. "I came to you with my intentions clear. My goal is to—"

Cornish's eyes snapped up from the ledger, pinning themselves to Annie. "Young. Angry. Brave. Bad combination for survival. The game, bigger than personal want. Kingdom represents greatest immediate threat. Let go of personal feelings."

A Red Winter in the West

"All I have left are my feelings, Mr. Cornish." Annie found herself wishing that Sarah was at the table with them. She had known Cornish longer, and Annie was sure she'd have taken her side.

"Larry," he said. "Larry to friends."

The word caught her off guard. Could a man like this have true friends? "Fine, Larry, all I have left are—"

"Health. Youth. Purpose. Acorns."

"Acorns?"

He nodded, his eyes coming up for but a moment from the ledger to give her an almost bashful look. "Currency stashed in tree of life. Winter of adulthood, and war slowly take them. Enjoy present moment."

"You mean like Julius taking his family to Canada. Is that what you think he was doing? Taking his acorns and running."

Cornish's brow sloped, annoyed. "Julius made choice. You, yours. Only making observation. Anger for want of revenge is corrosive. Poisons tree, enters roots, kills all. Unsustainable."

Annie leaned forward, her voice low and angry. "Then I best be about my business as quick as possible. Good morning to you, Mr. *Cornish*."

She sulked away from the table, her food uneaten, and went back to her bunk.

Inside the cabin, she opened her mouth in a furious silent scream. Who was Larry goddamn Cornish to tell her what her priorities should be? The man with no human feeling at all—a cold machine without the capability to feel loss or pain.

Well, it didn't matter what he'd said. He and Sarah would get her close to Sigurd, and when the right moment came, she would take her revenge. Until that moment, she'd play his 'game' his way.

Chapter Twenty-Four

CHICAGO, ILLINOIS

———————

CARSON STEPPED OUT into the sunlight for the first time in days. He winced against the brightness. Doctor Van Horn and the behemoth Walther stood next to him as they waited for the carriage to pull around the street corner. Carson leaned into the man's huge shadow to block out the accosting sun. He wiped his watering eyes against his sleeve. "Where are we going?" he asked.

"Shut up," said Walther.

"Mr. Rose," cut in Doctor Van Horn. "There's no need to be an asshole all the time."

Walther sneered at her.

The doctor then turned to Carson. "I see you're getting a feel for the dentures," she said. "Good."

It was a strange feeling, but the artificial teeth did fit well, and they provided an artifice of normalcy that Carson welcomed. "Thank you again," he said. "Now, if someone could tell me what the hell we're—"

The voice of the High Priest floated out from behind him. "It's too beautiful a day to be cooped up inside, Mr. Ptolemy."

Carson turned and, for the first time, saw the man. He gasped at the sight. No longer veiled in the firelight shadow, the man's face was a desolation. Long deep scars ran from the tip of his lumpy bare skull into curved red canyons along his chin and throat. They were knife wounds, and they were very, very old. He wore a simple black suit, closed at the throat by a pearl button big as a sugar cube. In his hands he clutched a walking stick topped by a great green jewel too dark to be emerald or jade.

The priest tilted his head at Carson and smiled at him with chipped teeth. "See the face of the man whom you have hunted so long, Mr. Ptolemy. I do not take offense at the shock. See the freak. The face of the man who will change the world."

"Sir, our carriage," announced Walther.

"Let this one go by, good brother. We will take the next one."

"Yes, sir."

"There's something I want to show you, Mr. Ptolemy. A gift. Something I believe will be the first beams of the bridge I hope to build between us."

"If it's friendship you're after," said Carson, watching another carriage roll up, "there's only disappointment waiting for you."

"Perhaps," said the priest.

Walther flagged the oncoming coachman. "Here we are, sir."

The black carriage, pulled by two dark mules, rolled to a stop before them. Van Horn went first, then Carson, Walther behind him, and last the priest. Satin curtains, blue as moonlit clouds passing in the dead of night, draped themselves over the windows, and so again, the high priest was comfortably cast in shadow where he sat.

"Walther, if you please," said the priest.

A Red Winter in the West

The big man, sitting opposite of Carson, lightly banged his fist on the driver-side wall of the carriage. They began to roll down the streets of Chicago.

The High Priest spoke. "Like you, Carson, I never knew my mother. My visage is a testament to her...disfavor of the son she bore. Amelia, was her name. The wife of a member of our society. When my father told her my preordained purpose, that I should be a herald of destruction, she despaired. Her heart was turned away from the rightness of things, and so, she plotted. When the time came for me to come into the world, she went to her bedchamber. With the help of her midwife, they fled to the emptied slave quarters. I was pulled from her womb, and then, amid our mutual screams, she took a pair of sterling sewing sheers and desperately tried to end my life. Luckily, my father's men had heard her cries and stopped her just before her work could be completed." He leaned forward, letting the slanting sunlight illuminate the wreckage of his face. "She was afraid, Carson. Fearful of the change I might bring to bear."

Carson listened, his finger working in the dark at the manacles on his wrists. But they were too tight for him to slip out of. Without a tool of some kind to work the lock, he couldn't free himself.

The High Priest leaned forward, closer. "My father punished her for her apostasy."

"Why are you telling me this?" asked Carson.

He smiled. "Because our stories are not so terribly different. We share an innate gift, a cosmic boon. Your father knew this. He worked with me, believed as deeply as any of us have ever believed— but he, like my mother, was weak in the end."

"I don't understand."

The priest lifted his walking stick, examining the dark green jewel perched at its top. "Ezra knew the Black Manuscript better than any of us, Carson. He was able to decipher an alchemy from its pages, a ritual that would take the life of his son, but in its completion it would forever seal off our world from the beautiful creatures our species so desperately need to remind us of our place in the universe."

Carson's mind began to spin.

"Yes, I can see it now on your face. Only now do you come to understand."

"My father—"

"At some point during his travels and his experiences, he fell from enlightenment. He began to see humanity in a false light. Training you in the language of the manuscript, he discerned a way to transform you into what you are now. And so, he put you before the black obelisk and began the work that would ruin the Society of Prometheus forever. He would kill his son, one of the two conduits required to see our own duty complete. I am one of those conduits. You, Carson Watts Ptolemy, are the other."

"That's...you're lying."

"I have no use for lies, Carson. Had it not been for Gilbert Ptolemy, you would have perished, and with you, our chance at the final victory. Our hopes of a world unchained...unfettered from all these contrivances of human supremacy. Fate spared you for this moment, this one grand purpose. Judge Ellison and your father conspired, both of them traitors to our cause. And now, both of them are dead."

Carson's heart fell, as if thrown from a cliff into a black ocean of despair, into a sunken place. "No."

"I'm afraid so. The Peregrine Estate made too many enemies, and one of those enemies put an end to him and to every living soul in Abilene where he was hiding."

A Red Winter in the West

Carson opened his mouth, but there were no words. Only the dark waters of his despair, fathoms deep, drowning his heart.

"A pity," said the High Priest. "I had deeply hoped for the Judge to see the coming day of transformation, that his belief might return to him in those final moments."

All the pain and suffering and memories came crowding over Carson. He began to weep.

Doctor Van Horn placed her hand on his sobbing shoulders. "Shh, it's alright. Everything is going to be alright."

"It was never our plan to take the lives of those we have for so long hoped to save." The High Priest's voice was so soft, so comforting. "And now, with the scales thrown from your eyes, you see. And as a man's wisdom increases, so too does his sorrow. Now you see why we never tried to kill you; and trust me, we held many chances to do so."

Carson, gathering his composure, wiped his eyes and looked at the dark outline of the priest. He wanted to say something so true and so hurtful that it would cut through the man's confidence. Something that would make him afraid of the pain Carson would put upon him. But nothing came, and so he just stared at the man, his unspoken thoughts drowning in the priest's darkness.

"Just think, Carson," Doctor Van Horn's kind voice filled his ears. "How all of this will be bathed in a cloak of night when the winter chases away all our present suffering. The Earth shall shed its summer flesh and find a skin of frost beneath the heat of war and hatred. It will be a world of cold certainty. Absolute. No more false gods. No more illusion. The true world we lost but are destined to regain. You can help us bring it to fruition."

The carriage came to a halt.

"He will," said Walther.

"Yes," echoed the High Priest. "He will."

"I'll die first," said Carson, defiant.

The dark priest shook his head. "So too shall I, Carson. But not for our own sake. We shall die together. Now come, let me show you my gift."

The carriage door opened, flooding the space with light. They exited, one by one, out into the busy street.

Before them was a brick church. Three-stories tall, it rose higher than any of the surrounding buildings. From the bell tower came a bright peal announcing the noon hour. The great wooden doors, cut into the stone archways, topped with triangular patterns pointing toward swooping arches, opened before them. A robed man stood in the open door.

He said nothing as he bowed before the High Priest.

"You even think of running," said Walther coldly, "and I'll make the beating you got on the train feel like a first kiss."

That made Carson think of Annie Miller. Had she been killed too?

A thin man holding a stack of newspapers came rushing up to them. "Howdy folks," he said. "Howdy, howdy! Have you seen the latest edition?"

Carson turned toward him.

"You sir," he said, shoving a paper into Carson's hands, "have you read the latest? The *Chicago Enquirer* is happy to report that Buffalo Bill and his traveling band are coming soon!" The man paused and looked Carson square in the eye, his brow twisting in confusion, then in recognition. "Say, don't I know you? Are you Bill Tomlinson's boy?"

Carson opened his mouth to speak.

"Walther," said the High Priest."

Walther gave the man a shove. "Sell your shit someplace else, urchin."

A Red Winter in the West

"Easy, friend," the man said, putting his hands up as if being robbed at gunpoint. "Just trying' to make a living! Yeesh, you're a big one, aren't you."

"Buzz off!"

"I'm goin', I'm goin', you ape. Keep the paper, friend," the man said to Carson before scurrying back into the crowd.

The curious thing that Carson saw was that once the man was deep into the herd of skirted ladies and bowler hatted men, he dropped his stack of papers and ducked away, running down an alley.

"Inside," the priest demanded.

Carson took a half step toward the crowd, but Walter slapped a hand onto his shoulder, sending a lance of pain all the way to Carson's rib cage.

"Not a chance, kid," said Walther, then guided Carson up to the entrance under the archway.

Cut into the white stone were the words 'Revelation 12:7.' Carson wasn't familiar with the passage, and so he passed under its sign into the sanctuary.

Inside, he looked up to see a great fresco painted into the central panel of the Church's ceiling: there, stroked in autumn colors, was Michael the Archangel casting the Serpent from the gates of Paradise. Carson looked at it for a long time, passing under the shadow of its beauty. It reminded him of years prior, when dark clouds, their swollen curves pregnant with rain, rolled in just outside of Big Spring. They had saved him and Mr. Ptolemy from the cooking heat of the West Texas sun like angels sent from Heaven itself.

West Texas was certainly no kind of paradise, what with the hard caliche and sand…but the clouds. The clouds, he thought, bursting from the sky like wedding-white wings thrust over the whole span of the choking desert—like the archangel. With lances of thunder and

245

sheets of rain, those wings beat the devil heat out for a blessed while. It had saved their lives. Remembering that sweet memory, Carson grieved his Gilbert's death again.

The great oaken doors groaned shut behind them.

There was a tremendousness to the sanctuary, a power rooted its foundation. No matter what befell the Earth or the people living on it, Carson thought, this building would stand resolute for all time.

Perched on the altar was a massive oak table. A white sheet lay across the center. Under the sheet, a round object bulged.

"Carson, come please." The High Priest stepped up to the altar, where he placed his hands on the table.

Carson hesitated, but Walther gave him a shove, and he walked up the steps to stand next to the High Priest.

"What do you think?" the priest asked, gazing up at the fresco, arms stretched wide.

"I've never seen anything like it."

"We love to build great real things to honor the imaginary, don't we? Look at those windows." He pointed up to the Passion play etched in sparkling glass at the tip of the altar's height. "Look at all the beauty they've wrapped around a lie. A little lie almost two thousand years old, and oh, how it has grown in the telling. One has to admire the belief in such a falseness and the hope it conjures. A hope just as counterfeit as the man they shackle it to. A hope as false as those new teeth of yours. Sure, they will do the job your old ones did, and they look real enough from a distance, but they aren't yours; and anyone who gets close enough will see through the artifice."

"There's a truth in all that glory," said Carson.

The ruined face of the priest looked bemused. "Spoken like a true Watts. Your father had a flair for the poetic, too. How does it make you feel, to now know the truth: that the father you despised was actually working toward the same goal you now have?"

Carson looked at a section of the glass window displaying Judas kissing Christ. "I don't know," he said.

"Does it make you love him again?"

Carson let the question swirl in his mind. He followed the story above from drawn lots to the scourging, angry crowd to the upward climb of Golgotha. "He was going to kill me for the sake of everyone else. I'm not quite sure how to feel about that."

"Neither did he," said the priest. "In the story, Christ welcomed the sacrifice, though near the end, he too felt betrayed by his parent. You and I both know that same wound. My mother. Your father. They tried to choose the world over their own children. Now we have a chance to choose the sacrifice for ourselves. A sacrifice in ritual that will change the course of human history. It makes me quite happy to be capable of such a work."

"Sacrifice in ritual?"

"On this, the manuscript is quite clear. Should we simply perish, the conduit that exists inside of us will pass to another, staving off the true gods' reclamation of our world for a time. But should we perish in the ritual, our sacrifice will allow the Earth's axis to tilt once again. The stars will align. All the great gates shall be sundered, and our true masters will make their triumphal reentry. And that knowledge, given to you in this place, is my gift to you Carson. If you simply end your own life, that great power in you, a power I am sure you see as a curse, will transfer itself to another. As it has since the cosmic gates first closed, before the recording of human history. You have an opportunity to strip humankind of the lie. You have seen Alitranz—seen his awesome power—and so you no longer believe, because you *know*. You know the truth."

Carson, looking at Christ crucified, turned his eyes to the scared eyes of the High Priest. "Gilbert talked about a higher cosmology. He told me that there were the powers of destruction and the powers of creation, and that your gods were only harbingers of death and sorrow. He said that God was real and that goodness and charity were his sign on the world."

"A brave theology," the High Priest remarked. "Encouraging, but a part of the lie. People do not work toward goodness in their lives; they work toward comfort in their minds, hearts, and souls. They crave it like a babe craves mother's milk. The nourishment of the breast is for the child, not the adult. Then the child grows up, and the coldness of reality is the only comfort the world affords. Humanity has lost that truth: the truth that we are not born of some grand maker but are a species wholly subjugate to a higher race. That cosmological truth will always be greater than the lie of the carpenter's son. Because the old gods are fact, and Christ's resurrection is a fable."

They stood there in silence, both of them looking up at the sunlight streaming in through the windows.

"Let me read it for myself," said Carson. "Give me the manuscript. If its words are real, as you say they are, let me find the truth for myself."

The priest nodded. "Time grows thin, and the stars will not wait on us much longer, but I will give this to you, Carson. I know that once you feel the truth in the manuscript's power, you will willingly come to me. You'll be ready to walk with me. Hand in hand, into the truth."

Chapter Twenty-Five

BLACK WELLS, COLORADO

DENVER'S ROCKY MOUNTAINS were cut from pure splendor. Their white-capped crowns ran a jagged slope down into a palisade of evergreens. The girth of the crag was painted the color of a stormy day, where blistering winds cut over the prongs of the mountain's peaks to assail the world with winter's fist.

To see the Rockies for the first time was a glory. Awe inspiring.

The Astolats, near Black Wells, Colorado, were an entirely different kind of wonder. They were blue-skinned monstrosities that struck out of the black soil like the crown of some dark tyrant slowly standing from a throne at the center of the Earth. His exodus from that place would irreparably wound the world. The mountain rose, wreathed in storm, claiming primacy over all other mountains near or far. From out of the clouds came a wide lavender line—a purpling river. It slithered down the mountain into a wide expanse, a body of water that blackened as it curled around the city sitting in the shadow of the mountain.

Carried there in the coach, Annie felt the terrible sense of her own immediate smallness in the world. Not only because of the greatness of the mountain but also for the vast predatory kingdom she knew rested beneath it. Sigurd was there, hidden in the belly of that giant. The thought of him ignited her anger, rekindled her desire to see him pay blood for blood. Life for life.

"I hate this place," said Sarah, her voice breaking the silence.

"You've been here before?" asked Annie.

"Mmhmm. Came by this way a few years back. Helped my friend settle a conflict between two packs of werewolves… Well," she corrected herself, "two families who happened to be werewolves. It was the Slaver's Revolt that caused it. One pack believed every creature deserved to roam free, the other believed that which could be subjugated by a stronger force deserved their chains. You'd be surprised to know, I bet, that the idea of abolition split the supernatural part of the country too." She smiled. "Not all the creatures who walk among us are malicious like those from the Red Kingdom. Some of them are just trying to live in the world, like we are." She pointed at the massive river hooking around Black Wells. "I almost drowned in the Cam River there. If it hadn't been for Conner, one of the aforementioned werewolves, I'd have been dead for sure."

"Like that story," said Larry. He was staring out the window at the mountain. "Should tell it."

"Some other time, when there's more of it. We're coming up on Black Wells. But, like I said, I hate this place. They don't take much of a shine to seeing an armed Black woman step out onto their streets."

"If anyone tries to give you trouble, I'll be there for you." Annie said. "We just need to find Sven."

Sarah shook her head, happy and content. "You are just filled with young dedication, aren't you. Your heart is quick to care. I like that about you, Annie Miller."

A Red Winter in the West

Annie blushed. "You did the same. You saw I needed help, and you came with me. You give me your help, I give you mine."

Sarah looked over to Larry, who was still staring out the window. "Getting butterflies yet?"

Larry didn't respond.

"Butterflies?" asked Annie. "Why would he be nervous?"

"Well, Larry here—"

"Sarah." He cut her off, the word soft and absolute. "Focus. The kingdom has servants. Not all of them walk in the dark."

The Cam River rushed forth, dark as night where it did not cap white among sharp black stones. They crossed over that torrent in the buggy and made their way along the deep rivets cut into the muddy slush of the city street.

"Hoooo," cried the coachman, as he pulled the carriage to a stop.

"Why's he stopping?" Sarah asked, mostly to herself. She thought about it a moment and then rapped on the roof. "Hey, we're supposed to be dropped off at the Imperial Hotel!"

"Yes, ma'am," the man said, his voice muffled. "Street is occupied by two fellas. Reckon with the crowd teaming on the sidewalks and posture of those fellas in the street, they're about to settle something with bullets."

Larry Cornish was out of the buggy in a flash, leaving his ledger and pencil behind.

"Wait!" Sarah called after him, but the door was already slapping shut.

"What's gotten into him?"

"No time. Grab his stuff."

They climbed down from the buggy and followed Cornish as he rushed out onto the walkway that ran along the center of the main street.

A few onlookers huddled next to one of the general stores, all of them watching the street with great interest. One of the women in the crowd, hearing their footfalls on the wooden planks, turned and put her hands out to caution them.

"Hold on, folks. Guild business."

"You mean the Gunfighter's Guild?" asked Annie. "Like, here in the middle of town?"

The woman looked at Annie and nodded gravely.

From over her shoulder, one of the two men in the street called out to the crowd: "My name is Stephen Lee Walker. As eight, I challenge Sven Erickson, the seven. I've approached this son of a bitch in honor, within the rules of our association, and I challenge him forthwith to a contest of the gun. I'm here to take your life, Sven, and with it, your title. What say you?"

Annie looked at Cornish. His eyes were glassy, wet, and his normally flat expression was grim as death.

"We have to stop this," said Annie, pleading. They couldn't have come so far only to have Sven die at their arrival.

Cornish ignored her.

"Once the challenge goes out," Sarah said, "there's no stopping it."

Annie peered around the crowd to see the two men standing in the otherwise empty street. Walker was medium height, skinny from shoulder to hip. Walker was medium height, slender from shoulder to waist, standing with a strong wide-legged stance, two pistols on his hips.. Closer to the crowd, with his back to Annie, was Sven Erikson. He was tall and thick as a bull all over. The man cast a long black shadow that ran the length of the snow-blanketed street.

The gunfighters stood like two dark pillars on a beam of white.

"My name is Sven Erikson," the man said, his accent as thick as he was, his vowels over pronounced. "As seven, I accept the challenge of the slaving marauder here before me. Let all witnesses know that I accept it in honor, and that should I die, this man may collect my guns and the guild pin I wear.

"Twenty-three have come before you, Walker. You have aims to be seven, but I fear you'll only be counted as twenty-four. And though you don't deserve it, you bloody bastard, I offer you this one chance to recant your challenge and walk away with your life."

Annie jumped when the crowd suddenly erupted in applause at Sven's words.

"The challenge stands," said Walker, popping the knuckles of his right hand into the palm of his left.

"Good," said Sven. "I commence the contest into action, with you knowing that every hand you've ever cut down in cold blood draws down on you now."

The street fell silent, save for the cold biting wind swirling from the Astolats. Snow fell, fluttering between the two gunfighters like white fireflies.

Time passed. The men did not move.

Annie's fingers were trembling. She had to remind herself to breathe.

A sound.

Metal sliding from leather.

The silence snapped with the crack of gunfire. A single shot. A hot, red mist sprayed out in a cloud behind Walker, mingling with the swirling drift of snow. His eyes shot skyward, wide as if he were answering a call from on high. His mouth yawned, silent in disbelief.

Sven flourished his revolver and holstered it. Walker fell backward, his hands clamped on the butts of his guns.

It was the fastest draw Annie had ever seen. One moment the revolver had been in Sven's belt, then, as if she'd missed a moment in time, it was smoking in the air.

Sven's boots crunched through the snow toward his victim. He crouched over the fallen man, stood again, then turned to face the crowd.

"Stephen Lee Walker was a murdering bastard, and it would not surprise me if the ground will spit him back out after he's buried. I've removed his guild pin and will be happy to see it worn by a man or woman worthy of its—" He fell silent and stared at Larry Cornish.

Larry swallowed hard. His chest rose and fell heavily.

Sven shook his head and continued: "Worthy of its station." The big man smiled, relieved. "Guild business is concluded. You folks can go on about your day, happy that a plague no longer walks among you."

The crowd applauded again. The woman who had stopped Annie and the other agents shuddered at the shoulders. "What a man," she said.

Sarah laughed and clapped Cornish on the shoulder. "Sure is, ain't he, Larry?"

The man said nothing but stepped away from them and walked slowly out into the snowy street to approach Sven.

The crowd had begun to disperse, but some paused to watch Cornish move toward the gunfighter.

Then Larry broke into a run.

The two embraced, and the shape of their desperate affection cast upon the pure white beneath them, kissed under a gunmetal sky.

A few in the crowd gasped.

"Oh…" the woman next to Annie said.

"Yeah," said Sarah happily. "Ain't love beautiful."

The woman gave Sarah a sideways glance and sneered.

Sven wrapped his arms around Larry's shoulders and leaned his cheek against him. He whispered something into his ear. Whatever secret was spoken there caused their embrace to tighten.

A Red Winter in the West

Sarah turned to Annie. "Come on, let's celebrate with them."

Annie followed her out into the street.

As they drew near, Sven reached out with a big hand and pulled Sarah into their hug. "Sarah Lockhart," he exclaimed.

"Good to see you, handsome." She kissed him on the cheek. "Glad to see you're still as slow as I remember."

Sven laughed. It was a big uninhibited sound. "I'm so glad you're here…and who is this young pup following you?"

"Annie Miller, Mr. Erikson. It was me who sent you the telegram about…about what happened in Abilene."

The man's mirth diminished, but only a little. "It's Sven to you, ma'am. And I am glad to meet you, Annie. Come on," he said, then planted a big kiss on Larry's cheek. "Let's go mourn and celebrate as only friends and lovers can."

They had their bags taken to the hotel and their mounts stocked at the livery stable.

Sven led the three of them toward the north end of the street. There, with a flourish of his hand, he gestured toward an omnibus. "Shall we?" he said, and opened the ornate door for Annie.

"Of course," said Sarah, laughing. "You wouldn't travel any other way."

"Not if I can help it." Sven guided them all inside. "My trade is a rough one that affords me to roam in leisure."

Carried forth by a quartet of midnight black Morgan's, the omnibus was a fine, regal thing with its cool green paint, sterling brass inlaid over every section of trim and plush leather seats. The gunfighter's cabin was just on the outskirts of Black Wells, he told them. On their way there, cradled in opulence, they told Sven of the fate of the Judge and those poor souls who'd perished during Sigurd's assault on Peregrine House. He listened intently, his hand laid over Larry's.

255

When Annie made clear her intent for Sigurd, Sven simply shook his head. "I am bereaved for you, Ms. Miller, I truly am, so I hate to be the one to tell you that your plan is set upon failure at the outset."

Those words sank Annie's heart.

"Don't let it wound you," he said. "The kingdom is too large, their power too great, for a band such as we are. A direct assault will garner little success. And of your enemy Sigurd, I have neither heard word nor seen any sight of him these last few weeks. Even if we had at our disposal the entire agency of the Peregrine Estate, I would not wager for a victory. The Red Kingdom is very old, and they have not survived this long by allowing themselves to become vulnerable."

"There has to be some way, something you know that can help us," pleaded Annie, desperate.

"We've come all this way to aid her in her revenge, Sven," said Sarah. "Give the girl something."

"Anything," said Annie.

"One of the human servants of the vampires does speak to me, sends me notes. He says there is a passage into the mountains whereby a force might seize the advantage of a surprise attack, but their numbers are in the hundreds, maybe more than a thousand. You must understand, these are creatures of pure perception, and our only advantage is silver and sunlight. Neither of which are in rich supply in the Astolats. With proper planning and preparation, we could build a force and strategy that might swing the effort in our favor. But now? It is an impossible task."

"Where is the path?" asked Annie.

"I know what it is like to want for something so dearly that you would be willing to place yourself at great peril to have it." At that, he looked at Larry longingly.

A Red Winter in the West

Astonishingly, Larry Cornish blushed.

"I promise you, Annie," he said, turning back to her, "we will work to do this thing. But it cannot be now. The kingdom is set in their mountain. They aren't going anywhere."

Sven's promise failed to soothe the anger and sorrow festering in her mind. "That is not a comfort to me, Mr. Erickson," she said.

"Well then you have my most sincere apology," he said. He rubbed his smooth chin, considering. His countenance darkened. "I have other news for you all, but it's also mixed. Got word this morning from one of our men in Chicago. It seems our young friend Mr. Carson Ptolemy is alive."

Annie's heart leaped at that good word. "He's okay?"

Sven's face remained reserved, grim. "He's been captured by those he sought to destroy," he said in a grim tone. "They have not been kind to him. The Society has him captive and are carrying him around Chicago. To what end , we do not know."

"Your man in Chicago is sure that it was Ezra's boy?" asked Sarah.

Sven nodded. "I trust his eye."

Annie produced her pipe, packed it to the brim. "Why take him prisoner?" she asked. "Why keep him alive?" She lit the bowl, taking in the sweet smoke.

"Who can say," said Sven.

Annie blew the smoke out.

"What I do know is that our late friend Judge Ellison was keen on finding him and insisted that, should Carson reappear, we should bring him back into the Peregrine fold. Though the Judge is gone, I am still eager to follow his last command. Along with that, Ezra Watts was my friend, and, though he betrayed us in the end, I feel a great compassion for his son. Should we reclaim him, he would be a strong ally. He has waged a one-man war on the Society of

Prometheus and made them bleed. He's exactly the kind of man you're looking to recruit when wanting to take on a whole mountain of vampires."

Annie nodded. "Carson is my friend. If it hadn't been for him, my family would never have made it out of Yellow Hill."

"Essential to mission," said Cornish.

Sven nodded. "I agree, Six."

Annie's pipe almost fell out of her mouth. *"You're* in the Gunfighter's Guild too?"

"Long time ago. Stopped climbing the ladder."

"We both did." Sven squeezed Cornish's hand.

"You're protecting him," said Annie.

"Larry doesn't need my protection. But yes, we are both in the guild, and because the rules of the association refuse us the ability to retire, we simply maintain our current positions."

Sarah laughed. "Which pisses off the guild something fierce, I'm guessing."

"We do not concern ourselves with the guild's position on the issue. All someone has to do to get to Larry is go through me. Technically, we aren't breaking any rules."

"If Carson is alive," said Annie, "then he deserves protection too. He needs us to help him, just like he helped me."

"Priorities," said Cornish, giving Annie a single resolute nod.

She let the smoke from her pipe billow out her mouth, speaking through clenched teeth. "Priorities."

Chapter Twenty-Six
CHICAGO, ILLINOIS

IN CARSON'S MIND, the library which held the Black Manuscript would be a dark and dreary place filled with flaming braziers and dripping stone ceilings. A hidden place for hidden things. But the personal library of the High Priest was brightly lit with grand glass windows. Light streamed into that place bright and clear. The priest's copy of the tome lay on a chest-high wooden pedestal, bathed in the glowing beams of the noonday sun.

The priest stood next to him in the sunshine, smiling. They were alone.

"Who would have thought that the two of us should ever be standing here, together, ready to embark on such a journey," said the priest.

Carson approached the stand where the book lay waiting. How could such a small thing, he thought, be filled with so much potential calamity.

"Does it hurt you too when you read the words?" he asked.

"Pain is the price of knowledge."

"I've never been able to read more than a page or two at a time."

"Your capacity will increase, such as it did with me. As you grow closer to the text, your knowledge of its power will grow too, and even greater truths will be revealed. Let it take you—it will show you many harrowing things. Far-off places and those waiting kings and queens of the space between the stars."

Carson stood now before the manuscript and, even without touching it, he could feel its irrepressible force.

"Don't be afraid," said the High Priest.

But he was afraid. So very afraid that that the book would claim him long before he could find the thing he was actually looking for. The ritual. The ritual that could end his life in such a fashion that the world would be made safer in his death. The ritual his father, Ezra, had sought to employ.

Carson looked at the manuscript for what felt like a very long time, one hand nervously rubbing his brow, the other, bandaged and still trying to mend, dangled at his side.

Was this his true purpose?

Was this the thing God willed him into the world to accomplish?

His heart bucked at the unfairness of it. The unjustness to be placed in such a position. Gilbert had often spoken of the importance of the calling put upon them: the calling to carry the light into dark places, shouldering the secret burdens of a world ignorant of the dangers beset upon it.

"Is this all I am," said Carson.

The High Priest remained silent.

"A device meant for suffering."

"We are conduits, Carson. We are built for suffering. It is the suffering that gives the bread of life its rise. The greater the suffering, the greater the earned joy. This is the truth humanity has

A Red Winter in the West

lost among the wasteland of its decadence. To live is to suffer and endure."

Carson watched the hand, which did not seem like his own, reach out and open the book's cover. In opening it, Carson felt something unlock inside him—an old door in the architecture of his heart he had tried so hard to forget. The door swung wide, and the memory of his life before came crowding over him. The struggle against the Society. The deaths of his fathers. The blood and the terror.

And, surprisingly, the face of Annie Miller came to him too. The kiss she had given him. That soft, grand gesture, so simple a thing. A gift given with such ease that it lifted all the weight of his journey from his shoulders. He thought about how poor the world would be without such a kindness. Such a power. He would give anything to feel that simple sweetness now, anything just to hear her voice say his name through her summertime smile.

His eyes went to the page. Immediately, the malice in the slashes of written language stamped down on him like a strike of lightning. He fell from the perch of his waking mind like a stone thrown from a cliff. The trajectory of his consciousness tumbled end over end into a pit of darkness. Strange, jagged shapes of indeterminable colors flew past him, their gloomy iridescence unable to pierce the darkness.

There was nothing in this place.

Nothing but darkness and the chill of death.

Then, from the vast and impenetrable black came a sound not unlike a voice and yet nothing like the sound of beast or man.

It was a presence of sound that pitched itself up to an unbearable intensity. From gale to whirlwind, hurricane to roar, it grew. The sound overwhelmed him.

It was the voice of the Black Manuscript.

A voice like the voice of God, he thought. A terrible, incomprehensible sounding of…what? What was this piercing noise? Words came in measured upticks of time, loose and long in their meter.

Then, Carson realized that he was not hearing speech.

It was a song.

A dark hymn that he could not remember knowing but which still bore the trappings of familiarity. It was old. Older than man. Older than measured time, and the sound of it crushed him.

This was a mistake, he thought. A terrible error to try and use the Black Manuscript as his father had.

It was only in that moment that Carson realized, as he fell further and further into the midnight song of the ancient, that he should have left the Society of Prometheus behind the day he survived Ezra's attempt on his life. Revenge had led him to this place. Revenge and his want for it.

He tried to scream.

The roiling song, so tremendous in its effect, filled his mouth. The notes filled him up like brackish water funneled into a wine skin, bloating the vessel that was Carson Watts Ptolemy.

Then, in the vast cosmic distance of the fall, there came a single shaft of light. A bullet hole punched into the fabric of night. The hole swung left and right, bending at its center. The song climbed higher and higher, from bass to tenor, alto, then soprano.

The hole expanded. Opened.

Immolating light, green and sickly, dawned in that dark place to reveal not a star—but an eye.

The eye of something huge.

To call the thing gigantic would be to undo all human reasoning of the word. A slumbering planet woke. And its terrible eye fell upon him.

A Red Winter in the West

Still the singing grew and grew, filling his stomach, his bowels, all of him.

The language, millions of years in its making, became clear to him. The words translated into concepts he could understand.

The Black Manuscript spoke its secrets.

Carson, though he tried with all his strength to refuse, heard every word. Every note, every word, he heard. He knew its melody

The song that would end the world.

Part III

THE LAST OBELISK

"Man believes he exists unto himself as an island, wholly concerned with himself and his fate. But there is no fate. There is no island. There is only a black ocean of stars, the Nine monarchs, and their cosmic song."

Principe of the Society of Prometheus,
Lucio Gandolfi, *Illimitable Primacy*

Chapter Twenty-Seven

ABOARD THE STEAM TRAIN *MONARCH*, EN ROUTE FROM DENVER TO CHICAGO

O N THE BACKS of their ponies, the four agents rode their horses hard away from Black Wells. A quartet of shadows cut a hard slender line, escaping the dreadful eye of the Astolats, painfully distancing Annie Miller from the Red Kingdom. From Sigurd. From revenge.

It was hard for her to accept what Sven had said. But if she were only ever going to get one chance at killing her mother's murderer, she told herself as Starchild tramped over that worn trail toward the Rockies, she would do it when success was certain. Getting Carson back would aid in that purpose. Still she feared they would not reach Chicago with time enough to find and rescue him from the hands of his enemies.

In truth, Carson's own choice to take on the Society alone was likely the error that facilitated his capture. If there were to be a victory over such a conspiracy, it would be accomplished by a company of capable fighters and not just one person alone. She would learn from his mistake.

She was grateful now, especially, that Sarah, Cornish, and Sven had taken her seriously and thrown themselves in with her. She did not know why—not totally, anyway—Carson had gone his way by himself, but she knew the lust of revenge, and certainly she could empathize.

They had Sven Erikson now and, from the man's display on the streets of Black Wells, Annie was confident that whatever was put in front of them, they had a chance to defeat.

The four of them arrived in Denver late in the evening, rode down and ragged from the hard journey. They purchased their train tickets for Chicago, and there at the livery stable, and with great reservation, Annie gave Starchild's reins to a young boy who, if she squinted hard enough, managed to look like Georgie. Sun-kissed cheeks, bright hair and bright-eyed. An innocent face.

Before she let him guide the horse into the stable, she gave the little boy a hug and told him to take care of Starchild. "I'll be back for her, but until then, take care of her as if she were your own." The boy looked at her bashfully, turning a toe in the dirt, he promised that he would.

Annie believed him.

The *Monarch*, a brown and regal machine, was like the shaft of a spear ready to pierce the night. Annie went to her car, entered her room, and watched the engine's steam flow past her window like spectral memories.

The engine churned, and they began to roll. She locked the door. And then, surprising herself once again, Annie cried silent tears as the tremendous blue face of the Rocky Mountains fell into the landscape like a setting sun. Three days in Colorado without even a chance to strike at her mother's killer. That was it. Now they were moving on, all her hopes of vengeance placed aside for the sake of a boy…no, she corrected herself—for a young man. Carson was not the shy boy who had come to Yellow Hill. She wondered what had happened to him during the time between. How had he changed? Would he still remember her? She certainly remembered him.

Her own struggles had changed her and done so right quick. She was the last living member of the Miller family, in the same way that Carson was the last of his own line.

A knock came at the door.

Annie brushed the tears from her face and cinched her hat down onto her head.

It was Sarah Lockhart. "We're gonna take a late dinner," she said, and then smiled. "Or a very early breakfast, depending on how you see it. We'd be glad for you to take the meal with us. Unless you're tired…?"

"No," said Annie. "I'd love some company. It doesn't feel good to be by myself, you know?"

"I know exactly what you mean, friend."

They walked together to the diner car, where they found Erikson and Cornish sitting next to each other. The big gunfighter was leaning close to his man, and he glowed with the kind of happiness that comes only from a reunion long overdue.

They sat together and ate a big meal, and Annie smoked her father's pipe. Sarah had a few beers, and Cornish and Erikson enjoyed cigars and something called cognac. Annie tried it but didn't care for it, and Erikson got a big laugh out of that. They talked about each other's lives. Not about the war, and not about Sigurd or the Red Kingdom; they just enjoyed the warmth of one another.

It was Cornish who finally broached the subject of Carson's rescue. "Chicago is dangerous," he said. "Many, many agents under Promethean command."

"Do we know where they're holding him?" asked Annie.

"I checked with the wire in Denver," said Erikson. "No update," He swirled the bulbous glass, and the dark liquid inside became a tiny whirlpool. "Chicago is a big place, but I figure we'll find them quick enough once we meet with our agent. What we do know is that they took him to a church. We'll start our investigation there."

"And when we find them?" Annie asked.

"We kill every last one of them." Sarah's words were blunt, unashamed.

"Hasty," said Cornish. "Cannot be reasoned with, true."

"Judge Ellison spent a long time thinking about this question," said Erikson. "From the way he would tell it, there were many opportunities to simply kill members of the Society, but he always pointed back to himself to express that every person can change,"

"Hellfire they can," said Sarah, her tone sharpening. "These people are insane. They won't stand to listen to reason, and you know it, Sven."

"Perhaps."

"If we just go in shooting, how do we know they won't just kill Carson?" asked Annie.

Sven nodded and took his cigar from his lips. "She's got a point."

"We have one chance at this," said Sarah. "One opportunity to catch them in surprise. If we fail and they scatter to the wind, there is no telling how long it might be before we get another chance. If ever."

"Carson is priority," said Cornish.

"On that we agree, Larry," Sarah said, "but—"

"No."

A Red Winter in the West

"Don't cut me off." Sarah knifed her eyes over at him. "The Society is a snake in the cradle of the world. You don't charm the viper; you cut its goddamn head off."

"Variables exist," said Cornish. He looked at Sven.

"The Society is not only comprised of adults," said Erickson. "There are children among them. If we go in and turn it into a battlefield, those who've never known a chance at a better way will be caught in the crossfire."

"Maybe," said Sarah.

"No maybe, Sarah. They will be. The Society's agents have families, this we know." Erikson let out a sigh. "I believe that's why the Judge chose to wield his own people like a skinning knife, not a hatchet."

Sarah slapped her palm on the table, rattling the silverware and glasses. "Look where that got him. He's dead, Sven. So is the Professor and this girl's friend and her mother. The leader of the Peregrine Estate is dead in the ground because he was slow to act with the kind of finality these animals deserve."

Annie watched the anger boiling off Sarah—a pure rage that frightened her. "They aren't animals," she said.

Her companions looked at her, Sarah looking almost shocked at the statement.

"Ain't that an interesting comment coming from the girl who not three days ago was ready to kill the citizens of the Red Kingdom." It was the first unkind words that Sarah had spoken to Annie.

"That's different," Annie shot back.

"Yeah? What makes them so different? Is it that they drink blood or can do things no human can do? Would it make it different in your mind if they ate people instead?"

The question cut Annie to the quick, but Sarah gave her no chance to respond.

"No, it's not one damn bit different. They're monstrous for what they do. How they treat people. It ain't claws and inhuman appearance that makes a monster, Annie. It's intent. It's the desire to dominate those who they see as inferior. A monster is not a monster because of what it looks like; a monster is a monster because of what it does."

"But the children of monsters need not become monsters themselves," Erikson said as he placed his big hand gently on the table as if to steady himself and his words. The thick fingers of that hand trembled, so did his voice. "Carson himself is proof of that truth."

"A hard truth," said Larry.

Sarah took a deep breath, calming herself. "I don't want to go in and just go shooting kids. Obviously. I'm not insane. The only point I'm making is that we have the opportunity to take these people by surprise. Because make no mistake, they won't be giving us a chance to try and sway their life philosophy."

The group talked and planned long into the waking hours, until sunrise became late morning. Then, as the *Monarch* thundered down the cold track toward Chicago, they pushed off to rest.

Annie slept a dreamless sleep. It was a welcome reprieve from her waking mind, which was always on the ghosts of her mother, Judge Ellison, and Orrin.

What Sarah said about the Red Kingdom made her think long and hard about the people of that vampiric race. They were human once. How much of that humanity remained? How many of them had chosen that life for themselves? They couldn't all be like Sigurd, could they?

What *was* a vampire?

Did they retain their souls after transformation? If not, then what made them animate?

A Red Winter in the West

Her mother had often spoken to her about God's love for all living creatures. Did God love vampires? If He did, that meant it would be murder to kill one.

She smoked her father's pipe, watching the black landscape of the Illinois hills drift past, asking herself questions she never dreamed would be hers to ask.

Sigurd would die, that much she knew. If it was a sin to kill him in revenge, then Annie would take that up with God on the Day of Judgment. Such a creature could not be allowed to exist. The rest of the Red Kingdom? Well, she'd deal with that when the time came. For now, there was only Chicago and, she hoped, the rescue of Carson Ptolemy.

Chapter Twenty-Eight

THE BLACK MANUSCRIPT

CARSON STOOD IN the light of the god's eye. There, in a language made up of suffering, he learned many old things. Time became nothing in that place. There was only the voice and the inescapable sight of that colossal orb. He saw many visions of what would come when the stars aligned, all of them culminated in a singular idea.

Eternal living destruction.

The bloody subjugation of every man, woman, and child that stepped upon the Earth.

The rape of human hope.

Slowly, so very slowly, over what felt a lifetime to him, Carson eclipsed the corona of the eye. In that passing, Carson left a piece of himself in that place; a part of him was ripped away, stolen by the mere contact with such a dark marvel.

He came to his senses sometime later, and when he did, he found himself looking at that terrible language. The language his father had taught him when he was too young. The Black Manuscript had swallowed him whole, and now, standing in the library of the High Priest, Carson read its pages.

He understood.

Among the tattered pages, Carson found the ritual his father had enacted to try and end his only son's life. In that moment, inside the beating heart of that revelation, Carson forgave his father, and he charged himself to finish that good work Ezra Watts started so many years ago.

"You have seen," said the High Priest, his voice soft and warm. "You see now, as so few of us have been privileged to see. You've seen what only the sacrifice can see in the moment before execution. The beauty that can only be found in the anticipation before the cut."

"Yes," said Carson. "I saw."

"And you now believe."

"I do."

"The time is soon upon us, Carson. Soon, we shall make our way to that holy place and give the world its just penalty for ever believing that such a grand thing ever belonged to us. That was our unpardonable sin—our unwarranted vanity."

"When?" Carson said this word slowly, carefully. It was essential to his plans that he appeared to convert to their thinking, all while planning their annihilation. And his own.

"The tenth of October. Which leaves us little time for our preparations."

Carson turned to face the half-ruined man. The High Priest stood before Carson, hunched at the shoulders. He wore his frailty proudly, but Carson now knew better. In the gloomy prison of his room, Carson had felt the power of the man's touch and the darkness inside him. That self-same darkness was in Carson now, he knew. Whatever part of him the god's eye stole had left a gaping void. There would be no escape from it. Not now, not ever. It was inside the Carson, and what it took, it would never give back.

"Preparations?" Carson asked.

The High Priest waved the question away. "You are young," he said, as he turned to exit. "It gives you a stamina for questions I am no longer afforded. Go, now. Rest. For tomorrow we will begin the long, hard work of purification."

Carson did as he was instructed. It was true: he was tired. More than fatigue gripped him though. The shadow of death was on him. No, it was inside him.

Down dark steps, through long stone hallways, he found Walther Rose waiting outside his door. Walther pinched his cigarette between his fingers and took a long drag. The ember of the cylinder burned red hot. He blew out the smoke, his eyes closing in deep satisfaction.

"Doctor Van Horn wants a word," he said.

"In the morning," answered Carson. "I'm tired."

Walther stepped in front of the door before Carson could enter. "Now."

Carson wiggled his fingers, searching for strength there. It was returning to him, but not enough to challenge the man before him. "Well, since you asked so nicely."

Walther dropped his cigarette on the ground, stamped it out. "This way."

He guided Carson further down the hall to another set of steps. This staircase spun around and around, climbing higher and higher, until it terminated at an open room filled with all manner of machinery.

They found the doctor standing near a long table. On the table was the naked body of a young woman, her blue-gray flesh split open at the breastbone. Upon hearing their footsteps, Van Horn turned to face them. She held a small saw in her bloody hands.

Her smile of excitement greeted them. "Carson. Excellent."

"Want me to stay?" asked Walther.

"I don't think that's necessary. Carson?"

"You saved my life," he said as he approached. "You have nothing to fear from me."

"See, Walther? You really must learn to see the goodness in people; even animals such as we know kindness."

The big man scoffed. Then, shaking his head, he left and headed back down the stairwell.

"Come, take a look see," said Van Horn

Carson stepped closer to her.

The woman's flesh had been shaved clean all over. From pubis to scalp, she was as smooth as a river stone. A long red line opened into a widened gap between her breasts.

It was the first woman Carson had ever seen naked.

Van Horn turned the saw, placing the teeth of the blade against her raw breastbone. A soft, grinding crunch filled the room as she pulled the saw back and forth. "I was thinking," she said, mindlessly sawing, "about our conversation from the other day. The one about books. Verne and Shelley." She grunted, plunging the saw deep into the woman's chest. "When we were at the church, while you were speaking with the High Priest, I thought to myself how strange this must all be to you, how much conflict must be inside of you."

She pulled and pushed, the woman's body bumping up and down as the blade bit into bone. "This part is always the dregs. Almost there. Anyway, I was thinking of just how wonderful a story this will make when it is all over. Maybe, just maybe," she said, turning to Carson, "I'll be the one to write the history of what's soon to come." She ran her sleeve across her brow, which was damp from exertion. "I've always fancied myself something of a hobbyist writer, just dabbling, you know?" She shrugged playfully, then went back to the saw. "And I thought to myself how lucky you are to be at the center of all of it." The last bit of the sternum gave way. The woman's rib cage split violently, revealing the glistening heart beneath.

"What are you doing to her?"

Van Horn looked at him, confused. "Her?" Then she rolled her eyes, understanding. "Oh, this? When you said 'her,' I was confused. But it makes sense that you'd still identify this as a person. This vessel is empty. Whatever once made it a 'her' has long since gone to… well, wherever the hims and hers go at the end."

"Who was she?"

"What an interesting question. I have no clue. But, to our purpose, the pile of what was once a beautiful woman has a place in our story, too. Would you hand me that scalpel, please? No, not that one—just to the left. Ah, yes. Thank you."

Carson watched the doctor. Her hands, meticulous, made three cuts. A singular scooping motion of her left hand produced the woman's heart.

"A portion at least has an important role. I have spent many years trying to decipher the alchemy of the manuscript, but alas…" She trailed off as she peered at the heart, pure wonder in her eyes. "There are mysteries that still evade those of us dedicated to its illuminating purpose. Why are the hearts of women needed for the ritual? Why nine?" Her eyes snapped over to Carson. "Why that number? Hmm?"

The answer sprang from Carson's mind. His words exited his mouth before he knew why. "Nine for the Brothers and Sisters exiled from the human perch. Nine for the nine names. Nine gentle hearts to be filled with the blood of the two keys. Two keys, for the nine skyward doors, turned open."

Van Horn's eyes brightened at that recitation. "You *can* read the manuscript."

Carson shook his head, then turned away from the still heart uplifted between them. "You don't read it; it puts itself upon you. Forces you into its secrets."

"Amazing," she said. "You are such a fortunate man to see what so many of us wish to see."

Carson's eyes were heavy, and his head felt like a boulder on his neck. He just wanted to sleep. "Fortunate. That's a strange word for it."

"I have so many questions," she said. "The High Priest shares only selected sections from the manuscript pages. Maybe—" She stopped herself. Her eyes went over to the open doorway where the stairwell yawned at them. She lowered her voice: "Perhaps, when you are rested, we could enjoy a meal and…you could answer some of my deeper inquiries?"

Carson considered her invitation. "On two conditions," he said. "One, I want a bottle of bourbon."

"Easily done!" She was as giddy as a child.

"Two. Among my effects there was a pipe and tobacco…."

"I shall bring them, posthaste. Tonight?"

"Tonight."

Carson left Doctor Van Horn to the rest of her bloody work and descended the stairs. There was no guard on duty at his door. Either they no longer sensed he was at risk of attempting to escape or they knew that any attempt was futile.

He entered his room and, finding it empty, lay on the bed. He stared long and hard into the fire, thinking of the woman splayed out and butchered on Van Horn's operating table. He thought of the eight others he hoped to never see.

The language of the Black Manuscript was imprinted on his mind now, and he searched those internalized pages, forgoing sleep. And it was there that he focused not on the ritual that would unlock the doors of oblivion, but on the one that could end his life. The ritual that would seal the nine names for all time.

Chapter Twenty-Nine

CHICAGO, ILLINOIS

CHICAGO WAS UNLIKE anything Annie had ever seen. Big and bustling, streaming with row after row of white buildings a metropolis. The walkways teemed with the hurried feet of men and women living in an absolute marvel of white stone buildings and stream after stream of black cobblestone streets. The train station ran not one or two lines but seven. Trains blew in and out of Chicago in the way that carriages ran in and out of smaller towns. Chicago had a Texas kind of bigness to it. People had told her Chicago was a huge city, but now that she found herself in it, she was redefining what the idea of a city meant to her.

A word fell out of her mouth.

"What was that, sugar?" asked Sarah as they made their way to the cargo car where their effects were stowed.

"Amazing."

"It is something, ain't it," said Erikson, tipping one of the cargo attendants a silver dollar. "I was here, about two years ago, I reckon. Yes, ma'am, this place is booming."

"Huron Street," said Cornish.

"What's there?" asked Annie.

"Newspaper man."

They gathered their luggage, most of which belonged to Erikson, but also the bags that contained what Annie had taken from the Peregrine Estate, and loaded them onto a carriage.

Annie sat next to the window. As they passed through the city, she looked up at the towering buildings and wondered just what in the world the people inside them were doing. She thought of just how much her brother would have loved this place. The streetlamps in Abilene were nothing compared to the sight of all this stone and machinery, all this civilization.

The others rehashed their plan for Carson's rescue, but Annie deafened her ears to it. She wanted to see Chicago for the glory it had to offer, before she found herself in some dark place filled with gun smoke and blood. It *would* come to that. There was no getting around it. For now though, she just took it all in and let herself have this little calm before the inevitable storm.

The coachman pulled the carriage to a stop just outside a hotel set on the west side of Huron Street. Erikson found them rooms, but there was no time for rest.

They came to a building, five stories tall, set between two greater structures bearing a bronze plaque that read, 'The Chicago Enquirer. Founded—1865.' The four of them went inside.

The interior was elegant in its simplicity, wearing none of the brass trappings or finery the exterior had suggested. The bull pen, a wide grid of wooden desks clouded with smoke, writhed with men. Some were furiously typing, others were yelling, and many were doing both. Opinions flew with curses in their wake. They argued with cigarettes or china cups of coffee in their hands. It was as wild as a stampede but without any wranglers. Every man acted as though his voice was the most important.

A woman's bright green eyes looked up from the reception desk. "Excuse me. Can I help you folks?" She was stern but cordial.

Cornish led them up to the desk. "Looking to sell an article on peregrine falcons."

The woman's measured countenance shifted, her eyes widening. "I see." She peered around his shoulder, spying Annie and the rest of them. She collected herself, and the professional coolness returned. "I am given to understand that they are becoming more and more rare."

"Not so rare as some believe," he replied.

"You'll want to see Ollie. He's downstairs in the distribution pool."

Cornish tipped his hat. "Mary," he said.

"Mr. Cornish," she said knowingly, but then went back to sorting through documents on her desk. Her mouth pulled into a little smile.

They passed by the stable of arguing men, curving around a banister that led downstairs.

Annie walked beside Cornish. "She's an agent?"

"Mary O'Shea. Corresponded with her many times. Been with us a long time."

"A receptionist?"

"Former werewolf-skinner. Dangerous with a knife. Retired."

"I don't remember seeing her name in the ledger."

"Judge Ellison kept many ledgers. Me, too. Oversaw payment and other logistics."

Up from the throat of the stairwell rose a deafening roar of a colossal printing machine. Big and black as coal, the presses spit sheets of paper out onto a conveyor line. The room smelled of musky cedar and some sharp spice she could not place. A band of workers sorted the sheets. Hot and busy, lathered with sweat, they went about their work like machines themselves, moving in perfect syncopation.

"Well, shit fire, is that Larry Cornish I spy?" said a short man, skinny as a toothpick, coming around the towering press. He threw his arms around Cornish and slapped him on the back.

Cornish allowed the embrace but did not return it. "Ollie."

Ollie turned and extended his hand to Erikson. "You, Sven, I expected," said Ollie, "but not a whole passel such as this."

"Oliver," said Sven, shaking his hand happily.

"And who are these two beauties you've got with you?"

"Sarah Lockhart," she said, stepping forward to shake his hand.

He nodded, his big white smile almost sparkling. "Heard of you. I consider it an honor, Ms. Lockhart. And you, miss?"

"Annie Miller."

"*The* Annie Miller, from the telegram."

"The very same."

"It is a pleasure to make your acquaintance. Let's get out of this noise, huh? Y'all come into my office. We've got much to discuss."

Ollie's office was simple, and the closed door didn't do much to deafen the sound of printing and nothing to dull the scent of cedar. They sat down in chairs opposite his desk.

Cornish spoke first. "Carson?"

Ollie shook his head, despair in his eyes. "Haven't seen him since the church."

"And you're sure it was him?" asked Erikson.

"No doubt in my mind. Spitting image of Ezra. The folks with him, I know. Been keeping my eye on them for a while. Walther Rose and Doctor Clara Van Horn. Got lucky seeing that bunch out in the open; they don't often make such trips. Another fella was with them, scars all over his face, walks with a cane. I think he's the ringleader."

"What makes you say that?" asked Annie.

"The deference they showed him," said Ollie, falling into his chair. Light as he was, the wood didn't even creak. "I surveyed the interior of the church after they left, but I didn't find anything that would explain their purpose there."

"Where can we find them now?" Sarah asked eagerly.

"The Society has deep roots here and owns buildings all over town, but where they're keeping Carson, I cannot say."

"Less than helpful," said Cornish.

Ollie's smile twisted a bit at that. "Well, Larry, I'm sorry to be such a disappointment to you. I suppose it's hard for you to understand how figuring the Society's location from a little post in Fort Worth isn't exactly a piece of cake."

"Don't be salty, Oliver," said Erikson, flicking a dismissive hand. "You know what he means,"

Ollie sighed, the tune of unhappy memories in the sound. "Same old Larry. Happy to criticize a job he's taken no part in."

"Fact remains," said Larry, "seeing Carson was a stroke of luck."

"True," said Ollie, leaning back in his chair, putting his boots up on the desk. "But it weren't no stroke of luck that I built a map of the Society's landholdings. Nor was it any sort of providence that I gathered a list of Society members in Chicago. A few of which will be of note to the two of you."

"Why's that?" said Erikson.

"For what they've got pinned to their lapels."

"Guild members?"

"Mmhmm. Twenty-three, nine, and"—he looked directly at Cornish—"number five his own damn self."

"Paul Moody," said Cornish. The name rang cold from his lips.

"The other two are Roger Combs and Jorge Reyes. A bloody pair, to be sure."

"Moody we know. Never heard of those other two," Erikson said, again, dismissive.

"Well, for sure they've heard of you."

"Moody," Cornish said again. "Employed or part of the society?"

Ollie shrugged. "Not sure if he's a convert or a hired gun, but it's him all right. And from what I hear, Walther Rose ain't to be trifled with, either. The stories that follow him are filled with skulls crushed by bare hands, if you are inclined to regard such a things as gospel truth. Seeing as I don't believe much in the way of speculation, I'm of the mind that the man is quite dangerous."

"And who is this Clara Van Horn?" asked Sarah.

"A German doctor and a goddamn lunatic, if you ask me," said Ollie. "What we know about her is that she got kicked out of a university in Europe for performing experiments deemed too extreme to benefit modern medicine, and joined up with the Society soon after. Whatever she's up to, it ain't good."

"Get us a map of the Society's holdings, and we'll hit them one by one," said Sarah, then stood up, as if all through with talking.

Ollie snapped his eyes up at her. "Begging your pardon, Ms. Lockhart, but the hell you will."

She gave him a wilting stare.

Ollie brushed it off. "The Society is slippery like an eel. Time and time again, they've proven that the moment they feel our pressure, they scatter to deep water. The first place you go into will be the last you see of them. They've consolidated in Chicago for a reason. Something's coming. I don't know what, but I do know that we've never seen this large a number of them in one place. I don't intend to lose them all now."

"Damn you for not wanting to lose track of the Society. They have our friend."

"Agree with Sarah," said Cornish flatly.

"How are we supposed to find Carson if you won't tell us the locations you know about?" asked Annie, lowering her voice to try and temper the tension rising between Ollie and the others.

"By trusting me."

Erikson leaned his bulk forward in his chair, placed his big hands on the desk. "We're here, Oliver. You wrote, and we came. That should prove our trust."

"It did initially, but here you come into my city, trying to tell me when and which way things should be done. Judge Ellison knew that beating the Society would mean a singular strike on the head of the snake. He also told me to report any sign of Carson Ptolemy, which I did. The former, and I'm sorry to say this to each of you, is more important than the latter. Destroying the Society once and all is the primary concern. You go blasting Society members to Hell, and we stand to lose the whole thing. I won't gamble now. Not with this."

"You said you saw their carriage," Annie said, again trying to ease the tension. "Why didn't you follow them?"

Ollie let out a sigh, pulled his feet off his desk, and stamped them hard on the ground. "I got too close, Ms. Miller. They saw me. And Walther Rose got a damn good look. I couldn't risk following them, lest I look suspicious."

"Wasn't caution," said Cornish through gritted teeth. "Fear."

Ollie slashed his eyes over to Cornish. "We ain't all gunfighters, Larry. Some of us carry our use in different ways."

"Coward."

"Fuck you, you taciturn poof!"

A blur of motion came from Sven Erikson. His gun was out, pointed directly at Ollie's head.

Ollie's eyes swelled in shock.

"Take care, Oliver." Erikson's voice was calm, deliberate. "Won't have you talk to my husband in such a fashion."

Ollie's fear shifted to anger, his cheeks and forehead turning purple as a beet. "You gonna kill me, Sven? Huh? Gonna gun me down right here in my own damn paper? Then what? Kill your way outta Chicago? This ain't the wilds of Colorado. You go popping that pistol, and the police will have you right sure. Then the Society will get wind, and they'll disappear—along with Carson."

"Take care," Erikson warned again.

Annie had listened to just about all she was going to listen to. "Can everyone just calm the fuck down!"

They all turned to look at her.

"Grab the bull by the horns, right, Larry?" she said.

Larry Cornish nodded. "See that the two are one."

"Right," said Annie, looking back to Ollie and suddenly speaking quickly. "We watch each of the Society's holdings, and we wait until we see the doctor or the ringleader or any one of them we know were with Carson. Hell, they don't know what we look like. And that's when we make our play. It ain't that goddamn hard."

Ollie cocked an eyebrow at her.

Sven holstered his gun.

"I was going to suggest the same thing," said Ollie.

"Well then, why didn't you?"

Ollie's eyes drifted, searching for an answer. "Aw, I just got worked up is all. I think that's a fine plan. One I can agree with."

A Red Winter in the West

"Well, I'm so goddamn glad." Annie shook her head. "I keep seeing it over and over. All of you are supposed to be these talented agents, but none of you can work together worth a shit."

"Annie," Sarah said, trying to calm her.

"It is clear to me now why you all needed the Judge to direct you, because you all have your own vendettas, your own wants, and none of you can just see the thing right in front of you: the goddamn here and now. These people have my friend—*your* friend—and all you can talk about is what you aren't willing to do for the good of the whole."

A long silence hung over the room after her outburst.

"Right," said Cornish.

"Who the hell is this girl," said Ollie, his smile returning.

"The Red Kingdom murdered my family and my best friend," said Annie. "I'm the *girl* who left my desire for revenge behind, for the sake of you all. For this goddamn mission of yours. So stop being petty and start working together."

Sarah chuckled. "Now, who does that remind me of?"

"Hezekiah," said Cornish.

"Mmhmm."

"Well," said Ollie, standing up, "you certainly know how to command a room, Ms. Miller. I'll station my criers at the Society locations I know of. Sales will suffer, but we're making money hand over fist here anyway. I'll let you know if we spot any of those who hold Carson captive."

"And," said Sarah, glancing at Annie, "you'll give us a map of those locations, knowing that we won't move unless we're absolutely certain we're aiming for the head of the snake."

"That's fair," said Ollie. He then looked back over at Cornish. "My apologies for any offense I gave, Larry."

"Accepted."

"I'll set my people in their places and get that map for you," said Ollie, his convivial tone suddenly returning. "Also, let me make up my offense. What's say tonight you all join me at the Continental. Best food in town."

Erikson placed a hand on Annie's shoulder. "I think a little dinner fellowship will go a long way. Don't you?"

Chapter Thirty

THE SOCIETY
OF PROMETHEUS
CHICAGO, ILLINOIS

CARSON WAS SITTING at the small table next to the fire when a gentle knock came from the open doorway. Doctor Van Horn stood there, one half draped in shadow, the other lighted by the hanging lamps. She wrapped one white gloved hand around the door frame, her countenance almost bashful.

"May I come in?"

Carson, thrown off guard, said, "Of course."

She came through his door with hands clasped together over her belly, eyes cast downward at her feet. She was dressed in a golden evening gown, with her hair braided into a swirling knot to crown her head. Her glasses hung from a silver chain and rested in the V of the dress between her breasts, like a broach.

She looked up at him, her eyes wide and glassy. He'd never noticed how big and bright they were until that moment.

"I've had our meal prepared in the dining hall. I've ensured that we will not be interrupted. Would you join me?"

Carson stood up, and then just looked at her for a moment. "You…your dress is lovely."

She ran her hands over the ruffles of her skirt. "It's a lot, I know. But tonight felt…"—she looked away, then back to him—"special. We're so close to an unparalleled accomplishment." She smiled. "All because of you. I hope it's all right."

"Of course."

It was a strange feeling, such a contrast to his feelings in her laboratory. This woman, who was working to crush the world, looked beautiful. Gentle. A serenity played about her, and this, without question, disarmed him.

"I don't have any clothes to match…"

She blinked slowly, her eyes like widening pools. "I don't mind. I'm just glad to have your company, and for the chance to inquire about…" She turned back to look at the empty doorway. "To converse about what we talked about earlier. Can we?"

Carson went to her. They were almost of equal height, but somehow she found a way to look up at him. There was something there, between them. He didn't know what it was. Certainly not admiration or friendship, but something. It was in the way she looked at him. Longingly? Eagerly? It was elusive, alluring.

"Lead the way," he said.

She turned to face the door, sliding one of those gloved hands through the crook of his elbow, and led him out of the room and down the empty hall.

"Where is everyone?" he asked.

"The High Priest has called a special meeting in preparation for the ritual. I chose to give that time to you and our conversation."

A Red Winter in the West

Was he supposed to say thank you?

"Doctor Van Horn—"

"Please, call me Clara."

"Clara, I never did thank you for your help with my injuries. So, thank you. Without you, I certainly would have died." *And lost my chance to end all this madness,* he said in his mind.

"It was nothing. Really."

"It isn't nothing to me."

Again, her eyes fell to her feet, and she grinned. "Well, not to be too self-aggrandizing, but there are maybe two or three doctors who could have successfully done that surgery. We are both lucky that I am one of them. The procedure is a precarious one, and it speaks to your heartiness that you survived. Medicine can only do so much, and I believe there was a divine hand bringing about your recovery."

They entered a small dining room offset from the hallway. The table was small, lit by a pair of candelabra. A fireplace cast the rest of the room in a soft golden light that shimmered upon her dress like sunlight over a stream. Two silver domes sat next to each other on the table. Next to them, set on a silver runner, was a decanter and a pair of ornate whiskey glasses.

"This is very formal. I wasn't expecting anything like this."

Clara slipped her hand out of his arm, circled the table, and lifted the stopper from the decanter. "I think your recent suffering warrants a little luxury. I've seen many conversions to our philosophy, Carson. None of them so difficult as yours. It is one thing to read of Saul's conversion on the road to Damascus, but it is another thing entirely to see it unfold in waking life—to witness the blinding that leads to transformation." She poured the bourbon into one glass and then the other. Offering one to him, she said, "Reformation demands celebration."

Carson joined her at the table and took the glass from her hand.

Their fingers touched, briefly. "Is that how you see me now, Clara? A reformed enemy bent to the Society's leanings?"

She lifted her own glass. "I knew what would happen when the High Priest took you before the manuscript. We all did, except for Walther, of course. But he is slow to trust, even slower to understand."

"Understand what exactly?"

She clinked her glass against Carson's. "That when a person is confronted with the truth, they cannot help but be changed."

"I'll drink to change," he said.

The heat of the liquor warmed him, trailed down his throat and made a hearth of his stomach. He let out a long, satisfied sigh.

"It is good, isn't it?"

"Good is good," he said. "This is something else."

She laughed a girlish laugh. "Please, sit. You must be ready for a real meal. How are those dentures fitting?"

They sat in unison.

"Fine as they can be, I guess. My thanks again."

"Certainly," she said. She plucked the domes from the platters, unveiling a huge well-cooked steak next to a white slice of onion and steaming potatoes.

"I hope you like it. I chose the meal myself."

While the steak was a little sweeter than Carson expected, it went down quickly, along with the vegetables. He drank another glass of whiskey, savoring it.

"Where do you go," asked Clara, barely touching her own food, "when the manuscript takes you? I admit that I have seen the pages myself, but, as the High Priest says, only a conduit can see them fully. I know much of what it says, but only through second-hand recitations."

Carson leaned back in his chair, feeling bloated—almost sick. "Difficult to say. The pages disappeared. They drew me into another

A Red Winter in the West

place, a place outside my own mind. It was a fall into complete darkness. Every moment was—"

"Yes?" she asked breathlessly.

"Agony."

"Fascinating." A sigh escaped her. "Only through pain can we know wisdom."

"It was more than that, more than pain. It was a descent into destruction. I fell, and every moment I grew more and more fearful of what was pulling me down. And after a long, harrowing time, I saw something…something too big for words to describe."

"Oh," she said, placing a hand on his leg. Her fingers dug into the meat of his thigh. "Oh, but you must try."

Carson looked down at her hand, then back to her eyes.

She withdrew her hand, ashamed. "I'm sorry. Please, please go on."

"I saw one of them, but it was not like the one I saw in Yellow Hill."

"Alitranz…."

"This one was greater, and not just in size. It was in the thing's potency, in its…I don't know, its sheer visible weight. I realized that I was looking at a tremendous sheet of skin. I have ridden across the sweeping plains of Texas, Clara. On those plains, you can see out forever, so far that you think you might have spied the place where the earth and the sky meet. And what I saw, illuminated in the terminal darkness, was the lid of an eye that dwarfed everything."

Her eyes, wide and wet, sparkled against the light of the candelabra. "I have, for a very long time, wanted to see that place. To see a true god."

"I would be happy to have never seen what I saw."

Her wonder wrinkled into disappointment. "How can you say that? You saw something…divine. More than that…" She shook her head, searching for her next words. "You saw something true.

More true than our flesh and our minds. You saw the greatest of the Nine—"

"What I saw," he said, cutting her off, though not unkindly, "was a terror greater than anything any human should ever know. But," he said, now searching for his own words, carefully, "you are correct. It was true. More real than anything I have ever seen. God is the only word that comes close to describing it."

"And so, with that, you believe. You see now the facade of this mortal coil. We are meat with delusions of grandeur. Animals, all of us, wearing crowns we were never born for."

"I have seen, and I now know the way, yes."

A look of realization passed over Clara; she'd remembered something. "Ah, your pipe and tobacco!" She rose, went to the hearth, and from a small pouch she produced the pipe that had once been Gilbert's.

"A promise is a promise," she said, returning.

He took the tobacco and pipe from her, knowing immediately that with the damage to his hands, he would not be able to fill it.

"Would you mind?" he said, licking his lips at the vanilla smell wafting up from the pouch.

"Not at all," she said. She carefully loaded the pipe and handed it to him. Then, striking a match, she leaned close and helped him to light it.

The first pull was absolute bliss.

"It's rare to see a person savor something so deeply," she said. "I'm jealous."

He took another pull, this time letting the smoke dive deep into his lungs. "The little things are what make life so sweet. My father used to say that."

"Hard to imagine Ezra saying such a thing. No offense, I mean."

A Red Winter in the West

"None taken. It was my other father, Gilbert Ptolemy, who said it, anyhow."

"I would never suspect any man raised by two men to be so reflective."

Carson smiled for the first time in a very long time. "They were both remarkable, in their own ways."

"I can see how that's rubbed off on you. You're not like any man I've ever met. I am truly sorry for what the Baroness did to you, Carson. She's always been a cruel woman."

"I killed her friends. Not sure I could expect anything—" Carson was interrupted by a belch. The souring of his stomach was growing worse. Probably from the tobacco. He set the pipe down on the table, left it there with smoke drifting from the bowl.

"Excuse me," he said. "That was a rich meal, and the smoke must not be sitting well with me."

Her eyes darted away from his.

"Carson," she said, her voice low. "I want you to know that I'm sorry for all of this. For what we've done to you."

Carson narrowed his eyes. He'd seen that look before, knew it well. The look of oncoming confession.

"There are things we do for the sake of the world we hope to build. Everyone is guilty of that, I think, myself included. I…I—"

"Clara?"

"I see the purification is going well," the voice of the High Priest came from the open door. He stood there, leaning on his cane. That infuriating, satisfied smile on his face.

"Purification?"

"Oh, you'll forgive Doctor Van Horn, I'm sure. She was acting in my strictest confidence. But the deed is done. Done unknowingly, but done nevertheless, and that is truly what is important, my boy."

Carson shook his head. His stomach was in a knot, but he felt strong enough to rise. But when he did, his knees buckled.

Had they poisoned him?

No, they need him for the…the ritual.

"I'm sorry, Carson," said Clara. "But the ritual has certain alchemical demands. One of which is…dietary."

"What…what did you have me eat?"

"I'm sure you can guess, my boy. Walther himself told me that you visited the good doctor while she butchered the meat."

Carson began to sweat, and his hands trembled. The realization was too much.

"Oh, Doctor Van Horn told me you inquired about the girl's name. It was Diana Murray. You'll be glad to know that her father was compensated well. I hope she tasted delicious."

Chapter Thirty-One

OUTSIDE THE AESCHYLUS CLUB CHICAGO, ILLINOIS

────────

THE MARBLE EXTERIOR of the Aeschylus Club in the northern section of Chicago sparkled pink in the early October sunlight. White men in black suits, with unread newspapers stuffed under their arms, stepped through the massive mahogany doors. Doors were pulled open by Black men in white suits, their eyes thrown anywhere but into the eyes of the White men. The professional smiles of the Black men were lies. At least, that's what Sarah Lockhart said.

She and Annie were sitting at a little cafe opposite the club, sipping coffee. They watched the doors swing open out of the corner of their eyes. Long, frustrating days had passed since their arrival in Chicago. There had been no word from Ollie's newspaper men. No sign of Carson, the doctor, or Walther Rose. Annie tried to wrangle her fear, the gnawing dread that they were too late.

Cornish had tried to dismiss that fear over dinner at the Continental that first night.

"The Society's action, if successful, will be clear," he'd said.

Ollie had chimed in gloomily while swirling red wine in his glass. "Larry has the right of it. If the persistent rumors of Yellow Hill are true, and I believe they are, the Society's success will bring about a change that we would notice. Immediately."

"It stands to reason," said Sarah, "that Carson is alive. The Society members are aristocrats, the spiritually impoverished rich who could not stand to kill an enemy when they had a chance. They are grandstanders. A circus of occult elites. Carson is alive, I think, because they'll want him to see, with his final sight, that he failed. There is no more complete victory over an enemy than that."

Annie thought about those words for a long time as, each day, she went from place to place with Sarah or Erikson, spying on businesses and homes, clubs and rail yards. For days, there was nothing but eating and talking and waiting. And yet they saw nothing of note.

Annie could feel the anxiety growing within the group, especially from Ollie who, on more than one occasion, apologized to each of them for the failure of his own network to discover Carson's location.

"Look at these pampered shits," Sarah said, venting her frustration as they sat outside the Aeschylus Club.

The statement hit Annie so hard and so unexpectedly, she choked on her coffee. Coughing and rattling her cup onto its saucer, she managed, "W-what on earth?"

"Every one of them pretending that their wealth elevates them higher than the men opening the door. Can you imagine it?"

"Well, I can't say I imagined that or this sudden turn of conv—"

A Red Winter in the West

Sarah was a bull seeing red. "Imagine being a person so in love with the myth of birthright exceptionalism. We're all grown in the same darkness. None of those men walking into that building see that equality—the only true equality."

Annie scooted closer, drawn in. "Which is?"

Sarah, as if offended by the question, set her wide, angry gaze on Annie. "We are all born afraid. We all come out naked, screaming and afraid when light first abuses us. When we feel the pain of cold's first blow, before we are alighted into the warmth of our mother's arms. We all come from that place. That savage experience. Unable to understand the vastness of the world much less the universe we're born into," Sarah leaned in closer, her voice softening without losing any of its edge. "Each person is just a tiny thing, screaming to understand why the unfathomable event of birth befell us. It is why all of us are forever asking the question: Why was I born? And when that question goes unanswered by philosophy or religion, we move on to a more selfish question: What was I born for? We spend the rest of our mortality on a journey that we hope will answer the purpose of the former and fulfill the yearning of the latter."

Sarah shook her head, angry. "It will never make any sense to me."

"And still, despite their error," said Annie, "you are working to save their lives."

Sarah pulled back, her eyes growing glassy. "No. I am working to save the lives of the people they oppress. Not because the exceptionalists are worth saving but because the world is worth fighting for. The child born in the fever shack on some goddamn plantation deserves a chance to rise up, claim the life they are deserving of. Larry's always talking about the work of the Peregrine Estate, saying it's the only game worth playing. Well, I'm not in this game for the white club member; I'm in it for the doorman. I'm in the game because I think, eventually, those of us who believe in true equality will win out."

The woman's wet eyes flicked over Annie's shoulder and widened. "Oh, shit."

Annie went to look.

"Stop," said Sarah. "Wait, don't turn around."

Annie remained facing her. "What do you see?"

Sarah relaxed, her cool smile stretching across her face. "That's Paul Moody, and I'm guessing the two folks with him are Combs and Reyes."

"Do we go after them?"

Sarah snorted a laugh. "Honey, I'm good with a gun, and I'm sure you're pretty good, too, but those men are of a different breed of gunfighter. Even if—and it's the biggest fucking unlikely if—we were able to take them down, we'd be striking at the effect only to leave the cause unharmed. They're headed inside the club."

Annie nodded, an idea coming to her. She looked over at the boy standing nearby on the street corner. One of Ollie's boys. "Excuse me, paperboy," she said calmly, like any person looking to buy the afternoon edition.

The boy, built like a sewing thimble, looked up at her under a mop of curly brown hair. He rushed across the street toward them, deftly moving through traffic.

"Yes, ma'am," he said, his voice bright, tenor high.

"Be a doll, would you, and go tell Mr. Oliver that Ms. Miller and Ms. Lockhart said they've spotted three of Mr. Cornish's friends going into the Aeschylus Club. The faster you get there and back, the bigger the reward."

The boy nodded, confident. "I hope you've got a heavy coin purse, ma'am."

Annie smiled. "And why's that?"

A Red Winter in the West

"'Cause," he said, dropping the newspapers at Annie's feet, "I'm the fastest boy in Chicago."

"Well," said Annie, leaning close to him, "I've got enough money to pay for the fastest boy in the world. "

"Don't blink," he said, a grin of pure charm lifting his cheeks. And with that he exploded away from the table and disappeared at a full sprint.

"Nice," said Sarah.

"So," said Annie, "now we wait for them to come out and follow them."

"That's the plan."

"What are they doing inside a place like that?"

"Probably pulling each other's peckers."

"You do not like men, do you."

"I like men just fine. I just know them and judge them fairly."

The word 'judge' flashed the image of Judge Ellison's final moments. His head twisted around in Sigurd's grip. The moment appeared so clear in her mind that the taste of blood filled her mouth. She swallowed hard, closed her eyes.

"Hey," said Sarah. "Where'd you go?"

Annie, gritting her teeth, shoved the bitter memory and cold terror down into the secret place where she kept all the things that made her feel weak—incapable. And when she spoke, the truth of how she felt came rushing out. "I'm scared of what happens next."

"I am too, Annie, but you have to swallow that fear. Breathe. And if a ruckus breaks out today, stick close to me. Pull your pistol and don't stop shooting until we've succeeded."

At the chiming of the church bells, the newspaper boy came back. His hair was matted with sweat. "Mis—mister Olive— Mister Oliver, s-s-huh…"

"Slow down there, Mercury," said Sarah. "Catch your breath."

The boy took a few deep breaths, but before he could speak, Ollie came riding around the corner on a lathered gelding.

Annie handed her entire coin purse to the boy. Nine dollars in coin. "Fastest boy in Chicago? You sell your services too cheap." The purse fell into the boy's hands with a rattle. "Now, I need you to go somewhere else. Things might get dangerous."

The boy looked at the coin purse, his eyes wide.

"What's your name, kiddo?"

"Charlie," the boy said.

"I've met a Charlie before," she said. "They call that a coincidence. You got a last name, or should I just call you Second Charlie? Or maybe, Chicago Charlie."

"Comiskey," said the boy.

"Well, Charlie Comiskey, I'm Annie Miller, and I hope this won't be the last time we meet. Now, scoot."

"Take my horse, Charlie," said Ollie. "Seeing as you beat him here, you might as well take him back to the paper."

"*Your* horse, Mr. Oliver?"

"Hurry now."

The boy climbed onto the horse and trotted away.

"All three of them?" asked Ollie.

"Correct. Where're Larry and Sven?" asked Sarah.

"Not a good idea to have them here for this. Those three would spot fellow guild members in a heartbeat, and we can't be having a shootout out here in the street. It would spoil our chances."

"Good point," said Sarah.

"We'll follow them, one at a time, each of us moving in a rotation, so that none of us look too familiar along the way. I'll take the lead."

A Red Winter in the West

It was another hour before the three gunfighters emerged from the club, each of them freshly shaven. One of them, the Mexican Reyes, had his hair freshly pomaded.

"Give them a second," said Ollie. "I'll go first, then Annie, then Sarah. We'll rotate every three blocks or so. Keep your distance." Ollie picked up one of the newspapers that Charlie had dropped, opened it, then began to walk across the street, pretending to be a man without a care in the world.

They followed the three men for a time, stopping to wait as they visited several businesses, including a painfully long visit at a brothel. But eventually they came out, each of them looking flush with the relaxed redness of what Annie assumed was exertion and whiskey. Eventually, they made their way back east, where they entered a large building that bore a bronzed sign reading, 'The Academy for the Advancement of Human Endeavors.' Standing at the front door, guiding the men in, was a man so big that he dwarfed all three of the gunfighters. He carried his weight well, and he went inside with the three of them like a man expected.

Annie and the two Peregrine agents found a grocer to meet on an adjacent street.

"That big, bald son of a bitch," Ollie said. "That's Walther Rose."

"I didn't see any of your newspaper fellows out there," said Sarah.

"You wouldn't. Never seen that place before. But, seeing it now, it makes all the sense in the world as their base. Big, old building, east side of town close to Lake Michigan. The pier would give them access to a quick escape should they need to make a getaway. And if we'd hemmed them off there, there's still the rail line not five minutes ride from here. Let's go gather our people. It's time to bring about the end of the Society of Prometheus."

"You make it sound easy," said Annie.

"It's simple enough, Annie, but it sure as hell won't be easy."

Chapter Thirty-Two

THE ACADEMY FOR
THE ADVANCEMENT
OF HUMAN ENDEAVORS
CHICAGO, ILLINOIS

THE EATING OF human flesh was only the beginning of Carson's purification process. That night, after the meal, many strong men came to collect him. They pulled Carson into a torchlit chamber where, as they beat him and stripped him naked, the cold floor and stone walls rang with his protest. Though he tried to pull away, tried to fight them with all his strength, there were too many. They picked him up and carried him over to a large brass tub.

Just before they pitched him in, Carson saw the shimmer of what looked like grease and boiled white bones floating on the surface. He splashed down into the cold, oily fluid.

Carson thrashed, striking at them with his hands and trying to heave himself out of the tub, but they held him down and scrubbed him forehead to toe with sharp thorny branches that scraped his skin raw.

The taste of the human broth filled his mouth, and he vomited. Still they persisted in washing him in what he knew was the boiled fat and bones of nine women.

Finally, they took their hands off him and let him crawl out of the tub.

He lay on the cold stone floor, slathered in grease, gagging and cursing each of them. When he looked up, he recognized the Baroness's men, Combs and Reyes. The men who had beaten him on the train. The men who had stolen his father's gun from him, and who had taken joy in ripping his teeth out of his mouth. Combs was still wearing Carson's pistol. He appeared amused, chuckling to himself.

The High Priest loomed over Carson. "I can understand why this process offends your sensibilities, my boy, but you must trust me that it is necessary. I knew simply asking you would be of no use. You see, I know a lie when I see it. And the lie of your supposed conversion was easy to discern. Nevertheless," he said, hobbling over to the towering Walther Rose, "I am happy that the truth is now all that remains between us."

Carson, dripping in human fat, having nothing to say, erupted in ungovernable rage. He screamed unintelligibly at the High Priest and his followers, pushed himself to his feet, and rushed the son of a bitch.

Walther, showing his unnatural speed, stepped between them and hit Carson so hard that the world tilted and flashed.

While he was on the ground, the man's huge fingers pried Carson's mouth open and jerked his dentures out of his mouth. "Heel," said Walther.

"Now," said the priest, "if you're quite finished? What comes next will be unpleasant for you, and, honestly, for myself. But great

A Red Winter in the West

change requires great sacrifice, and so we will bear the load together, for the sake of all humanity."

Set before the Black Manuscript, Carson fell into the embrace of the god's eye over and over. He railed against it with his waking mind, but each time, less of him remained. On what was announced to be the advent of the ritual, Carson was placed on a great stone slab in a dim torch-lit antechamber. There, lashed on his stomach, he saw a woman enter. She was smiling, naked, tattooed from throat to navel in the harshly scrawled letters seen only in the manuscript.

She produced a small hammer and a strange knife that bore a blade on one end and a needle on the other. "And now, we shall make a manuscript of you, yes?" she said, as two men brought in a small table and set it down near Carson's head. Upon the table was placed a large, bulbous inkwell.

First, she slowly cut into his flesh, carving long deep lines along his back and thighs. He bled for them. Screamed at them. He kicked and twisted, but his bonds held him in place.

Over the sound of his wailing and cursing and protests and bargaining and cries for help, the woman hummed a tune while she worked. It was a gleeful, happy song Carson quickly grew to hate. Fully exhausted, drawn to the edges of his sanity and resolve, Carson Watts Ptolemy shamefully appealed to her to help him, to let him free. Begged.

She never responded, only working in his flesh like a tailor stitching a suit. Hundreds upon hundreds of painful pinpricks went down his spine, his shoulders.

Hours passed. Perhaps days.

The woman's work done, the men came and took him again. Their rough hands, made slick and bloodied by his excoriated flesh, washed his marred skin with something that burned cold as a winter wind, then like fire. And finally, as they scoured his wounds with the rough branches they'd used when bathing him, he mumbled through drooling lips and whined like a whipped dog.

Again the High Priest came, again he taunted Carson, though the words no longer bore any meaning.

Carson, exhausted from the pain, lifted his head to look at the horrid face of his chief captor. "Please," he said, his voice weak, his anger a broken thing. "Please stop."

The priest, without mortal pity in his eyes, leaned down and with cool, wormy lips, kissed Carson on the forehead.

"No," he said. "For the sake of the world, we endure this. But tonight," he whispered. "Tonight, it ends."

They took Carson to his room, where Combs, Reyes, and Walther guarded him. It was not sleep that found him, but a waking nightmare of the god's eye, its unbearable sight irrepressibly weighing upon him. The eye stared. Carson, unable to look away, stared back, screaming.

The giant's voice sang to him, and the longer it did, the more Carson grew to love that dark song he somehow knew was sung only for him.

He could no longer tell what was him and what was the influence of the Black Manuscript. He was lost inside himself. And though he closed his eyes, trying to recall the face of his fathers, his friends, and those he loved most, all he saw was the eye.

Ever expanding, the god's eye eclipsed him.

Soon it would darken everything Carson had once been and swallow everything he ever hoped to be.

The hour drew near.

They dressed Carson in a gray cloth robe and cut loose all his splints and bandages. A cold breeze touched his hands. Chills raked his spine.

A Red Winter in the West

"Day of judgment is here, dog," said Walther, as he tied a rope around Carson's waist. "Time for you to bleed for all the lives you told yourself were rightfully yours to take."

Carson mumbled a curse at Walther. He wasn't sure what the word was, but he tried to say it harshly.

"What's that, dog?"

Carson had no strength left to speak of. His head swam with hot, throbbing pain. His stomach churned with hunger, and his gums were raw.

"That's what I thought."

They took him out of the room and up the stairs that lead to the front entrance. There, in a large foyer, the High Priest, also garbed in gray, tottered over to Carson and embraced him. Nearby, looking entirely bored with the situation were Combs, Reyes, and another man Carson did not know. Just behind them stood Doctor Clara Van Horn, her golden curls almost silver in the flickering light of the entryway's ensconced lamps. To her left, leaning against a pillar with her arms crossed in deep satisfaction, was the Baroness, Gwendolyn.

"Oh," she said, "how low the proud are threshed."

"Perfect," said the High Priest. "Just perfect. Can you feel the power of chance upon you?"

Carson's eyes were heavy, unable to focus. He did not speak. His curses and protests were useless, carried no weight. *He* carried no weight. No fortitude to call upon, no strength to finish the mission he had promised Gilbert Ptolemy he would bring to fruition.

Carson Ptolemy had failed. The end of his life would not end in some grand triumph, but in the desolation of everything he hoped to save.

And it was his want for revenge that had brought it all, he thought. His great sin—an unyielding wrath that had laid him low as a worm. A worm now clutched in the beak of a titan bird, soon to be swallowed up.

"Don't worry," said the High Priest, releasing him. "I feel it, too. We are brothers of the same wound, you and I. And now, by our demise, we bring about a final revelation."

With weary hands, Carson tried to shove the High Priest. But his weakness denied him even the ability to move the man.

The priest laughed at him. "Still some fight in that husk, I see. Good. Now…" He patted Carson on the top of his head like a pet. "Let us make an end of all this vanity. All this ignorance. Let us usher forth the Nine."

They led Carson out the door and into the night. They moved along the walkway that terminated at the street, where a carriage was waiting.

With all that was left in him, Carson tried to run.

Walther snatched him by the collar and, with great ease, pulled him into his tremendous bulk. "I told you before, dog," said the man, lifting his hand to deal another blow. "To he—"

Walther's head snapped back, and the left side of his face bloomed open, red with gore. Blood and brains and skull sprayed into the open air. He let out a terrible noise as his eye flopped out of the socket. It dangled about his cheek as the man swayed, then fell. Walther's hand, still clutching Carson's robe, pulled both of them to the ground.

Someone screamed. "Ambush!"

Chapter Thirty-Three

THE BATTLE OF CHICAGO
CHICAGO, ILLINOIS

TWO HOURS BEFORE Annie Miller shot Walther Rose through the head, she was sitting at her bedside table cleaning the gun that would end him. Quietly smoking her pipe, she ran the plan through her mind. They would wait outside the Academy until dark. There, hidden among the oak trees at the building's perimeter, they would wait until 1 a.m., and then commence their assault. She ran the oil rag along the revolver's barrel, the weight of the gun heavy in her hands. The weight of killing heavy on her mind. The fear of losing Carson heavy on her heart.

Cornish had said it plainly. Said it best. "One chance. All things hinge on the now. Let us be our best."

Be our best.

Her mother used to say that. "Be our best for one another, because all we have is each other." Annie saw her mother's face in the shine of the revolver, saw the fanged mouth of Sigurd, and so too did she see the young, shy face of Carson Ptolemy. He was like her:

a survivor of Yellow Hill. She made a promise to him, in the quiet of that lonely space, that if he were still alive, she'd see that he outlived the Society.

Annie filled her father's gun—*her* gun. She spun the chamber, watching the brass fittings roll like a wagon wheel. Smooth as silk. The gun went into her holster, and she picked up the Henry repeater leaning against the wall.

Down the hall, she went to Sarah Lockhart's room and knocked.

"It's open," said Sarah behind the door.

"It's just me." Annie went in.

"Was wondering when you'd come my way." Sarah was tying her hair back with a black ribbon. "You know, I've been meaning to tell you how much I like that brown jacket of yours. I've always liked that cavalry styling, especially with those brass buttons. After all this, I might get me one, too."

Annie ran her fingers over the leather jacket she wore, touching the cool brass lines of buttons as if searching for something. "Oh, thank you."

"I saw one like it before, but it was white. You should consider that color. It'd look great."

"This was a gift. From Judge Ellison."

Sarah smiled that warm, knowing smile of hers, a smile with so many secrets. "Now there was a man who loved jackets. I remember he used to wear this ridiculous red smoking jacket. I gave him shit about it all the time and asked him why he wore it. And he'd say, *It's sophisticated*"—she mimicked the man's kind baritone voice—"*like me.*"

Annie's laughter at the joke was bittersweet. "I know the one you mean. He was wearing it the night that he offered me a chance to be one of his agents."

"Of course he was. Bet he was smoking that pipe of his, too."

A Red Winter in the West

"He was." Annie's eyes fell away from Sarah, remembering.

"Not yet, Annie Miller. Do not go to that place just yet. The time to remember the fallen is coming soon enough. The moment before us is not for mourning, it is for salvation."

"You really think he's still alive?"

"I do, honey. I really do. Carson Ptolemy was raised by a strong man. A man with endurance. Gilbert suffered a great deal during his life, and many of those sufferings were for his son's sake. Carson profited from that example. He's alive, Annie. He's alive, and we're going to take him back. Not because we want revenge, but because he is our friend. He doesn't belong to them. He belongs to us."

Annie looked back to her. "He does."

"I love that look," said Sarah. "You can't see it yourself, but I can tell you, without any aggrandizement, that your look of determination is a terrifying thing. You're meant for something big, Annie Miller. I don't know what it is, but I can't wait to find out."

They went to Cornish and Erikson's room, where the door was cracked open. As they approached, they heard the two men's voices.

"Two years."

"Still think you can shoot, my love?"

"Still can. Still faster than you."

There came the shuffling of feet, steps across the room.

"How glad I am that we'll never have to find out."

"I love you, Sven Erikson."

"I love you, too, Larry Cornish. And that love doesn't end today, not for either of us."

Sarah smiled at Annie.

She smiled back, realizing that they now shared a secret.

Sarah knocked hard enough so that the door swung open.

Cornish and Erikson did not end their embrace.

"It's a grand picture, don't you think, honey?" asked Sarah, not waiting for an answer. "Two of the most dangerous men alive, united against the world—not for money or personal gain but just for the sake of having each other."

Erikson smiled. "There is no love like ours."

It still amazed Annie when Cornish blushed.

"Whatever happens tonight," said Sarah, "I want you all to know, it has been my deepest joy to ride with you."

Cornish nodded. "Honored."

"Me, too," said Annie.

"The time is upon us, dear Peregrine agents. Let's go get our friend back."

Ollie was outside, sitting in the riding position on a carriage. He was dressed as a coachman, a blanket thrown over his knees. "All aboard," he said.

They climbed into the coach. Sarah sipped from a flask while Erikson and Annie smoked. Cornish studied his revolver. None of them spoke.

In the dark of night, the carriage jostled down the almost empty streets of the eastern end of Chicago. The cold wind rolled off Lake Michigan, whipping against the cabin. They deposited the carriage a block away from the Academy and made their way quietly toward the outcropping of sentinel oaks standing just outside the gate.

Annie expected to wait a long time, but they had only been in position for a few minutes when three coaches came riding up to the Academy. Maybe their assault wouldn't have to wait after all. Then, by stroke of luck or providence, the highest-ranking members of the Society of Prometheus emerged from the front door.

And for the first time in over three years, Annie Miller saw Carson Ptolemy.

A Red Winter in the West

Her mouth fell open at the sight of him. Her initial excitement at seeing him alive was quickly cut down by what she saw.

Oh, Carson. What have they done to you?

He did not so much walk as shuffle. Broken. He wore a gray robe belted at the waist. His shoulders were bent, his head shaven, and his cheeks sunken. And there was something about his lips that did not look right.

Anger filled Annie Miller. The same anger she'd felt in the alley when the man had attacked her. The same anger she knew for Sigurd of Antioch. It poured into her—overflowed.

She slid the Henry repeater up to her shoulder, setting it firmly in the cradle of her arm. If they got Carson into the coach, she would have no way of following without being seen. What if they were moving him to another building, or, worse, to another city?

Carson tried to run, but there was no chance. The attempt was desperate, almost pathetic. Walther Rose snatched him by the back of his robe, raised his arm to strike him.

Annie sucked in a big breath. Pulled back the hammer. She would not allow Walther Rose to ever strike Carson again.

The repeater kicked.

The shot landed true.

A woman screamed. "Ambush!"

All hell broke loose in the streets of Chicago.

The three Society gunfighters drew their pistols and immediately began to fire in Annie's direction. Their bullets exploded into the wooden flesh of the tree from where she fired.

Someone called out, "Moody, get him in the coach! Reyes, Combs, cover fire!"

The guns of the Peregrine Estate lit up the night, chipping marble, splintering wood, but finding no scoring hits. Combs and Reyes walked forward in tandem, taking no cover. They fired over and over in such a fashion that Annie could do nothing but keep her back against the oak.

The Peregrine agents all returned fire, their volley relentless. Annie swiveled around the oak tree, aimed at Reyes, fired. The man twisted, winged, but he spun with the momentum, turned and fired. The bullet clipped the trunk of the oak, sending splinters into Annie's face. She winced, rubbing the sleeve of her jacket against her cheek.

One of the coaches exploded forward in an attempt to escape. Annie racked the repeater, her back against the tree. She waited until the coach passed into her line of sight and fired, levering quickly. But in her rush, her shots sailed wide.

Something knocked Annie's rifle from her hands. She pulled her pistol. "They're getting away with Carson!"

"Goddamn you, Roger Combs," Erikson screamed.

"Hell fire," Combs called back. "Is that the voice of Sven Erikson I hear?" The man sounded elated.

"You're goddamn right it is. I'm here to kill you. You, too, Reyes."

"Piss on you, you Dutch son of a bitch."

Annie watched in horror as the horses of the coach carrying Carson turned the corner, out of sight.

"Ollie!" Sarah commanded, "you and Cornish take Annie. Get them! Sven and I have this!"

"The hell you do, bitch," said Reyes, cocking his gun. He fired again.

Sarah cried out, hit.

"Go," Sarah screamed. "Goddamn it, go!"

Annie, seeing Ollie and Cornish run toward their own carriage, fired her revolver, trying to get Combs and Reyes to take cover. Then

A Red Winter in the West

she bolted, staying as close to the trees as she could. Rounding the corner, she saw the coach carrying Carson bend around a street. Again, out of sight.

"I'll bet my life they're headed to that church," cried Ollie as he climbed up into the driver's seat.

Annie took the shotgun position next to him.

Cornish, grabbing the railing, commanded, "Go!"

Ollie whipped the horses, almost tipping the carriage as they turned it to give chase. Annie's hands shook violently as she tried to reload her revolver.

"Hyah, boys," Ollie screamed at the horses. "Run like the dogs of Hell!"

The horses responded, stretching their necks long, thundering to a gallop.

The wound on Annie's face had already swelled to the size of an apple, making it hard to see out of her left eye. She wiped the blood away on her sleeve. Her heart hammered in her chest.

Ollie took a turn so fast that had it not been for him grabbing Annie by the shoulder, she would have fallen onto the rushing street below.

"Stay with me, girl. Hold on. We're almost there"

They peeled around a corner, where a huge church came into view. The Society's coach was parked at the front steps. Ollie had been right.

"Now, be carefu—"

A crack of thunder. A single flash of light. Ollie let go of the reins, reaching for his throat. Blood rushed through his fingertips.

Twice the thunder sounded again, and the two horses rushing forward lost their legs. The carriage wheels hit the bodies of the horses and pitched forward, sending Annie flying out of the seat. She hit the cobblestone street, landing on her shoulder. Something inside her buckled. Another gunshot went off, not from an outside assailant but inside her mind.

She was hurt. Something was broken.

She tried to get up, but the world was spinning. Everything was happening so fast and so slowly all at the same time.

Something small pressed against the top of her skull. She turned her head to see the tips of boots. Her eyes followed those boots all the way up to a slender man with gray eyes.

"You've got sand, I'll give you that." He cocked the hammer of the revolver.

"Paul Moody!"

His eyes snapped wide, and he turned away from Annie.

Painfully, Annie turned to look back.

Cornish emerged from the wreckage of the carriage, his left arm hanging limp at his side. His other hand hovered over the butt of his revolver. "My name is Larry Joseph Cornish," he said, methodically walking toward them. "As six, I challenge five. Approach, in honor, within rules of our association." He brought himself to his full height, his eyes narrowing. "Challenge you, here and now, to a contest of the gun."

"You've no right, Cornish!" There was a cold confidence in Moody's voice. "You fired upon me without honor, a goddamn sneak-thief." Moody pressed his revolver hard into Annie's skull.

"Kill the girl and lose your life, Moody."

Moody laughed. "Renounce your challenge, Cornish. Walk away, and we'll have our business on another day."

"Unacceptable."

Annie searched the ground for her revolver. It was nowhere to be seen.

A Red Winter in the West

"Face me," said Cornish. "For her life, coward."

Moody looked away from Cornish, down to Annie. It was a cold look of pure confidence. "Tell your friend that if she moves to act, she'll get much worse than a bullet to the brain, Cornish."

"Annie," said Cornish. "Trust me."

Annie nodded.

Moody retracted his arm, the warm metal of the revolver lifted from her brow. He then holstered his revolver and took a step away from her, facing Cornish.

"Heard you retired," Moody said.

"I challenge you, here and now, Paul Moody, to a contest of the gun."

Moody nodded, holstering his revolver. "Challenge accepted."

Annie looked to the open door of the church. Was Carson okay? Were they too late? Her eyes went back to the two men.

The contest between them ached with motionless silence.

"Didn't think I'd get the chance, Cornish. Been looking forward to it, because once I kill you, that husband of yours will come running. Then it'll be his turn."

They drew. Both their pistols flashed.

Larry Cornish's head snapped back.

Moody bent at the waist.

Annie screamed.

Moody clutched his belly, staggered. Suddenly, Annie was moving, her hand jerking her boot knife free from its hidden place. Moody turned toward her, the pistol in his hand went off. Annie lifted her knife and brought it down hard into his shoulder.

Moody howled.

Annie, blind with rage, jerked the knife free. Over and over and over, like so many years ago, she stabbed the man's throat and face.

She could hear herself screaming, pumping her arm up and down, killing Paul Moody one bloody stroke at a time.

When she stopped, there was nothing recognizable left to call a human face. Only a pair of flat, gray eyes looking back at her from a ruin.

She clambered off the man and ran to Cornish.

His green eyes, eyes that had gazed with such tenderness upon Sven Erickson upon the snowy street in Black Wells, stared blankly at her. There was a single dime-sized hole in his head.

Annie grabbed his pistol. It felt so very heavy in her trembling hand. Then, suddenly, an explosion sent her flying. The night sky was made bright as day by a sickly green light.

A pillar of incandescent flame punched up from the church. It was unlike anything Annie had ever seen. From out of that tower of light came a sound, a terrible inhuman noise that threatened to break her mind. A gale of wind, colder than any blizzard storm, slashed through her jacket, cutting her to the bone.

"No," she said. "No!"

She gathered herself up from the ground, tried to run, but could only manage a slow, swaying hobble. Up the steps of the church, it took all her strength to stay on her feet.

She shoved the door open with one shoulder and stumbled inside. What she saw down the aisle froze her heart.

The two figures in gray robes floated above the ground. Between them was a luminous orb, from which came penetrating beams of light turning night into day.

Two women stood, transfixed, before the orb, their backs to Annie.

"Carson!"

A mistake.

A Red Winter in the West

One of the two women, a dark-haired creature, whirled on her heel. Weaponless, yet still unafraid, she charged up the aisle at Annie. Her face wore the mask of a maniac.

"Stop!" commanded Annie.

The woman only charged forward, her hands bent into claws.

Annie lifted the revolver.

The bullet took her in the woman in the chest, sending her tumbling into a pew face-first.

The harrowing sound booming from the lighted orb grew louder, threatening to burst Annie's ears. She fell to her knees, holding the sides of her throbbing head.

She was going to explode, she thought.

The orb throbbed, sending out a wave of cold power that frosted Annie's hair and sucked all the moisture from her mouth. She couldn't breathe.

Pulling herself down the aisle, Annie came to the front of the tabernacle. She looked up to see the other woman lift a long black knife. Annie tried to lift the gun, but she could not.

The light was so bright.

The cold so desolating.

The woman plunged the knife into the back of one of the figures in the gray robe. "Glory be," she railed.

Blood ran down the knife, then floated into the air like a scarlet ribbon. Twisting, swirling out of the man's body, the orb drank the blood.

It pulsed violently.

The maddening sound impossibly grew louder.

"Glory be," the woman screamed again, approaching the other figure.

Annie cinched her eyes shut and gathered all the strength within her. She pushed against all the sound, all the cold, all the pain in her shoulder and her face. Her heart was gripped by the blizzard inside her.

The woman lifted the knife, ready to plunge down. Annie lifted the gun, still so heavy in her quaking hand.

She fired.

The revolver shattered like glass in her hand.

The bullet took the woman in the side, and the knife slashed across the figure's back, cutting a long scarlet line. Blood flowed from the wound, trailing as the other had done, to flow into the orb.

"No," the woman screamed, looking over to Annie. "You will not stop this!" And she ran at Annie, the knife upraised.

Annie lifted her arms in defense.

Thunder cracked. The woman's scalp flapped open, and the red tissue of her brain splattered against the orb. The wounded figure, still levitating in the air, began to scream.

It was Carson.

Annie did not look back to see who had fired the shot that saved her life but instead ran for Carson. She wrapped her arms around his waist and pulled with all her strength. The light of the orb swallowed them both.

"Please," Annie screamed. "Please, help me!"

There came another set of arms. Then another. Those strong arms, together, pulled Carson out of the line of light. He fell on top of Annie with all his weight.

On her back, Annie watched the orb pulse once, twice. It rose into the air, throbbing with impossible waves of power. Then, as if shot from a cannon, it rocketed up through the stained glass, the visage of Christ crucified.

"Sven!" Sarah Lockhart called out from the ground next to Annie. "Help us!"

A Red Winter in the West

Annie looked at Carson, who lay face-down over her, his eyes closed. "Carson! Carson, it's me. It's Annie." She could feel his chest pressing against hers, still breathing.

But he did not wake.

Then, from above, came a tremendous explosion. The spectrum of green waves became white. The blizzard wrapped them up in its cold embrace.

Light swallowed the night.

Epilogue

TWO WEEKS LATER
ABILENE, TX

ANNIE MILLER STOOD on the porch of Peregrine House, a shawl wrapped around her shoulders. She smoked her pipe, watching the snow fall, and probed at the long scar on her cheek with the hand that wasn't in a sling.

Carson came out of the house, wrapped in a black winter coat that didn't fit him quite right. He put his own pipe in his mouth, struck a match on the porch post, and lit the pipe.

They didn't speak for a long time.

"Sarah says Erikson sent a telegram," he finally said. "Said that some of the trains are up and running. And that reports are coming in from everywhere about creatures streaming out from the gates. They're calling it the Great Blizzard of Chicago. President Grant has mobilized the army. No one knows what to do. Everything is in a panic."

Annie listened and smoked. The snow continued to fall, almost peacefully.

"I haven't had the chance to say thank you," he said.

"What's to thank?" she said. "We failed,"

"No," said Carson. "The world is still here. Our world is still here."

"It isn't ours anymore," said Annie. "We couldn't stop the Society. They won.

"I don't believe that. The ritual was supposed to bring forth something more. The Nine. Whatever is coming out of those gates, it isn't what I saw. If they'd been successful—if it hadn't been for you, Annie—I don't think we'd have survived. We would have seen the end."

"What if this is what the end looks like? You read the manuscript," she said, coldly. "What is supposed to come next?"

"Suffering," he said. "Other than that…."

She turned and looked at Carson. "You don't know."

He sighed, resigned to her. "I don't."

"Is there a way back?"

"I don't know that either." His voice was weary. "But if there is, we'll find it."

Annie looked out at the vast expanse of white, pulling her pipe from her mouth. She let out a big exhalation of smoke. "I'm scared, Carson."

He moved closer and wrapped an arm around her.

Annie felt his warmth.

"I am, too," he said.

She turned and embraced him.

They held each other.

The unyielding winter fell with an irrepressible weight on the Peregrine House. The two of them, with the warmth from the other, kept the cold at bay as best they could.

CEMETERY DANCE
PUBLICATIONS

We hope you enjoyed your Cemetery Dance Paperback! Share pictures of them online, and tag us!

Instagram: @cemeterydancepub
Twitter: @CemeteryEbook
TikTok: @cemeterydancepub
www.facebook.com/CDebookpaperbacks

Use the following tags!

#horrorbook #horror #horrorbooks
#bookstagram #horrorbookstagram
#horrorpaperbacks #horrorreads
#bookstagrammer #horrorcommunity
#cemeterydancepublications

SHARE THE HORROR!

CEMETERY DANCE PUBLICATIONS
PAPERBACKS AND EBOOKS!

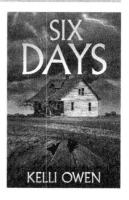

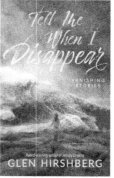

Printed in Great Britain
by Amazon